The Last Descendant

By

Shirley McCoy

Copyright © 2021 Shirley McCoy. All rights reserved.

Contents

PART ONE: FORMATION

Chapter One

Chapter Two

Chapter Three

Chapter Four

Chapter Five

PART TWO: FORTIFICATION

Chapter Six

Chapter Seven

Chapter Eight

Chapter Nine

Chapter Ten

Chapter Eleven

Chapter Twelve

Chapter Thirteen

Chapter Fourteen

Chapter Fifteen

PART THREE: CONFRONTATION

Chapter Sixteen

Chapter Seventeen

Chapter Eighteen

Chapter Nineteen

About the Author

PART ONE: FORMATION

Chapter One

Not for the first time since the phone call, Jessilyn wondered if she had gone crazy. She, a geneticist at the top of her game, was meeting a complete stranger. Sure, it was in a public place, but still. She had agreed to go to the middle of nowhere, or more precisely the 51 Diner (as in Area 51 for God's sake) in Roswell, New Mexico, on the mere possibility of a scientific breakthrough. On the basis of a deep, resonant, British-accented voice on the phone, she travelled over 1500 miles.

She was exaggerating a bit there, she admitted, which was most unlike her. She had, in fact, researched him thoroughly via social media, the internet and by reading the research, he himself had produced. She found his work to be insightful, detailed and intriguing in spite of, or perhaps because of, it not being in her field.

The pictures of him on social media had not done him justice, even as attractive as those had been, she noted as she caught sight of him at a booth in a far corner. When he rose to greet her, she saw he had black hair and was a well-muscled six feet.

As she approached, he turned his bright green eyes on her and gave her a jolt in more ways than one. Not only was he attractive, but the intense aura of power about him was palpable, almost mesmerizing. She had to swallow hard and clear her throat before speaking. "Dr. Avery?"

He nodded. "Dr. Matthews?" When she nodded in her turn, he put out a hand, she clasped it and they shook. "Nice to meet you. Please sit."

He indicated the booth he had just vacated and she slid in. Before doing likewise, he turned to signal a waitress and she observed he wore snug, faded jeans like they were meant to be worn, i.e. over a damn fine ass. A little shocked at herself for noticing at all much less feeling such a visceral physical attraction, she forced her mind back to the topic at hand and turned her gaze back to his face.

"Thank you for coming all this way. How was your trip?"

"Long, but otherwise enjoyable. I do have to get back as soon as possible, however, so if we could get down to business? Your research on the brain intrigued me and I would like to see more."

At this, he shifted in his seat then looked straight at her. "I am afraid I have you here under false pretenses, at least in a manner of speaking."

Jessilyn froze with her water glass halfway to her lips. "I'm sorry what?"

"There isn't any new research per se, although I do very much hope to work with you to produce some."

Surprise filled her but no undue alarm, so she said, "Okay, why not just tell me that when we spoke on the phone? I would consider working with you depending on the topic."

"Even if the field of study is an unconventional one?"

A little chill shivered down her spine at that, but she ignored it. "That depends. Exactly what field of study are we talking about?"

"Paranormal psychology also sometimes termed brain to brain communication."

Whatever she had been expecting, it had not been that. "Why in the world would you want to switch to that field of study? And I use the term loosely."

He took a deep breath. "Because I am the last descendent of Merlin, the magician."

Widening her eyes, she asked, "You're who?"

"I am the last direct descendent of Merlin, the magician. As such, I was born with certain abilities."

Jessilyn laughed outright. She couldn't help it, but she soon sobered. "Right. Let's be serious please. Why did you contact me? Why did you want to meet me? Why the hell did you insist on dragging me all the way out here from Princeton?"

"I am serious, doctor. I can prove it to you."

In spite of the fact that alarms were starting to ring in the distant recesses of her head, she decided to play along for the time being. "Okay. How? Wait, back up. First, what abilities?"

"Telepathy, telekinesis, precognition, and clairvoyance. At its base, it all comes down to being able to manipulate both matter and energy. Put simply, synapses fire in the brain when I want to do even something as simple as scratch an itch. When I read a person's mind, I am manipulating energy, electrical impulses. Each person's brain functions on a very specific, unique wavelength. Using my own energy, I tap into a person's particular wavelength or brain pattern, first to become aware of and then to interpret and finally perhaps even influence that energy, to, in essence, effect the thoughts of others, in theory. Telekinesis is a bit different. With that, I am using my energy to influence matter, but the basic principle is the same. To sum up, I have limited control over objects down to a molecular level. Scientifically speaking."

Fury erupted within Jessilyn without warning and she could not contain it. "Dr. Avery, I don't know what sort of game you are playing, but no matter what it is, I do not appreciate you wasting my time." Then as she gathered her things she muttered, more to herself than to him, "I traveled over 1500 miles for this?"

As she started to rise, he placed a hand over hers. "I told you I can prove it, remember? Please sit down."

She assessed him. He did appear to be serious as well as convincing. Although, if he weren't he would hardly be a good con artist now would he? Yet there was an air of sincerity she found hard to ignore. Against her better judgment and praying she would not regret it, she returned to her seat.

"I'll make you a bargain. If after I have given you a little demonstration, you still don't believe me, you can go and I'll never bother you again. I swear. But, if I do manage to convince you, then you stay and hear the rest of what I came to tell you."

Jessilyn glanced around the diner. While it wasn't exactly doing a brisk business, nor were they alone, so her safety wasn't an issue, just her sanity. She sighed and responded, "All right, you have five minutes, Dr. Avery. Dazzle me."

He did dazzle her with his grin, but it was fleeting. A moment later he was concentrating, his entire focus directed inward and his pupils dilated so much his eyes were almost black.

She waited with increasing impatience as nothing happened. When she was about to give it up as a bad job, the iced tea he had earlier ordered for himself heated then boiled. All she could manage to do was gape.

After a long moment, she did succeed in finding her voice. "How did you do that?"

This time his smile encompassed his eyes. "I told you. I have abilities."

"No," she shook her head and gestured at the glass. "No, that cannot be what it looks like."

He made no reply. Instead, he regarded her with his steady gaze.

When she made no further comment, he asked, "Do you want to see more? There are other things I can do."

Like a puppet on a string, she bobbed her head.

After he checked to be certain no one was paying them any attention whatsoever, cream and sugar floated through the air to her outstretched hand. Jessilyn gripped them in her now trembling fingers then returned both to the tabletop with great care.

"Still not convinced? Think of a number between one and one million."

"What?"

"Think of a number and with your permission, I will read your mind and tell you what number you chose."

"You have got to be kidding me. Anyway, that's an old trick."

"For some," he agreed. "Your number was 175,868 by the way." When her expression remained stony, he sighed. "Okay, then how about this? I want you to relax and think of your childhood home."

Shaking her head in disbelief, she complied nevertheless.

He got that focused look again, only more so. A few seconds later he murmured, "I see a pretty farmhouse painted yellow with a field of tall green grass surrounding it. It has white shutters and a red door. Inside there is a staircase with a bannister of smooth wood under my hand as I head upstairs. To the right is your room. It's painted a light green with pink roses climbing up the wall. The view from the window is of the cornfield behind the house. I see a pretty little girl about eight years old in her nightgown curled in the window seat looking up at the stars, so hopeful and –"

Abruptly, he stopped speaking and came back to the present. "I'm sorry. I did not mean to delve that far into your memories. Your mind is very open."

Lips stiff, mind and body rigid with shock, she managed a few words at last. "It's all right. It was a little… disconcerting, but I'm fine."

"So do you believe me now?"

"I think I'm starting to."

"Good, because I want you to study me."

Excitement shot through her before she could stop it. The mere thought of studying his powers had her adrenaline skyrocketing. "I'm sorry, I couldn't possibly have heard you right. You *want* to be experimented on?"

He grinned. "Want is too strong a word in this instance. I wouldn't go that far. I wouldn't say I want to be experimented on, no. I would say it is necessary. I want, no I need, to know if there are others like me."

"I see. So you don't know if there are others or if you are alone?"

"That's right. There are people who claim to have power and some of them may even be genuine. Most won't be. I need your help to develop a protocol to determine who has real power and who doesn't."

She fiddled with her straw a moment. "Let's say, for argument's sake, I was interested." She held up a hand to stop his enthusiastic response. "The sort of study you are suggesting requires equipment, facilities and capital, a great deal of it. Now, I don't know about you, but I haven't got anywhere near the kind of money it would take to –"

"I do," he interrupted. "It's not common knowledge, not by a long shot, but I am a billionaire. I already have my own facility set up. It's about thirty miles from here. That's why I dragged you all the way from Princeton instead of coming to you. I can take you there whenever you like. If you agree to come and work for me, you will have the run of the place and carte blanche as far as funding. Any equipment or anything else you need which isn't already there, I can get it."

"If you came to work for me, you would live and work at the facility I have built, it's called A Plus Labs Inc."

"Wow, okay."

He chuckled as he registered her nonplussed expression, then handed her a business card with his name. Avery industries, a website and contact information were also printed on it. "I realize this is a hell of a lot to process. I can see you still have doubts. You are thinking 'this guy is so.me crazy eccentric at best and a con-man at worst.' It's okay. I understand. Take your time, vet me however you like. I promise you I am legit, by the way. I will tell you this work is long term. It is also secret and that's the way it has to stay. Think about whether you want to get involved."

Without another word, he rose and left her.

****

Time would tell. Meanwhile, at least it was out there. Whether she would believe him or not, at least she knew his secret. He'd done all he could and he had to leave the rest up to fate. That's what Thomas tried to tell himself as he left the 51 Diner. Jessilyn (he already called her that, at least in his head) would, he hoped, be a valuable ally in his search. He prayed she could at least give him somewhere to start.

With little thought and even less hesitation, he gave up the internal battle and decided he couldn't, even now, perhaps especially now, leave everything up to fate after all. It went against his grain. He would do everything he could, use whatever gifts of his own came to hand or were required to achieve the outcome he wanted. The stakes were too high for him to do anything else.

As he put his jaguar into reverse, when he was half-in, half-out of his parking space, someone burst out of the front door of the diner. A flash of white top told him it was Jessilyn. He put his foot on the break and slid right back into his space as she approached.

A little breathless, she gasped out, "Okay, I'll do it." She handed him her card, which he accepted.

"Excellent." If his grin was from ear to ear, who the hell cared? "I'll call you tomorrow with the details."

As he pulled out of the lot and onto an all but deserted road, elation filled him up like a hot air balloon until he felt ready to take flight. Now the real work could and would begin. Samples, experiments, blood work, invasive questions, even more invasive procedures that would be as bad, probably worse. None of which he was looking forward to. Not so spending time in the company of the lovely Jessilyn. There would be some benefits after all and once it was done, he could be proud of what he achieved. In the end, he wouldn't have a care in the world. He'd have kept it safe after all.

****

It was essential everything was properly arranged for Jessilyn's arrival (God, he loved her name). Over the previous year, Thomas had caused the facility to be built then filled it with the finest scientific and medical equipment available. During that same period, he also gathered an elite group of scientists and doctors, but it was Jessilyn's participation in the project he most coveted. She would be his shining star even among others burning almost as bright. The elation of a few days ago when he had succeeded in convincing her to be a part of his life's work had not yet faded to a manageable level. Luckily, it came close because within twenty-four hours she would arrive. So, it was time for the most important bit of preparation yet.

The magical protection spell was one of his own devising. Added to it were ancient symbols to guard and augment its strength. He circled the facility as he chanted words of power.

Hold safe all who enter here

Bar any who wish to harm.

So all herein may know there is nothing to fear,

Steer all evil away with this charm.

This protection I fashion for mine and me

As I will, so mote it be

As he concluded the chant, a ring of bright blue magic surged up, surrounding the hidden facility like a wall then faded. The most important preparation for Jessilyn's arrival now complete, Thomas took a deep breath of the hot, dry desert wind as some of the tension drained out of him. Satisfied, he returned to the cooler air indoors.

As he entered, his butler, there was just no other word for him, approached. The man was younger than the common vision of a butler, being thirty at most, but in every other way, Jackson Styles conformed to the traditional picture of such a man with his elegant suit, snooty accent and impeccable grooming.

"Is everything on track for Dr. Matthews' arrival?"

Styles inclined his head. "Sir, her quarters are prepared, furnished in the most tasteful style, as you dictated. All the new lab equipment has been delivered, installed and is currently up and running, except the MRI machine. It has been delayed due to the specially requested modifications. The screen in the media room is functioning and various streaming platforms containing a variety of movies and television programs are available. The chef is prepared to serve a gourmet, four-star meal promptly a 7 o'clock tomorrow evening."

"Excellent."

Styles gave a little half-bow. "I will take the car and pick her up from her hotel at 9 –"

"No, I changed my mind, I'll fetch her."

Styles raised an eyebrow but said only, "Very good, sir." After a moment's hesitation, he ventured, "The protection spell is in place?" When Thomas nodded, the butler continued, "It went well then? It wasn't difficult?"

"Not any more than anything else? Why?"

"From what you've told me it's a very challenging piece of magic, complicated and demanding. I wanted to make sure you are all right, that's all."

"Nothing I can't handle." He clapped Styles on the shoulder. "You worry too much. Everything is falling into place at last."

"It certainly seems to be, sir."

"Well, I'd best be off to bed if I'm going to arrive to pick up Dr. Matthews in good time in the morning." He turned on his heal, leaving Styles to his other duties.

****

As arranged, the car arrived for her at the hotel at 9 a.m. on the dot. What Jessilyn hadn't expected was that Thomas would be behind the wheel or that the vehicle would be a fancy four-wheel drive rather than some dignified sedan. She had to admit he made an attractive picture in his khaki shorts, white shirt, open at the collar, and sunglasses. It was not such a bad beginning.

He rolled down the window as he braked to a stop in front of her. "Good morning, Dr. Matthews."

"Hi. Call me Jessilyn please. We are going to be working very closely together after all."

"Sure. And call me Thomas."

"When you said you would send a car for me I had no idea you would be driving it. Not that it isn't a nice surprise," she hastened to add.

"I don't do this sort of thing often to be honest, but I wanted to escort you personally to A Plus Labs. Hold on a second and I'll help you with your bags."

She smiled at the gesture; she couldn't help it. "Thanks."

When they were settled, he started down the road and she tried her best to make polite conversation, even though making small talk was not her favorite thing to do. Nor was she all that talented at it. Shop talk on the other hand…

"I am looking forward to seeing your facility."

"I'm glad to hear it." He proceeded to give her more details about the set up and those scientists she would find there as the car ate up the distance and the sun shined down in a brilliant blue sky.

After perhaps ten miles, they were well out of the town proper and on a road winding through desert with no signs of civilization. "When you told me this place was out in the middle of nowhere, you were not exaggerating."

"It had to be. It's all very top secret." He smiled at her and her heart skipped a beat. "I still can't get used to saying that. Even after all this time, I have to admit it gives me a thrill."

Time flew by and as Thomas had informed her, the facility was thirty miles away, so it was in fact a short trip. The road dead-ended and Thomas brought the car to a stop. There was a gray metal door attached to a room the size of small shed. Jessilyn pushed her sunglasses up and into her hair the better to study it. A bit surprised, she made no comment. What could she say after all? Where was the rest of it? That it was small? That was the obvious and probably false assumption, so she kept her lips shut.

As it happened, she didn't have to say anything, Thomas spoke instead. "From this angle, the outside is not very impressive, I know. But I promise, inside, it's quite something. C'mon."

They exited the car and he led her toward the door. The security system included a coded keypad, presumably for a keycard, a voice print match and finally a retinal scan.

"I see your security is state of the art as well."

"Oh, it is. I don't take chances."

As the door closed behind them, lights equipped with motion detectors blazed on to reveal an unimpressive set of concrete steps. Jessilyn shivered and the thought crossed her mind she might have made a terrible mistake and she could be walking into the lair of a serial killer. So far, the place sure as hell looked like every horror movie she'd ever seen after all. At this point, if she were watching this movie rather than participating in a real life scenario, she would have been screaming at the heroine not to go down into the dark, dank cellar. Following a relative stranger into a hole in the ground was never a good idea. Giving her over-active, not to say lurid, imagination a stern talking to, she followed him inside.

At the bottom of the staircase, there was a heavy steel door with the same sort of security set up beside it. Still uneasy, she studied the area in more detail while Thomas went through the whole security procedure again.

Seconds later the door opened and the last of Jessilyn's fears vanished. Shaking her head at her ridiculous fancies, she thanked God the stairs didn't end in some small concrete box of a room with manacles fixed to the walls. The room revealed was instead a massive circular atrium bordered with labs and full of people, most of them in white lab coats. From what she could see, the labs contained the most up to date equipment from microscopes to petri dishes, from beakers to Florence flasks. Counters of a pristine pearl gray held test tubes in neat racks. Everything she could even imagine needing was there.

"So, welcome. I'll show you to your quarters. Please make yourself at home. You can relax and unpack then maybe in an hour or so you could join me for a light lunch in the main dining room."

"Sure. I'd like that." She had to grin. A light lunch. He was so adorable, so English, so formal and polite. And for a second she wondered whether he was always like this or –. She shook her head inwardly to banish the wayward thought.

"Later this afternoon we can set you up with security passes etc. My chef is preparing a gourmet meal in honor of your arrival for 7 o'clock this evening. After that, we can both call it a night and get an early start in the morning. Sound good?"

"That sounds perfect. I can't wait to get started."

He led her down a long hallway away from the hustle and bustle of the common area to her rooms, which turned out to be as impressive as the rest of the space, if not more so. The 1000 square foot space had a floor of light gray tile and cream-colored walls. A sofa in a darker shade of gray sat beside occasional tables of glass. As she looked out of the floor to ceiling windows, she glimpsed a panorama of the entire facility. Very little showed above ground, as much of the place was located below the surface. What wasn't, the east side, looked out from the edge of the jagged desert canyon it had been carved from. In this way, it was concealed from civilization and could only be seen from the direction of the empty desert or from overhead.

Noticing her fascination, Thomas commented, "It's camouflaged with magic as well, a simple deflection spell to start with as well as various more complicated ones I won't go into. We are quite secret and very safe here."

A little dazed, Jessilyn nodded.

Glancing about the room, Thomas said, "I hope this will do."

"Oh, this will do very nicely. I expected much simpler accommodations, but seeing the rest of this place should have clued me in. You never skimp on anything." The lavish luxury combined with the understated elegance of the space suited her quite well. Who wouldn't enjoy such comfort?

He chuckled, she presumed at her use of such a very American idiom, but she didn't mind. The sound of his laugh was rather intoxicating, especially as she got the distinct impression he rarely did so.

Then he cleared his throat and his habitual serious demeanor returned. "My quarters are in the East Wing not too far from here."

So, close, but still allowing for plenty of privacy. That sounded perfect to her.

"If you want to change any of the décor or if you need anything," he continued, "let me or Styles know and you'll have it as soon as possible. I do hope you'll be comfortable here."

"I'm sure I will be. Thank you."

With a nod, he left her to get settled and she prepared to embark on a great adventure.

Chapter Two

By 8 o'clock the next morning Jessilyn had been in the lab for two hours when someone opened the door. As Thomas entered, he started in surprised to find the lights on, but when he caught sight of dark hair stark against a white coat, he grinned over at her.

"Good morning, Dr. Matthews. So, I'm guessing the facility and the lab in particular are acceptable since I see you are already making use of them."

She turned to him and offered him a beautiful smile. "More than. This lab is the best I have ever seen much less worked in. So, are you ready for our first experiment?"

He glanced over in surprise. "Already? You don't waste time."

"No, I do not. I've been here since six. Are you ready?"

"Right now?" When she nodded, he continued, "Of course. What will this first experiment involve?" Thomas asked.

"Hmm, something simple. How about moving that pencil? Can you do that?"

"Sure." With a gesture, he sent the pencil in question rolling across the table all on its own.

"Wait! Wait!" Jessilyn ordered, half-laughing. "I have to get you set up first. This is supposed to be an experiment and as such it has to be recorded."

"I know. I'm just keeping you on your toes. What do I need to do?"

"First, let me attach these electrodes." She placed the first two at his temples then asked, "Can you remove your shirt please? These have to go on your chest to monitor heart rate."

"Absolutely." The smile on his face was electric and very hard to ignore although she did her best.

As he discarded a very expensively tailored silk shirt and she positioned the electrodes, she tried not to notice the expanse of smooth skin and muscle revealed. Once done, she stepped back right away. Then she offered him a hat which consisted of similar electrodes. He put it on then gave her a brisk nod. "Okay, I'll go into the observation booth.

When I give you the go-ahead, you move the pencil again and we'll have our first look at your brain activity."

"Sounds great."

Jessilyn entered the observation booth and said into the mic for the recording. "This is experiment 1-A. Dr. Thomas Avery subject. Also present and conducting the experiment, Dr. Jessilyn Matthews. The date is April 18, 2028 and the time is 8:04 a.m. The subject will attempt to move the pencil that is on the table using telekinesis while his brain activity is monitored. Go ahead, Dr. Avery."

"Any special place you want me to move it to?"

She thought for a moment. "How about from its current position to the far edge of the table?"

"Will do."

Right away he got a look of intense concentration, the one she was beginning to recognize as an indicator he was preparing to do magic. Seconds later, the pencil vibrated then floated an inch or so above the table then across to the other side. Just when Jessilyn thought the momentum would carry it to the floor, it slowed and came to a stop mere centimeters from the edge.

When she tore her gaze away to glance at the monitors, she gasped. "Wow. This is amazing! Your parahippocampal gyrus is lit up like a Christmas tree. Move it again."

He grinned and obliged. The pencil rolled back and right to his hand.

"This is terrific! All right, Thomas, I want you to do one more thing for me and then we will be through with this part of the proceedings. Can you lift the pencil then hold it in the air? I want to know if things stay the same or if this requires more effort."

He did so.

"Slightly faster heartbeat and respiration but the brain scan remains the same. Okay. Thomas, that was great. Give me a second to jot down some notes and I'll be in to talk to you."

As promised, mere minutes later Jessilyn rejoined him.

"So, I'd like to ask you a few questions about what you did in experiment 1-A," she said.

"Of course."

"Can you describe the sensation? I can note your mental processes as well as your physical responses, but what does doing magic feel like?"

For a long moment, he paused, considering, then he shook his head, as if giving up. "I'm sorry, I don't have the words. It's difficult trying to describe the indescribable. I mean, it's like trying to describe sex to a teenager who's never had it. They can extrapolate, but they can only get a very vague idea which can't begin to touch the reality."

The next, most obvious question was one she wasn't sure she could or should ask but... "So, it feels good then?"

He shook his head. "No."

When she glanced up in surprise, he smiled and Jessilyn knew she was looking at pure temptation. "It feels bloody great."

She cleared her now dry throat. "That's what I thought," she murmured. Trying for a normal tone she said, "Okay, I'll draw some blood and we'll be done for today."

"For determining my genetic profile?"

Jessilyn nodded. "Tomorrow I'll also draw some prior to the experiment for comparison. I also want to see if there are any interesting changes to your blood when you practice magic."

"Excellent idea. I will focus on the neurological aspect and perhaps develop experiments for that area of study while you can focus on the genetics."

She found herself startled then impressed and soon she settled into pleased. "That sounds like the perfect area for you to concentrate on, considering your field."

"Well then I say let's get to work. The others will be arriving soon, but we can at least make a start."

All but bouncing on her toes like a little girl in anticipation, she gave him an eager nod and began.

****

As the weeks passed the experiments continued, many in the same vein as the first, others were developed to test different aspects of his magical ability. She became intimately acquainted with his body and mind, yet it was some time before Jessilyn felt justified in asking Thomas another personal question. Although it had occurred to her during their very first experiment together, she had hesitated to ask it, but now she would. After all, what she wanted to know was relevant. "Have you ever told anyone?"

"About what I can do? No. My parents always knew from the very beginning, of course, and one very close friend from childhood suspected and for a time he believed I'd grown out of it. Jackson saw me do things he couldn't explain before I learned to control my abilities fully. We got into an emergency situation a year ago, however, and he saw that I can still do what I used to."

"So, you've never told anyone else," she stated. "You've never been able to confide in anyone else or be truly yourself?"

"No," he confirmed, expression solemn.

She tilted her head to one side like a curious, excited sparrow. "Do you find it a relief to talk about it now or is it difficult?"

He considered. "Secrecy had become such a habit with me that, I'll admit, at first, it was difficult. But now? To be known is… intoxicating."

Jessilyn locked her gaze with his. "I can imagine."

She blinked and tried to pull herself together. A person could get lost in those powerful green eyes of his so easily. He was mesmerizing and magnetic without a doubt. But she had a job to do and allowing herself to become distracted by Dr. Avery had no part in it, she told herself in her sternest mental voice.

All of a sudden, she realized the silence had stretched too long and she cleared her throat. "Sorry, I just wanted to get a clearer picture of you and what your life has been like. We might see the same things in the others we find."

"You may be right. There's no need to apologize. Ask me anything you like. It's why I'm here."

"I'll keep that in mind." She pulled up his chart on her I-pad and scrolled to her notes for the next experiment.

****

"Thomas, I would like to go over my preliminary findings with you. After studying you for two months now, I can venture a few basic conclusions and more than a few areas of study to pursue further. That having been said, I would like to hear your thoughts and observations first."

Thomas sat back in the comfortable visitor's chair in Jessilyn's office as she gestured for him to begin.

"First, the most exciting observation is when I do magic I use an area of the brain the average person never uses. I mean this area of the typical human brain lies entirely fallow, or at least that is what we have been able to observe until now. Which makes perfect sense, considering most people cannot do what I do."

"Which area?

"The right parahippocampal gyrus." He pointed to an image of his brain in which an area at the front right of his skull was lit up like a ride at a fairground. "This was taken the first day when I moved the pencil. Various types of magic make greater use of one segment of this bright area or another but all activity remains in this quadrant. As we continue with our research, I will eventually be able to pinpoint to the centimeter which area is in use for any magical task. It's simple brain mapping."

"That's ambitious and exciting, I must say," she commented.

"So, what about you? What have you discovered? What conclusions have you come to?"

Jessilyn pulled up a document on her I-pad then handed it to him. "When I tested your blood, certain blood cells were active while you were doing magic as well as for some time after. I put this fact against our control group and found this particular type of cell is all but nonexistent in that group. Now we still have to determine causality, but a simple blood test can confirm potential. Added to that, and the piece d'resistance, your DNA has several specific genetic markers not seen in our control group or anywhere else for that matter. Which means we have two ways of confirming potential and we can now begin to study causality."

Thomas sat back, impressed as well as intrigued. "You are saying everything we hypothesized is true so far."

"Yes. We have far more work to do and still need to keep testing our theory, but the preliminary results support our hypothesis."

"That is excellent. I'll start working on a protocol to find others."

"Then all I have to do is use my clearance to access private medical and genetic records and bing, bang, boom, we're good to go."

He glanced over at her and saw the tension investing her features. "You having second thoughts? It's okay if you are. We are going to be violating people's privacy and committing about ten felonies at a guess."

"I'm not having second thoughts. That doesn't mean I like the idea of invading people's privacy. Privacy people legally and ethically have a right to. As for breaking the law, that doesn't worry me per se, at least not in this instance. I make my own rules and my own decisions on how to live. And anyway, I found a legal loop hole."

"Really? Tell me." He leaned forward, not conscious of the movement until after completing it.

"Statute 1593-A of the United States Criminal Code. 'If genetic information is used solely for the purpose of scientific, not-for-profit, academic research, then it may be used at the sole discretion of the scientists responsible for the research without the consent of the individuals involved,'" she quoted. "There was some more legal terminology, but that's the basic gist of it."

"That's great but there are still other statutes involved," he reminded her.

She acknowledged this with an inclination of the head. "I know. I will worry about that if and when. I want this to happen and I want to be part of it. I believe in this study."

"Look, so far no one's broken any laws. If you want out though, now's the time."

Jessilyn shook her head. "I'm all in."

Thomas beamed at her. "Good."

****

Thomas had not slept well, an unusual occurrence for him. For that reason and several others, his mood was foul. Over the past few weeks their progress had stalled on every front and he had no idea how to kick-start it again. The experiments were going well and they were collecting a large amount of raw data, but it was clear to him the data would need to be sorted, put into a coherent format and a protocol for their search would have to be developed from that. Although he had been prepared from the first to do this, it would all take far more time than he would have liked. Time was of the essence and he wished there was more of it.

Added to that, Jessilyn was driving him mad. The look of her was always before him. The scent of her was soaking into every cell of his body until all he wanted was to be able to bury himself in her, let her surround him and forget about the rest of the world. He wanted to let all of it go. It was a battle every day to remember who she was, his research partner and nothing more. It was a battle he was beginning to fear he would lose. Today, with his defenses down and exhaustion clawing at him, he was having trouble remembering why he was fighting so hard against the inevitable. To hell with it, he decided on impulse. No more.

Instead of keeping his longing for her on a tight leash as he normally did, especially when she was physically close to him, he let a fraction of it loose. When she stepped over to hand him the electrodes for him to place on his chest, he accepted them but then let his hand trail down her arm. A combination of triumph and raw lust tightened his every muscle when she shivered at the contact.

As she shot him one startled look then turned away, ready to head into observation, he tangled his fingers with hers.

"What?" Her voice was a bare whisper, but he heard her. When he said nothing, just looked at her and let his desire show, she barked, "What are you doing, Thomas?"

****

"What are you doing, Thomas?" Jessilyn's tone was harsh, but she could not help it. It was all she could do to speak even those few words past the lump in her throat and the rapid beat of her heart. When he looked at her that way she could barely remember her own name. She caught flashes of that hungry look before and that had been difficult enough. Now, he seemed to be making no effort to mask his craving for her and so all she could see or feel or know was him.

For a moment, he tried to form words but then he gave up and covered her mouth with his. Her gasp was smothered and heat shot down her veins as his lips firmed. The next thing she knew, she parted her own lips and granted him entry. In response, he groaned and wrapped his arms tightly around her.

For long while she savored the kiss. When he broke it, they were both breathing heavily and as her mind cleared she wondered whether he would pull away now. He didn't. Instead, he placed hot, open-mouthed kisses down her neck. Every rational thought was wiped away, every single cell in her body responded and she shuddered. The giving and receiving of pleasure was all that was left.

With swift clarity, she was certain she was no longer alone inside of her own head. She could feel him there, entering her mind as he had her mouth. For one searing instant, she could feel his pleasure almost as if it were her own and it was overwhelming. Then she sensed his clear intent to give her more and take more for himself. This astonished her enough that her eyes, which had been closed in ecstasy, popped open.

With a supreme effort of will, she pulled back from him, mentally as well as physically, something she was only able to do because she was frightened. Not of him, or only a little. No, more than anything she was shocked by the enticement he offered and alarmed at how tempted she was to accept it.

In a voice far too breathless for her liking, she managed to gasp, "What the hell was that?!" When he didn't respond, she asked, "You do realize that you were…"

His head shot up and his eyes when they fixed on hers were blazing. "Inside of you in more ways than one? Yes." He broke the contact, took a deep breath, then ran a hand through his hair, destroying its usual tidiness. When he met her gaze again, his was somewhat calmer and rock steady. "I apologize. What I did was inexcusable. To do that without your express permission was unforgiveable. Most of the time I have a lot more control."

Jessilyn took a deep breath of her own. "Apology accepted. I was startled, that's all. You didn't force me and I wasn't exactly complaining."

He accepted this with a grateful nod then spoke again. "Still, I feel I owe you an explanation. We have been working closely together and from the beginning I found you attractive. So that kiss was a long time in coming, at least for me." After a pause, he rose, unearthed a bottle of whiskey from a top shelf of one of the cabinets scattered around the lab and poured himself a glass. "Some people are easier to read, did you know? You fall into that category. When I kissed you, your thoughts and feelings were right there, so close I could almost taste them. Only the smallest barrier concealed them. It was like brushing aside a curtain instead of going through a door or trying to break through a wall. Christ, I barely even realized I was doing it until I had. It was instinctive, natural. Even so, that's no excuse. I can promise you I won't ever do that again. Not unless you ask me to."

The idea of that had Jessilyn trembling and not from fear. "Well, I won't."

"Why not?" He looked away. "Stupid question. It's because I scared you. If so, I apologize again. I am sorry for it with all my heart."

After a long pause while she tried to convince herself to let it go at that and to let him believe fear was the reason for her retreat, she gave up the fight. "It's not that," she admitted. "It's... our relationship needs to remain strictly professional. Neither of us needs the complication of sex or romance."

When she sent a sidelong glance his way, he grinned. "Or both, God forbid."

"Right," she replied. Her tone was brisk and she ignored the comment, although her lips twitched in spite of herself.

"So, we pretend this didn't happen?"

There was something in the tone of his voice which made her heart pound but... "No... we process it and move on."

His jaw tensed. "I see. Good luck with that."

Without further comment, he held out his wrist for her to take his pulse and begin the day's tests.

****

For a week he did his best to honor her wishes, but on day eight he cracked. "Jess, we need to talk."

"About what?" She asked the question absently as she continued readying the equipment for more tests, more monitoring.

"The kiss. What else? I can't stand acting like it never happened."

"There is no need to discuss it. I told you that. You kissed me. It won't happen again. End of story." She did not look up as she said all this.

"Wrong. *We* kissed. You participated fully."

Although her voice wanted to tremble, she held it steady. "You're right. I did. That doesn't mean it would be wise to do it again."

"I'm in no mood to be wise."

"Thomas, I –"

He sighed with an edge of impatience. "Indulge me then."

"What?"

"Indulge me. Let me kiss you again, because I can't get you or that kiss out of my head."

"Thomas, I can't do that and you know why."

"No, Jess, I don't."

"Damn it, Thomas, I am not going to have this conversation with you again."

He shrugged. "Okay, I am tired of talking and this was a boring conversation anyway." Without further comment or warning, he kissed her again.

In a sudden rush, she found herself doing as he asked, indulging him and, in the process, indulging herself. So, when he drew away she was a bit surprised; he was the one who kissed her after all.

"I'm not sure I can do this," he breathed the words. "I can't be around you and not want to kiss you and touch you and…"

"This attraction between us is difficult to cope with, I know, but we have to find a way. Because what about all the work we've done? I won't quit and I won't let it all be for nothing. It isn't near finished and I am not going anywhere until it is. We should focus on that." She was babbling and she knew it, but she couldn't seem to stop herself. "All we've worked for could go up in flames if things don't work out between us. Besides, what we have right now is precious to me and I don't want to screw it up. Just because we are attracted to each other doesn't mean we should..."

Slowly, he ran a hand through her hair. "Act on it? Why not? Give me one good reason."

Jessilyn couldn't and if she was being brutally honest with herself, she didn't really want to.

Encouraged by her silence, Thomas took her hand. "These feelings, I've been fighting them for a long time. I don't want to fight them anymore. They aren't going away and not acting on them is driving me out of my mind. Can we at least try? See where things go?"

"You do understand if we do that, we are risking everything?"

"Yes and I don't care. All that matters right now is this: do you want me?"

"Yes, I do." If she were being honest, what else could she say?

"Then have dinner with me tonight and hopefully, eventually breakfast."

"We're both insane. You do realize that?"

"I do. At the risk of repeating myself, I don't care."

Temptation beckoned and Jessilyn could not resist him, not along with herself. He was everything she ever wanted and she would be damned if she'd let this opportunity, or him, go. "All right, dinner. *Just* dinner."

Thomas gave her a satisfied smile as he kissed her hand then he let her go so they could begin the day's work.

****

Thomas had it all planned. He had no intention of going casual for their first date. There was nothing casual about this, not anymore, at least not for him. They would share excellent food prepared by his personal chef along with the perfect accompanying wine she would bring to his candlelit dining room. Then they would enjoy dessert and the moonlight on his terrace and he would kiss her again. Afterward, if he was lucky, they might do a bit more. The sound of a knock interrupted that train of thought and he tried to convince himself it was just as well.

She was as sweet and pretty as a spring morning in a summer dress of some light fabric in pale blue. A moment to drink in her beauty was all he allowed himself before he forced himself to speak coherently. "You look amazing." He stepped away to allow her to enter. "Please, come in."

"You don't look so bad yourself."

The simple compliment pleased him far more than it should have. The same way seeing her in his space did. Watching her as she glanced here and there cataloging details felt curiously intimate and he relished the feeling.

"I brought this. I hope it goes well with whatever we'll be eating. I'm afraid I don't know much about wine." She lifted a hand to indicate the bottle of Sauvignon Blanc she was holding.

"This is perfect," he replied. He set the wine on the counter, rummaged for a corkscrew and opened it. Then he poured them each a glass. "We should let this stuff breathe, but what the hell."

Handing one to her, he lifted his own in toast. "Here's to new beginnings."

"To new beginnings," she agreed, and smiled at him as they clinked glasses.

He set his wine aside then brushed a hand over her cheek. "I promised myself I'd wait to do this too, but…" Giving her plenty of time to back away if she wanted to, he edged nearer and nearer, until their lips were all but touching. She stayed right where she was and he was drawn to her, like magnet to steel.

"What the hell," she finished for him. So, in the end it was she who crossed that last bit of space between them and pressed her lips to his.

The kiss was sweet, slow and languorous with a touch of heat. Before that heat could begin to burn, however, he hauled himself away. That it was more difficult to do than he expected surprised him. The realization he was already at the limits of his control from one kiss astounded him, in fact, and he shivered in reaction. For one searing moment, their gazes met and he thought from the greedy look in hers she would tug him back to her mouth. If she did, he would never be able to resist her and the knowledge rocked him. The unfamiliar urge to lay back and let her take him roared through his body, shocking the hell out of him. Normally he did the taking, but not tonight, not with her. With her he wanted something entirely different. But she blinked then stepped out of his arms, breaking the spell at least for the moment.

He had to take a second before he was lucid again. He cleared his now parched throat then said, "Dinner should be ready in a few minutes. Why don't you make yourself comfortable at the breakfast bar here while I finish up?"

"Sure. That sounds great."

He was as good as his word and within ten minutes they were seated at a charming dining table with baked chicken, potatoes au gratin and fresh green salad in front of them.

The first bite had her eyes going wide then closing in ecstasy. He'd had no idea how sexy it would be just to watch her enjoy the food he cooked for her. When she made a little humming noise in her throat the sound made him tense in the best way and he took a large sip of wine.

"This tastes so good," she informed him.

He sampled the chicken and decided she was right. "It did turn out well didn't it?"

She nodded and drank more wine.

"So, how are the search protocols coming?" she asked once they had made a decent start on their meal.

He shook his head. "No shop talk, not tonight."

She twinkled at him like bloody Tinkerbell and he found it irresistible. "Okay then, I have to ask, where did you learn to cook like this? I swear I've had meals at some of the best restaurants in the world that were not this good."

"My mother taught me. It's become a hobby of mine in fact."

After that the conversation naturally turned to family, his then hers. They spoke of early life then of what they studied at college and Thomas found the time flying by. Already aware of her intelligence, he had to admit he was surprised by her charm. He'd seen flashes of it before of course, but it had never been so much on display. In addition, she was more relaxed than he had ever seen her, as was he. It seemed they were both enjoying themselves.

Once dinner was over, he insisted they leave the mess and he coaxed her out on the terrace. And was glad he did when her eyes brightened.

"Look at that sky. I'm still not used to the nights here. The stars are so bright and close. It's beautiful."

He couldn't help smiling. "Yeah, it is." Her hand rested on the railing and he placed his own over it.

For a while they stood star-gazing and enjoying the cool desert breeze.

With the press of a button, he turned on the sound system and a soft, jazzy melody played from the strategically placed outdoor speakers. He held out a hand to her and she placed hers in his. They swayed in time, mostly, to the music. Since he was no dancer, he kept the steps simple and they did well enough. With their bodies close, he felt her warmth not to mention the shape of her and knew how well they would fit together. And once his mind strayed to that tack it was time to bring the evening to a close.

The song ended and he murmured, "As wonderful as this has been, I think I had better take you back to your rooms."

"To my rooms? You... don't want me to stay?"

She gazed quizzically at him with such a compelling mixture of shyness and allure, he almost caved but... "I do want you to stay very much. Believe me. But this is our first date and I am a gentleman. It's about respect but also about taking our time. Before, you said what we have is precious to you and you don't want to screw it up. I guess this is my way of saying, neither do I."

"Well, that's lovely. I appreciate that and I am very flattered. So…"

"So…"

She sighed, "So, as much as I would love to spend the night in your bed, you should take me back to my rooms."

Somehow, knowing she was as reluctant as he made it a little easier to leave her. A little.

Chapter Three

As a scientist, it was Jessilyn's job to ask questions then to answer them. Sometimes that was easier than at other times, like today. Even so, there were things she needed to know and still didn't, even after studying Thomas for months. So, it was time she asked point-blank.

"As far as telepathy, what are your limits? Or to be more accurate, what limits have you observed so far?"

"Well, it's not a power I use often, but I've observed closer is better and to have physical contact is best. I'm not sure of the precise distance it ceases to work since I haven't ever tested it though."

Jessilyn noted that down then fixed him with a direct stare. He was not going to like this next question, her instincts told her, but it had to be asked. "What about controlling someone's thoughts?"

His entire body went rigid and he shook his head. "Never. I have never and would never do that."

"But you could." When he nodded, she asked, "I believe you absolutely when you say you never have, but how do you know you could?"

For a time, he seemed to struggle for the proper words then at last, he spoke. "There's a potential there I can feel. When I'm riding the wave of someone's thoughts I know all it would take is a little push of my own to change their direction. That's the best way I know to describe it."

She bit her lip. "I very much want to test that theory."

"No! Not just no, but hell no." His voice was harsh, absolute and very unlike his own.

In truth, she had never heard him sound like that before, so stern and so uncompromising and the experience was a bit unnerving. Yet, her scientific curiosity was enough to trump her unease. "I know this is an ethical line you don't want to cross, but I think in this controlled environment we could risk it."

"I said no and if you ever ask again, we are done, do you understand?"

Jessilyn wanted to plead, but she knew better. The look in his eyes now forbade it, so she nodded.

"Today's experiment is over." With a jerk, he pulled off the already attached electrodes and strode away without another word.

****

By the afternoon, some common sense tempered his fury. What she said about the safety of a controlled environment was true, at least up to a point. Up to a point was to him the key, of course. More important, however, he knew her. No matter the depth and strength of her scientific inquisitiveness, she would never do anything unethical. He believed that absolutely and trusted that to his core, in fact, it was a large part of why he'd chosen her, and yet he had behaved as if she were some crazy mad scientist. He had been wrong and he owed her an apology.

So, at 7 o'clock he knocked on her door with a bottle of pinot grigio. After an appreciable pause, she opened the door.

Before she could say a word, he blurted out, "I'm sorry. Sincerely. I never meant to sound so accusing."

When her stiff posture eased somewhat and she stepped back to let him enter, he breathed a small sigh of relief.

"I'm sorry as well," she said, surprising him.

"What on earth do you have to be sorry for?"

"I never should have suggested something I was aware crossed your personal ethical lines. So, I will accept your apology if you will accept mine."

He smiled. "Deal." He held out the wine. "I brought this as a peace offering. I thought we might have some along with a working dinner? I make a very good steak."

"That sounds wonderful." She smiled as she stepped back to let him in.

****

The 'working dinner' went far better than expected. As a consequence, Thomas was in an excellent mood when he walked into the lab the next morning. He greeted Jessilyn with a smile and a quick kiss then was about to settle down to work when her voice caught his attention.

"Thomas, I'd like your permission to do another experiment."

Thomas glanced over at Jessilyn, eyebrow raised. "You know you have carte blanche. I trust you."

Jessilyn bit her lip and said nothing. Thomas was quite prepared to wait. After no little hesitation, she murmured, "This experiment comes under the heading of extremely personal."

"You mean invasive?" He could not help but tense a little at the thought.

"Not physically no. I would use the word intimate."

Thomas stilled. "What do you want to do to me, Jessilyn?" He could imagine so many things, all of them deeply pleasurable.

She took a deep breath and burst out, "I want you to read my mind."

Confusion added to the tension he was feeling. "Weren't we done with the telepathy experiments for now?"

"We were, but I want a better idea of your abilities and the way to get that is to run deeper tests. Tests a lot more complicated than 'Do you know what card I'm holding'. What do you think?"

What did he think? What he thought was that she was temptation incarnate. He'd been careful to avoid any contact at all with her mind aside from that very first day at the 51 Diner and during their first kiss. Since then he'd resisted the lure of her, even in their more, to use her word, intimate moments, and with good reason, because for the first time he was unsure of his control.

"I get you want to know my full strength, Jess, but in this area that is not a good idea." He stopped her protests with a hand. "I could go deeper. If that's what you want."

"Deeper but not full strength. Why?"

He made a frustrated sound. "Because, it's like you said. Telepathy, especially full strength, is intimate. In some ways, it's more intimate than having sex. It's not something I'm willing to do with anyone else. I very much want to do it with you. Are you ready for that?"

"I... I," she stammered.

Unable to resist he took a single step closer to her then another until he was no more than an inch away from her. "Are you ready for me to be inside your body and your mind? Because that's what I want. I want that so much I can barely think straight sometimes. That's why I haven't even skimmed your mind since our first kiss."

Her mouth formed a little oh, but she did not answer. Still, her eyes spoke for her. When he looked into them, he saw raw desire, eager anticipation and some trepidation.

She looked down then stepped back, breaking the connection and he could hardly breathe through the pain of unfulfilled desire. "Maybe you're right. It's too much."

He nodded, then silently added, 'At least for now'.

****

A few days later the silence in the lab was broken by an inarticulate whoop uttered at top volume into the stillness. Hearing it, Thomas jumped about a foot. He was surprised he hadn't jumped right out of his skin. "Jesus, what the hell, Jess?"

"Sorry, sorry. I didn't mean to startle you, it's... I've found one."

"Someone with abilities? Show me." Even as he said the words, he rushed over to her workstation.

With one hasty motion, she tilted her computer screen so he could see. "Hannah Barnes of Scranton, Ohio. She's fourteen and she has all the genetic markers we've been looking for."

"But we both know this doesn't mean she has power."

"Maybe not, but I think this makes it a pretty safe bet she does."

Clicking with her mouse, she brought up a news story from several months before with the headline, 'Local girl survives fire, police baffled.' Thomas read.

Against all odds Hannah Barnes, fourteen, of Scranton, Ohio survived a house fire which killed her father and would have killed her mother and younger brother if she had not braved the flames to rescue them. Barely burned and with no ill-effects from smoke inhalation despite being exposed to the fire, it is not known how Miss Barnes survived. Physicians say it should not have been possible, but Hannah is alive and well and by all accounts is in perfect health.

"After this story ran they had to disappear from Scranton. They attracted far too much of the wrong sort of attention. It took a while, but I found her living with her mother and brother in, wait for it, right here in New Mexico with her maternal grandmother. Their house is only about a two-hour drive from here."

A slow grin spread across his face. "This is good. This is very good. I can't believe we've found someone else with power and so close by too." He trapped her gaze with his. "You are amazing."

"Thank you. I can't take all the credit though. We developed the list of genetic markers together."

"But you coordinated and organized it all. You really are astonishing." The kiss he gave her then was gentle and sweet, almost reverent, and over far too soon.

When he broke the kiss, she grinned at him. "Should I start a list of all possible candidates?"

He grinned right back at her. "Absolutely."

****

Alone for the evening as she readied herself for bed, Jessilyn hummed under her breath without even being aware of it. Once she realized what she was doing, she paused a moment, shrugged, spat out toothpaste then continued. She was happier than she had ever been in her life so why shouldn't she enjoy the feeling for once?

The attack came out of nowhere. Jessilyn was knocked off her feet by a dark cloud of some unknown substance. It was unexpectedly solid, not to mention possessed of unprecedented strength. With an abrupt force which shocked her, she hit her forehead on the edge of the porcelain sink as she went down. She saw stars and was stunned a moment. Disoriented just long enough, a tendril of cloud coiled tightly around her ankle and dragged her across the bathroom floor before she could even struggle.

****

The hot water of the shower eased Thomas's aching neck and shoulders and it felt incredible. He lingered a bit, enjoying the sensation, but then picked up the bar of soap. Rubbing the fresh, lemon-smelling stuff over his body, he imagined Jessilyn's hands on him instead. Groaning, he braced his arms on the wall in front of him and bowed his head under the spray. Feet wide apart and planted firmly on the tile, he took a deep breath and attempted to calm himself with little success. Trying to resist the temptation to make do with the feel of his own hands, he was occupied with this thankless task, when without warning, all his senses were bombarded by a vision of Jessilyn being dragged across the floor by the dark force. In a flash, he saw as well as sensed she was in pain and bleeding from the head. Incipient rage warred with abject panic as he flew into action. With one hand, he smacked off the water, while with the other he grabbed a towel to wrap around himself. He yanked pants onto his still damp body and seconds later, he raced down the hall to her apartment.

When he reached it, he found her door locked. With a swift gesture and a murmured spell, he turned the lock and opened things up. The sound of running water filled his ears and, remembering his vision of white tile framing dark hair and red blood, he dashed for the bathroom.

The door was ajar and he could see a rope of swirling dark wrapped around one white ankle. He pushed the door fully open and came face to face with a formless darkness nevertheless growing more solid by the second. The wisp of the smoky, murky, rancid cloud he had glimpsed was dragging the woman he loved toward a portal, or more like a dark void as black as obsidian. Fully conscious now, she was kicking and screaming and doing her best to halt her forward motion, but eventually, the dark force would win. It meant to leave and take her with it. Well, he would not let that happen, not, by God, without a fight.

Steeling himself and calling on all his faculties, he summoned up every bit of his power and focused every ounce of his strength on freeing her. His voice was a command.

Unexpected Dark, go and leave no mark.

The one I hold dear, leave untouched.

Do not stand against my power, but set her free.

As I will, so mote it be.

The light of his magic burst forth and when it touched the dark, a terrible shriek, like that of a wounded bird of prey, filled the space. The dark force shrank back and loosened its hold on her somewhat but did not let her go. Instead, it moved more quickly toward the abyss still dragging her with it. He did not let up, but concentrated his power on her leg, determined to force it to release her. The noise was a cacophony now, but Thomas could feel the dark force weakening in the face of his power. At last, he broke its hold on her and it retreated into the chasm. Then the void collapsed in on itself and disappeared.

In the ringing silence, it was all Thomas could do to remain on his feet between the amount of energy expended, the rush of adrenaline now ebbing and the sheer relief coursing through him. As he gave himself a moment to breathe, he realized he had in fact beaten back the dark force and more importantly, Jessilyn was safe.

****

Jessilyn returned to her senses to find herself being dragged across the cold tile of her bathroom toward what looked like a mini black hole. With a wild shriek she struggled, but to no avail. She did all she could, but she could feel herself, everything she was, slipping away. She didn't have much time, maybe mere seconds, before she was dragged into the abyss. Then she heard Thomas's voice chanting. In her heightened state of agitation, she couldn't make out the words, but from the tone of Thomas's voice, she could tell it was a spell of immense power.

Almost as soon as his words died away, the dark force's hold on her loosened. Fighting with renewed strength, she did her best to free herself. With all the force of her considerable will she tried to push it away. The darkness receded in slow increments, then as quickly as it had come, it was gone.

****

"What the hell was that? What is going on? And don't you dare tell me it was nothing!"

Jessilyn shouted into the silence of her living room and Thomas admitted to himself that it was time, long past time, to tell her the whole story. Judging from the stubborn fury on Jessilyn's face that fact was clear, so he sat down on the sofa beside her, took a deep breath and began. "Certain myths are present in every culture throughout the centuries with varying degrees of truth to each. You find the same forces under so many different names. Some myths have more truth than others and some forces are stronger. So, let me tell you what I believe. There is an ebb and flow in everything. In nature as well as in magic there is a balance that must be maintained. The ancient Celts believed the universe is divided into three realms, Albios, what most people would call heaven, or the upper-world. Then there is Bitu, this world, or the world of living beings. Last, there's hell, the dark-world, Dubnos. To me, these represent what we would call dimensions today. These dimensions exist in a very delicate equilibrium that is tested once every millennia. Accordingly, every one thousand years, dark magics, dark forces or demons, call them what you like, rise out of a rift between this world and Dubnos, to battle with the forces of light from Albios for dominion over the earth. The ruler of these dark forces is called Baylor. One thousand years ago, the leader of the forces of light was Merlin. My direct ancestor."

Her pretty eyes went round at his words, but all she said was, "Let me guess, the time for this battle is again fast approaching."

"Yes. What's more, that rift is located in the center of a stone circle on my estate in England."

"So that's why I've sensed some sort of clock running out for you," she mused. "It all makes sense now. You've been on a time constraint all these months."

He nodded. "That's why I need to find the others like me. I need as much help as I can get if I am going to stop dark magic and the demons who practice it from taking over the world just as my ancestor Merlin did a thousand years ago. He managed it, but it cost King Arthur his life and destroyed Camelot. I am not sure if I am strong enough. I cannot do it alone. Baylor must be defeated without the mass destruction this time."

Jessilyn let him speak and took it all in, for the moment saying nothing, but then she murmured, "My God, you haven't been searching for your kin or even for students, you've been recruiting for an army." Shock and horror filled her voice, replacing the numbness she exhibited before. "And I've been helping you. I've been instrumental. You couldn't have done any of this without me." She gestured a little wildly and turned from him.

"Jessilyn –"

He stretched out his hand to her, but she shook him off. Without saying another word, she stalked out of the living room and headed toward the kitchen.

"No! You have been lying to all of us. You've been lying to me not for days or weeks but months! And that's not even mentioning the fact that some of these recruits are kids! Children, Thomas."

"You think I don't know that?! I have no choice. Ask yourself, is it better for them to fight or is it better for them and everyone else to die?!"

When she did not answer, he muttered, resentment coloring his tone, "That's what I thought."

She shook her head in denial of him and his reasoning. "I don't know you at all."

"You do know me. I didn't lie. I didn't tell you everything, I admit. Not because I didn't want to or because I was trying to manipulate you. I did it to protect you. The less you knew the better."

"Who the hell ever said I need your protection! If I had known what was happening I could have defended myself tonight. Instead, I almost died because I had no idea what was going on!"

"I realize that now. It was my hope it wouldn't come after you, that you wouldn't be connected to this or me. I must've gotten careless or perhaps it's getting stronger. I don't know which. What I do know is I never wanted this to happen. Everything I have ever done has been to protect you and everyone else in this whole bloody world!"

"Well then stop!" She was shouting at the top of her lungs now, but she couldn't seem to prevent it. "Let people help you for once. Let me help you! I can study these dark forces like I've studied you and we can figure out a way to defeat them together. We might even have already figured out a solution to this problem if you had come to me."

"Because together we are unstoppable." His lips twitched in the ghost of a smile, but he was dead serious.

When he glanced over, hers were pressed together in a tight line. "You're damned right."

She took a deep breath and poured them both a glass of wine. "Drink this and start talking," she ordered. "Don't stop until you tell me all of it. And Thomas, one thing, no more lies including ones of omission. One more, just one, and we're through. Done. Finished. Got it?"

With a sigh of great relief, Thomas nodded his agreement and did as he was told.

It took time, but he related the whole story. He related the entire history and his part in it. He spoke of forces of darkness which must be defeated by him and anyone else willing to help. He told her what said dark forces were made up of and how they could perhaps be conquered, as well as their origins and capabilities. All he knew poured out.

"Do you understand now?"

"I think I might be beginning to." Her tone was careful, neutral and he took hope.

"I'm glad."

When he reached out to take her hand, she evaded him and her expression was sterner than he had ever seen it. "I meant what I said though. No more lies, no more omissions."

"I promise."

This time when he reached for her hand, she let him take it and bring it to his lips.

****

"We need to study it, you know." When Jessilyn said this to him a few days later in the lab, her tone was casual. With deliberate movements, he set down the test tube in his hand, left what he was working on and gave her an intense, not at all pleased look.

She glanced over at him and saw the expression on his face. "You seem surprised and I don't know why. I want to help."

"I'm not sure that it is a good idea," he told her.

"My helping or studying it at all?"

"Both."

"Why not? The thing tried to murder me after all. I don't want it hurting anyone else. The best way I know to stop that from happening is to study it. Its strengths and, even better, its weaknesses."

"No."

She made an impatient noise low in her throat. "You know I'm very good at what I do. I can help. So, I'm going to ask again, why not?"

"Because I don't want you anywhere near that thing, okay!" The words ended on a shout. He took a deep breath and did his best to get himself under control. Accomplishing this was vital and, after a monumental effort, he did. A moment later, he drew near and took her face gently in his hands. "Baylor came so close to killing you, Jess. I'm not ever going to let that happen again, especially not now."

"What, since we're seeing each other now you mean? Well, to use a British expression, bollocks to that. I want to be more than your star scientist on tap or your friend or even your lover. I want to be your partner. I want, no I need, you to understand I am your equal, even if in many ways, I am your opposite."

"My equal? Sometimes I can barely keep up with you. You are so smart and so strong. You are the strongest woman I know and I admire you in so many ways. But that aside, I need to protect you."

"I've told you before, I don't need you to protect me. I need you to trust me. I need you to trust I am strong enough to stand beside you."

"I do trust you."

The words spilled out before he could stop them. Then he clamped his mouth shut because he wasn't ready to tell her the rest of what he was beginning to feel. He was falling in love with her. Hell, he was probably already there. Admitting to himself and to her that he trusted her was a huge step off that particular emotional cliff, he was well aware. He couldn't deny he was bloody terrified and for now one step was quite enough for him.

The smile she gave him was well worth it. "Good."

She grabbed her tablet and woke it up. As he watched her, he hoped and prayed, no, he vowed, their trust in one another and his protective instincts would not be mutually exclusive. He would keep her safe, he would retain her trust and he would make sure she was a part of all of this, even dangerous as it was, no matter what.

Still beaming, she said, "Let's get started."

****

Their first date had been the beginning, but after the attempted abduction, they became even more of a tightknit unit. Over the next weeks, they spent more and more time together, until all their waking hours and some when they should have been sleeping were spent with each other. After their first date, caution ruled Jessilyn. She was wary of jumping into anything too soon despite all the fun she was having.

So, they availed themselves of all the entertainment they could and sampled every bit of what Thomas's world had to offer. The facility had a movie theater, miniature golf, a skating rink, even a small bowling alley and they enjoyed them all. They also made use of the Olympic sized pool, the gym and even the sauna once or twice. They took turns cooking each other meals. They did all of that and at the end of every date they stayed at second base.

It was rather high school, but Jessilyn also found it to be interesting. Dating him without sharing his bed was exciting, tantalizing, but, it had to be said, also frustrating. Still, a whole month was about enough of that and she would tell him, or better yet show him, soon.

She was even surer of that when they ended up on her sofa and he was touching her.

"If you don't let me have you soon, I think I'm going to go insane." He murmured the words against her ear then grazed his teeth down the side of her neck.

She gasped and shifted against him. In response, he groaned and moved over her.

"If you don't let *me* have *you* soon, I'm the one who's going to go insane," she whispered back.

Never taking his gaze from hers, he trailed his fingertips in a slow path up her thigh then inward until his hand was between her legs. She twined her fingers with his then arched into their joined hands.

Her ecstatic moan was cut off by a knock at the door. A deep, strangled noise emanated from Thomas's throat and he let his head fall to her shoulder, but after taking a second or two, he got to his feet then helped her to a sitting position.

"I'll get rid of them. Give me a sec." With a quick, hard kiss, he started toward the door.

Jessilyn registered the murmur of voices in a vague way as she tried to collect herself. Her entire body was still burning from his touch and she was finding it hard to think. Then Thomas spoke, in a louder, altogether different tone of voice. "Damn it!" Her would-be lover let out an exasperated groan then said, "Fine. Give me a few minutes and I'll be right there."

He rejoined her on the couch and brushed his hands back and forth from her shoulders to her elbows. "I am so sorry. There's been an accident at the lab."

Concern eclipsed her frustration and focused her mind. "Oh no, is everyone okay? Is anyone hurt?"

"No one is hurt, but they need my help sorting things out," he admitted.

"I'll come with you if you want. I'd like to help."

"I would appreciate that. I could use all the help I can get." He brushed a hand over her cheek and sighed. "This is not at all what I had in mind for an end to the evening."

"Me either, but what can you do?" She shrugged, took the interruption philosophically, then rose.

And found herself caught up in a brief but intense kiss that heated her blood right back up again.

"To be continued." He said the words against her lips, then pulled away.

"Definitely," she agreed and followed him out.

Chapter Four

Thomas all but lived in his office over the next weeks. Filled with sleek, cutting edge equipment, state of the art computers and an ergonomic chair covered in black leather, it more than suited his needs. Whenever he entered, he experienced a certain satisfaction knowing he had all his tools at his disposal, as he did in his lab.

As he settled to work, he reflected that sitting in his new office designing a series of tests for prospective students was something he never thought he would enjoy doing so much. Any person with the genetic markers for magical ability would be contacted, but as Jessilyn pointed out, that didn't mean they could actually do magic. Thus, the tests. In spite of all the other balls he had in the air, he made time to create these assessments and then conduct them on himself because he considered them a priority. Each exam would gauge various skill levels. Areas of expertise in different types of magic would be evaluated, first and foremost, pure magic (He might as well call it the pure power inherent in the very cells of the mage's body, if he wanted to get technical). This power could be and often was channeled into areas such as healing, divination, and finally spells/potions. He suspected, and as yet this was all theory, each person's talents would be most apparent and manifest most strongly in one or perhaps two of these areas.

The whole process was fascinating and at times even tipped over into entertaining because he was not alone. In addition to being both scientist and subject, he had Jessilyn there for him to bounce ideas off of. She had plenty of her own thoughts regarding their experiments. Everything from how to conduct them, to what type, to when. It soon became abundantly clear to him that professionally they were better together than apart. As for personally? He felt drawn to her more and more every day. Particularly after their interrupted evening, he was certain she was his ideal partner.

Shaking his head to clear it, he tried to focus on his task and not the beautiful woman captivating him. It seemed as though every waking moment his thoughts threatened to drift to Jessilyn without his constant supervision. He closed his eyes, took a deep breath and directed his attention to the new test he was devising to measure healing gifts.

****

"I want to show you something I've been working on," Jessilyn told Thomas some days later. She led him over to a small clear box about as large as a jewelry case. "It's a contained dampening field or, as I like to call it, a CDF for short."

"There is an inner and outer wall and molecules are sent round and round in between that inner and outer wall in waves. If I am right, the speed and density of the molecules will act as a barrier through which no magic can penetrate."

He picked up the clear 8"x8"x8" cube to study it in more detail. "I am intrigued."

"So, in your expert opinion as a scientist and magician, the theory is sound?

"It is. As a scientist and magician, I am hugely impressed," he admitted.

"Thank you. I need your help though. I need your help to build it, test it and, ideally, modify it."

"Modify it how?"

"First, it's size. It's far too small of course. Second, I wonder even about the basic design. It would be far better if we could also come up with something less locked into one fixed area. Something more portable, a movable device of some sort would be preferable. Which brings me to problem number three. As of now, this will work on any type of magic. I want something that will work on dark magic only." She glanced over at him. "Is that even possible?"

"The origin of all magic is the same. It all comes from the same root. You are asking whether we can determine where, when and how it splits into two distinct branches, dark and light."

"Yes." She beamed at him, pleased beyond words he understood.

"It seems to me you are also asking several even more complicated questions."

"Such as?"

"Can magic itself be separated from its intent? Are light and dark magic inherently different or it is all perception? Does it all have to do with the motive or object of the magician? Is magic a tool that becomes a weapon when in the wrong hands, like a gun? Or is it evil or good in and of itself?"

"Exactly." She paused and looked at him, her expression full of expectation. "So, you're the magician. You've practiced all your life. What do you think?"

"I think the question is a fascinating one. One I've often tried to answer but never have, not fully and not at all to my satisfaction. In my experience, to some degree, the spell itself, along with the elements used to cast it, determines the type of magic practiced. For example, if I am doing a simple scrying spell, all I need is a crystal and a map. On the other hand, if I am seeking to harm that usually requires blood. The more harmful the spell, the more power needed and the more blood magic required, the ultimate being the torture and death of multiple victims."

Jessilyn swallowed hard. "Mass human sacrifice."

Thomas inclined his head. "But there's more to it. I think when a person casts a spell or works any bit of magic there is a statement of intent, separate from the elements of the spell, which the universe can recognize and respond to."

"You think it is possible then? To come up with something that will limit magic of evil intent, black magic for want of a better term?"

He shrugged. "I have no idea, but I think it's worth a try."

"Well, we'll work on it. For now, let's test this prototype and see if it works. I want you to try to move this pencil." She placed the pencil inside of the CDF.

As the memory of their first experiment together flitted through his mind, his lips curved for a moment. He stilled then focused his mind and nothing happened. What should have been a simple matter was impossible. The pencil stirred not one inch in spite of the fact that he was expending more energy than he would normally have needed to move a car. After several minutes of hard effort, he gave it up. Sweat prickled on his skin and his breathing was heavy when he admitted the truth. "It works and damned well too."

"Really?" Her face lit up. "That's great! It's a place to start anyway."

He studied the device with a combination of fascination and wariness. "You think you can adapt it to a larger area then? Create something for an average size room maybe?"

"With the help of your engineers? Absolutely." She furrowed her brow the way she did when, he now recognized, she was thinking very hard. "I still say we need something more portable in addition to this. Now I have the basic principle down, I'll work on designing something."

"How about I work on the dark magic only aspect starting with your prototype?"

"Hmmm, that sounds like a good idea."

Her hesitation was slight, but it was loud and clear to one who knew her well. "Except?"

"Except how will you or I or any of us truly test the CDF against dark magic? You are so strong, but you are a white wizard to your core."

"Thank you for the compliment. There are certain gray areas I could explore for the sake of science."

"But there is a world of difference between the two. Gray is not dark."

He shrugged. "I know, but like you said, it's a start. We'll worry about the rest later."

"One thing at a time," Jessilyn agreed.

****

"Are you sure about this? You're sure this will contain it?" Thomas studied the room with an anxious expression. It had taken several weeks of uninterrupted effort to create the CDF in its current form, which was large enough to encompass the entirety of what they were calling the holding room.

"As sure as I can be. Baylor and his dark forces are the source of all dark magic, so this should work fine, in theory at least. Besides there is no time limit here, even if all we can keep it contained for is a matter of seconds then send it back to hell, we will obtain valuable data which will help us defeat it. Why?"

"We're taking a huge risk. I've studied this thing all my life and I've tangled with it a few times, while you've gone up against it once. I'm not sure you realize how powerful the dark forces are."

She narrowed her eyes at him. "It did try to kill me remember? I have some idea." Her expression softened a bit as she caught and held his gaze. "Trust, remember? You need to trust me. Trust this force field I've created will contain Baylor and all his dark forces at least temporarily and I will trust you to use your power if and when the CDF fails."

He kissed her long and slow and said the words that came a little easier now. "I trust you."

She gave him that sweet smile again then nodded, her expression turning deadly serious. "Call him."

She stepped into observation, flipped the switch to activate the CDF then signaled him to begin. He centered himself, raised his arms and did as instructed. Using a combination of an ancient spell and his own power, he called Baylor and his dark forces.

The shriek that filled his ears was of a bird of prey swooping in for its kill or maybe a thousand damned souls crying out in agony all at once. Along with this sound came a rising wind and the ground shook under his feet. Although it was at its heart unchanged, this time the dark force was less dense but more all-pervasive. It gained strength by the second, and worse, it also solidified. Within moments, it blew the connecting door between the holding room and observation off its hinges. It rushed into observation as if the CDF were not even there.

Right away, it made for Jessilyn, swirling around her like some dark hurricane.

Instinct kicked in as soon as he saw her in danger. It was clear to him that the dark forces were not going down without a fight. With every bit of strength he had, he began to force it back into the void that was its home. Naturally, it resisted. In response to his interference, it shattered the thick glass between the lab and observation. Anything not nailed down flew at him, but he deflected the objects to either side of himself before impact. The walls shuddered and the floor buckled the same way it had when the dark forces had tried to take Jessilyn weeks before.

Even in the midst of all that, Baylor tried to tempt him. It called to the blackest part of his soul, but he was unmoved. He must contain it or all was lost.

Somehow, he managed it. Even though it felt like trying to hold back the ocean and its tide, gradually, he pushed it back. In the end, the last remnants of the dark forces disappeared back into the void.

"Jessilyn?!" Thomas croaked. He could not see through the dust and debris, but sheer panic propelled him blindly forward.

Coughing echoed and he lurched toward the sound. "I'm okay. I'm over here," Jessilyn called.

At last, he reached her. For one blissful second, he wrapped her in his arms, but then he drew away to run his hands over her, checking for injury.

"I'm okay," she assured him again. "I'm a little bruised, but I'm fine. What about you? Are you all right?

"Yeah." He took stock of a few minor injuries. "I'm still on my feet anyway."

"You were amazing. Your power was... I've never seen anything like it. You saved us both."

Something hot and primal surged through him, but he tamped it down. Instead, he offered her his hand. "C'mon, let me take you to your quarters so you can clean up." She gripped his hand and he led her down the corridor.

When they arrived at her rooms and she reached to open her door, he put out a hand to stop her. "Let me in." They both knew he wasn't just talking about into her room. "Please."

"Absolutely." Without another word, she opened the door and she was his.

"We almost died," he murmured. "I'll be damned if I'll die without ever having done this."

"I feel the same way."

His desire slammed into her body and mind simultaneously and she gasped.

"Tell me you want this," he demanded in a hoarse whisper.

He knew her answer, experienced the upsurge of desire in her mind, even before she spoke. "God, yes."

Those two words were more than enough and he stopped thinking. All he could do was feel. He gorged himself on a million different sensual impressions. To be specific, he breathed in the clean scent of her hair. The warmth of her skin reached him even through layers of clothing and he basked in it.

All that was for a start. It was not even mentioning the electric sensations coursing through his own body. Sharp pleasure rose everywhere she touched him. When he touched her, Jessilyn's pleasure surged and, connected as they were, it filled his mind, all but swamped him, until he could barely breathe. He didn't care; he was happy to die in her arms.

Desire, he'd never desired anyone so much. He was half-blind with it. Naked, he needed her naked right now, so he pulled the soft blue cotton t-shirt she wore up and over her head then he damn well got rid of his own. The touch of her bare skin all but drove him over the edge and he was fine with that. Urgency filled him, telling him he had to be inside of her now, in every possible way, body as well as mind.

****

Taking one brief second to savor the prospect, she opened the door then closed it behind them and a moment later he was on her. All restraint gone, he kissed her with unprecedented openness. There was passion and carnality and an uprush of something, some emotion, only an undercurrent before, and Jessilyn reveled in it. She had, of course, had sex before, but it had never been like this for her. She didn't feel he was intent on just shagging her; she felt... owned on every level and in the best possible way.

Because of his telepathy, he could and would give her everything she could dream of. He would be everything she could ever want in a lover. All she had to do was think it and it was done. All of it was hers for the taking. All this time she had known that, even experienced it to some extent. With each kiss, each touch, she had felt it. But this? This level of utter possession was something she never imagined. It was outside the realm of her experience, but that didn't mean she wasn't enjoying it immensely.

As attuned to her as he was, he very quickly learned exactly what gave her the most pleasure. She did her level best to respond in kind and she found, somewhat to her surprise, it wasn't so very hard. If she was open to him, he was open to her as well. In fact, he was the most open lover she had ever had, willing to be totally vulnerable. So, she was visited by a fierce wish to know his mind, to know him the same way he now knew her. Understanding there was no sense longing for what could never be, she tried to put the idea out of her mind and content herself with what was. Not all that difficult to do since what was, the reality right in front of her, was amazing. Maybe she would never be able to read his mind, but she could read his eyes. As for his body, well, she intended to learn every inch of it.

For a start, she kissed him. Then she ran her hands over his torso, pleased beyond measure with his sculpted chest, broad shoulders and muscled abs.

God, she loved the way he touched her, like he couldn't get enough. When his hand glided between her legs, she let out a moan then without warning the words, 'I have to be inside of her right now.' echoed through her head as clear as a bell. Shock diverted her attention from the amazing things he was doing to her at least for a moment because he hadn't spoken. It was his thoughts, she realized. For one electric moment, she had been able to hear his thoughts.

Could she again? To get his attention, she took hold of his face, and tilted it up from where it was buried in her neck so they were eye to eye. She projected her own thoughts to him as best she could. 'I heard you.' Then she listened as hard as she could for his voice in her mind. Unlike before, it came from a great distance, but she heard, 'What?'

At that she laughed, because even in her mind, his voice was breathless.

'I heard you,' she repeated.

His jaw went slack as what she was trying to tell him clicked. 'How?'

He looked so adorably, endearingly, downright charmingly dazed that she kissed him. She couldn't stop herself.

When their lips met, she was hit with a wave of desire so intense she shook with it. It rolled through her and she gasped. Even though she swallowed hard, when she spoke her voice was low and husky. "I don't know, but will you kiss me again? I'm pretty sure I felt –"

Heat rushed up her cheeks as he obeyed. After one fiery instant, she tore her mouth from his. "Oh Lord, I can feel what you feel," she told him. Now it was her turn to feel stunned. "How the hell can this be happening?"

****

Thomas felt like he was dreaming, but Jessilyn's question forced his mind back into working order and he made his lips form words. "Hell if I know, but I am not inclined to question it. Not right now." Then he took her mouth while his hand plunged back between her legs to caress and arouse. In response, she moaned and reached for him. She managed one long, languid stroke over his rock-hard prick before he stilled her hand.

Gaze locked to his, she tightened her grip on him. Even through layers of clothing the sensation was so intense the hand restraining hers loosened just enough and she caressed him firmly.

"Christ!" The exclamation tore from him as his body arched, an involuntary motion he had no hope of controlling. In one lightning fast move, he had her in his arms and strode purposefully to her bed.

A soft laugh filled his ears as she repeated the caress once he laid her down on the mattress, but more slowly, prolonging the sensation. "Do you like that?" she teased as she did it a third time. And then another and another. He groaned and almost came right then and there.

It was long past time for more clothes to come off. With his mind, he started to unbutton her jeans while his hands went to his own. Her gaze shot down her body to the now gaping garment and watched for a long moment. After which she raised her eyes and examined the bare flesh he was revealing. Then at last, he was rewarded with her hands fumbling at the waistband of his boxers. After that, things got a bit blurry for him until all their clothes were gone.

He took one swift moment to look his fill, to worship her with his eyes then did what he'd ached to do for so long and worshipped her with his body. He communicated his adoration in every way he could think of, by kneading, caressing even licking beautiful breasts, by grasping a sleek hip, kissing the pulse at her neck and most of all, by living and breathing for her response.

Response which was not long in coming and was exquisite. Now she could read his mind, she was learning in short order every way he liked to be touched and he was utterly captivated. How could he not be? To keep things quite equal between them, however, he slid his fingers in and out of her wet heat as he simultaneously rubbed his palm over her mons until she let out a whimper and whispered, "Please." He took her right to the edge, but he would not let her go over, not until she pleaded with him, body and mind.

Being inside of her mind, even while touching her was not new to him. Not for the first time, he felt her pleasure even as he experienced his own and, as always, it was a gift. Yet having her inside his mind was a novel experience. The searing intimacy of it all left him emotionally unsteady. It made him yearn. And by God it made him feel reckless and eager to explore all the implications of their new link.

Deliberately, he sent her an image of the two of them in her bed, him above her, plunging into her over and over. In answer, she sent him an image of her astride him, his mouth at her breast. Already stiff as iron, he got even harder and brought the image from her mind to life.

Unable and unwilling to hide anything from her, he let his passion show on his face and rein free through his mind. She was the only woman he could ever imagine being this close to and he wanted her to know it. At last, as he entered her, inch by delicious inch, the world fell away until it was the two of them alone. The love he had been experiencing for weeks, even months now, swamped him and he found he also didn't want to die without speaking the words.

"I love you," he whispered.

She gasped and her pretty eyes widened then went soft and dreamy. "I love you too."

****

Wordlessly, those beautiful eyes of Thomas's asked if she was all right. The question in them made Jessilyn smile gently and her heart glow. In answer, she arched into him, taking him deeper. With a groan, he began an enthralling rocking motion. She lost every inhibition she ever had as she met his movements with her own. Opening her mind to him, she did her best to give him everything he wanted. His mind was beautiful, she realized, full of intelligence and life. There was such sweet tenderness and love for her inside of him, along with a healthy dose of pure lust. One body, one soul, one mind, she thought, dazed. As at last he joined his body with hers, he gave her his heart and his soul as well and she marveled at the gift. She was swept up in a wave of love and desire and longing unlike anything she had ever felt before. As he thrust into her over and over, she climaxed and he was a heartbeat behind her.

****

Minutes or maybe hours later, she had no idea which since time had ceased to have any meaning for her, Jessilyn stretched, one languorous motion, then asked, "God, why didn't we do this ages ago?"

"You had lots of rational reasons as I recall," Thomas replied as his hand drifted through her hair in a lazy way.

"Rational reasons?" She feigned a puzzled expression. "Hmm, I don't remember that."

He chuckled. "Oh, you did."

"I was a fool," she informed him. "Let me make it up to you."

Being no fool himself, he let her.

Quite some time later, with the aftermath still racing through their veins, he returned to the subject of rational reasons. "Waiting so long, it wasn't because I didn't want you. I hope you know that."

"Hmm, I do. I hope you know the same."

"I do." He kissed the top of her head. "Do you know why I think we waited? I have a theory."

"Oh? I'd love to hear it."

"I think we waited so long because we both wanted it to be right. The right time, the right moment, *right* for both of us. Then tonight, we both could've died and I thought, if not now, when?"

"I thought the same." She paused a moment then continued, "When you touched me and I could feel what you felt? I've never felt so in sync with another human being in my life. How is this even possible?

I've never had any extra sensory perception before. As far as I knew, I was non-magical."

"I've been thinking about that. Jess, have you run our protocols on yourself? It is clear you have some magic in your blood."

"I never thought to, but I will now. As soon as we are back in the lab tomorrow morning, I should say. I still can't believe it." She turned on her side to face him and he mirrored her movement. Then she said in a confessional sort of way, "You know, right before it happened, I was thinking about how much I wanted to know your mind the way you know mine. It was like I willed it to happen."

"Or maybe we both did. I was thinking the same thing. Oh not about E.S.P. particularly, but that I wanted you to know me as much as possible, on every level, in every way a human being can know another."

"Really? So that was as new to you as it was to me?" Jessilyn asked, shy.

"Mmm hmm. I've never shared my mind like that with another human being. I've never even wanted to."

"And now?"

"Now, I wouldn't have it any other way and, however it happened, I'm glad. This has been amazing."

"It has." She placed a hand dead center of his chest. "Does it have to be over? It's... I'm not ready for this night to end yet."

"Neither am I. I'm not going anywhere. Not ever."

His lips met hers, sealing the bargain, and he made love to her one more time.

Chapter Five

From that night on, they spent every evening together, either in Thomas's rooms or in hers, whichever place they found themselves in after a long day of work. So a week later, Jessilyn was surprised to wake after an hour of fitful sleep to find herself in his bed alone. The clock on the mantelpiece chimed midnight as she wandered into the living room toward the soft lamplight expecting to find him. She was not disappointed. He looked almost unbearably sexy in green boxers and a white t-shirt as he sat staring at a laptop screen. She put a hand on his shoulder to get his attention and he carried it to his lips.

"It's late, sweetheart," she murmured. "What are you working on?"

He ran a hand through his hair and stifled a yawn. "Right now? I'm working on turning my ancestral home, the family estate, into a school."

He tapped a notepad with a long list written on the first page. "Extensive renovation and repurposing will have to be done, requiring a massive amount of paperwork, permits for a start. In addition, I have to make provisions for the care and safety of all the future inhabitants."

He turned to her and there was an earnest, determined expression on his face she found most appealing. "You see I am not only thinking of the war. The one great battle we will fight is the most important thing, of course, because if we don't win that then none of the rest will follow. But I am also thinking long term. I want this school to be around to educate young magicians long after the battle is won. Hell, I'd like it to be around until the next great battle a thousand years from now."

"That is an ambitious and noble goal. What can I do to help?"

"I'm glad you asked. Tomorrow I'd like you to take a look at the ideas I have so far about the renovations, the structure of the school and a thousand other things and then tell me your own. I value your opinion and would love your take."

"Done."

He rose from his chair. "Right now, however…" He captured her hand and led her to his bed. More than willing, she followed.

****

Months passed as they engaged in challenging research and enjoyed each other. The one dark spot on Jessilyn's horizon was she was back to square one with the CDF. Since she had to start from scratch after their spectacular failure with the dark forces, she had her work cut out for her. It was months of covering the same ground, refining and improving. Even so, she was happier than she had ever been in her life. Sadly, all good things come to an end and Jessilyn should have remembered that. Instead, she was stunned when Thomas sat her down, not only to a meal at his table, but to talk about next steps.

"Jess, I think it's about time to leave here," he began.

Surprise shot through Jessilyn, but it shouldn't have. Their research was all but done and his home was in the U.K. after all.

In a matter-of-fact way, he continued, "We've got a working protocol and we are finding other descendants. More to the point, I can feel the time drawing nearer every day and I can feel the deep-seated need to fight the dark forces calling me home. That's where this all has to happen. Not here, but in Kent, at home, right on my doorstep."

She cleared her throat and took a bold leap. "Well then, I'm coming with you."

"Of course you are." That he spoke as though her coming with him wasn't even a question eased her fluttery stomach. "As long as you're sure this is what you want. This life is dark and dangerous and it won't be easy."

"What do I care about danger? This life is what I want as long as it's with you."

The serious lines of his face eased as he captured her hand in his and kissed it. "Well, that's all right then."

"Besides, I want to see this through. After all our work, after everything we've already been through, good and bad, I wouldn't miss this for the world."

"Brilliant. I'll start making our travel arrangements."

****

The next day, while Jessilyn compiled data, Thomas drove the thirty miles into Roswell to shop for the perfect ring for the woman he wanted to marry. He was damned nervous and although he felt like a bit of a fool for feeling that way, he tried to cut himself some slack. He was about to ask the most important question of his life; he had a right to be nervous. No matter what, no matter her answer, his life would never be the same. Such a big step ought to give a man pause, he reasoned. Oddly, he didn't question what her answer would be. He believed deep in his heart she would say yes.

He stepped into J & L Jewelers and took in the sand colored tile, the wood and glass of the cases but most of all the top-quality gems. Gorgeous diamonds, rubies and sapphires in elegant settings impressed him. Taking a deep breath, he headed straight to the first salesperson he saw.

"Hi, how may I help you?" The elegant, middle-aged woman behind the counter inquired.

"Good morning. I am here to buy an engagement ring for the most amazing woman in the world. Can you show me all of your custom-made pieces to start? If I don't find something suitable then I'll have a look at any designs you might have."

She beamed. "Of course, sir. I am Harriet Johnson and I will help you find the perfect ring for your fiancée, Mr. …"

He took a deep breath. "Dr. Thomas Avery. I place myself in your very capable hands, Ms. Johnson."

****

After a long day of wrapping things up at the lab, Jessilyn was looking forward to a quiet evening at home, snuggled up with Thomas and a good book. Instead, she opened the door to find her apartment transformed by the soft glow of countless candles.

Her face broke into a slow smile as she asked, "What's all this?"

He held out both hands to her and she took them. "It's to thank you for all your hard work at the lab. It's to spoil you and to show you how wonderful I think you are. It's to celebrate finishing what we first set out to do. And it's to commemorate the start of a new journey, the Avery Institute and… our marriage. If you'll have me."

Jessilyn drew in a huge lungful of air then stopped breathing altogether as Thomas got down on one knee and produced a velvet ring box from his pocket. He lifted the lid on a flawless three caret diamond with platinum band that sparkled in the candlelight.

"Jess, this past year with you, has been the happiest of my life. Getting to know you has been my very great privilege because you are a woman of unimaginable beauty as well as formidable intelligence, fierce loyalty and unfathomable joy. Jessilyn Elizabeth Matthews, will you be my wife?"

Tears of the unfathomable joy he mentioned rolled down her cheeks and she didn't bother to stop them or even wipe them away, she let them fall. She couldn't have held them back even if she'd tried. "Yes," she whispered. Then, more loudly, "Yes, yes, yes!" An instant later she was caught up in his arms, he spun her around and they were both laughing, crying and kissing all at the same time.

His hands were trembling as much as hers were as he slipped the ring onto her finger. "You have made me the happiest man alive. I love you. I love you so much." He punctuated the words with kisses and she responded in kind, pressing her lips to every bit of him she could reach.

His kisses slowed then his hands got busy unbuttoning her shirt. "Let me show you how much, wife."

Jessilyn's mind started to cloud with desire, but she managed to point out, "I'm not your wife yet."

He shrugged. "It might not be official yet, but in my heart, we're already husband and wife."

"In mine as well."

"Well, then let's celebrate." He refilled both champagne glasses, handed her one, kept hold of his own, snagged the half-empty bottle and took her to bed.

****

If their relationship had progressed at a pace as slow as molasses up to that point, after their engagement the very opposite became true. Later, Jessilyn described the time as a whirlwind of work, play (whenever they could manage it, which wasn't often) and preparation. Mere weeks later, they married in a tiny church on the outskirts of Roswell. They decided on a very small but joyous affair, with guests including the team of scientists working with them attending along with a few close friends and immediate family. In total, forty people were present for the ceremony, but for Jessilyn that made it all the more special because those most important to her were a part of it.

In spite of the small number of guests, their wedding was a celebration for all that and as she waited at the rear of the church to join Thomas, her heart overflowed with happiness. They would belong to each other. She would be his and he would be hers as never before. She walked down the aisle toward him with a sense of utter rightness unlike anything she had ever felt in her life.

The minister said the traditional words of the ceremony and then they promised to spend their lives together. Her life with all of its ups and downs, hits and misses, pain and sorrow and above all, love and joy would be hers to share with him. A year ago, she never could have imagined it, but now here she was on the cusp of a whole new journey. She could hardly wait. The adventure had only just begun.

****

It was done. They were married. Thomas could barely believe it. Pure, untainted, wholesome, innocent joy of a kind he hadn't felt since childhood filled him. That elation was coupled with desire for her, his beautiful wife, which was far from innocent. It ebbed and flowed through him as she chatted with their co-workers then danced with her father. This incandescent creature was his to love and cherish and even, or hell, if he was honest, especially, to revere.

At long last, he was able to tear her away for another dance, their second as a married couple. The band played something soft, low and romantic, a song she loved to hear and he was pleased with it and the world in general.

As he swept her onto the floor, he drew her close and murmured, "Hello, wife."

"Hello, husband," she replied with a breathy laugh.

He took in her simple white chiffon gown and the spray of pink roses and baby's breath in her hair then said, "Have I told you how lovely you look?" When she said nothing, he continued, "No? Well, I've never seen you look more beautiful."

She beamed up at him. "Now you have." Looking him over from head to toe, she added, "You don't look so bad yourself, handsome."

While taking her through the steps of the dance, he held her close and she clung to him. As the music faded, Jessilyn whispered, "I so want to be alone with you."

"Say the word and I can make that happen." Deliberately, via telepathy, he sent her one hot image of the two of them alone, naked and in his bed, for encouragement.

She sucked in a breath then let it out. "Very tempting. This isn't some party, it is our wedding reception and we can't leave yet."

"Okay, when?"

"Uhmm…" Her voice trailed off as he nibbled her earlobe.

He bit just hard enough then demanded in harsh whisper, "When?"

"Oh, Lord… not for… a least another hour maybe two."

He swore. "Are you sure about that?" For further incentive, he sent a wave of pleasure through her mind, making them both tremble. "Maybe we could slip away for a few minutes?"

"Thomas!" Shocked amusement along with pure yearning crossed her face and her cheeks heated to as pale a pink as the roses in her hair, charming him. "This is our wedding day; ergo we are the guests of honor. Ergo we can't disappear, not even for a few minutes."

He groaned into her hair. "One hour then. After that…"

She fixed him with her gaze. "One hour," she promised.

****

One hour had never seemed longer to Thomas in his life, but at last it was over. The cake was cut, the bouquet thrown and they were sent off with bubbles bursting off his wife's gleaming hair. After all the traditions were observed, they were alone in a limo rented for the occasion and on their way to the best hotel in Roswell. The drive was a short one, ten minutes no more. Yet, it was long enough for a few breathless kisses.

When they arrived, he checked them into the hotel as quickly as possible. The bellhop followed with their bags. Once the young employee was in possession of a generous tip, he left them and they were alone.

As he had earlier in the afternoon, Thomas smiled at her and said, "Hello again, wife."

She responded in kind. "Hello, husband."

Thomas took his new bride's hand and pressed his lips to her knuckles. He let his fingers skim up her arm, but resisted the almost overwhelming urge to touch her anywhere else. Keeping himself under tight rein right now was imperative because he was afraid of what would happen if he didn't. His control was hanging by a thread as it was. "I thought this day would never end. All I could think about when we were at the reception was you." With deliberate care, he unbuttoned his shirt. "I don't think I can wait one more minute to be inside of you."

■■

Her smile was wicked and sensual and everything a man could want. "Good, because I feel the same way." She reached behind her back and in one deft motion, dealt with the zipper of the simple cotton dress she had changed into for the short journey. "I feel impatient." She let the dress skim down her body and drop to the floor.

"Come here then."

****

"Come here then."

Jessilyn heard the words and a shiver passed through every inch of her. The words were command and seduction combined, both mingled in equal measure, and she could not have resisted him if her life had depended on it. With all her senses heightened, she obeyed.

Over the past seven months, they had made love countless times until the point where she was as familiar with him as she was with herself. Yet, tonight the intensity was sharper, the attraction deeper, more overtly sensual, than ever before. She was well acquainted with the taste of his mouth, the feel of his skin and she craved both. And, God, how she wanted to touch him.

So, she did. In no mood to deny herself, she let her hands and mouth roam over him, pausing at the places which brought him the most pleasure. Pressing her lips to the juncture of his neck and shoulder caused a hum of appreciation. Flicking her tongue over flat nipples elicited a gasp and so she lavished rapt attention on them. When she got a firm grip on his well-muscled ass and hauled him flush against her, a sound of satisfaction originated from deep in his throat.

He copied her movement and not only got his hands on her butt, but lifted her up and into him and then it was her turn to gasp. Unable to help himself or wait any longer, he braced her against a wall and kissed her hard until she was absolutely riveted.

Out of nowhere, her world tilted and she found herself easily supported in arms of corded steel as he carried her to the bed. Never breaking the kiss, he placed her on the king-sized mattress. Kneeling over her, he all but ripped his open shirt off the rest of the way then lifted her to undo the catch of her bra. Her body burned everywhere he touched her and his heated look held her so enthralled she moved not a muscle when he rose to rid himself of the last of his clothes. Instead, she remained sprawled back on the bed the better to enjoy the sight of him and all that gorgeous bare skin.

****

Feeling his wife's eyes on him was the most erotic experience of Thomas's life. So far. If having her eyes alone on him could make him feel this aroused, thinking of what would happen once she actually touched him sent tremors of need running through him. Being inside of her, mind and body? The mere thought of it brought him to the brink of climax.

"You are the sexiest, most beautiful man I have ever seen."

He tried to think up some sophisticated answer, but nothing came to mind. An irresistible urge to return the compliment rushed through him, but his brain was far too clouded with raw desire for him to come up with anything coherent much less eloquent.

Instead, he showed her. Determined to give all, to give everything, he opened his mind completely. As always, his body was hers to do with as she wished. It seemed she wanted to lavish as much pleasure on him as he lavished on her. Each caress became a back and forth interaction between them. Communication in its purest form. He swept his tongue over her pert nipple and she arched, telling him she wanted more. She rocked against his stunning erection and they both moaned.

Before her, he'd believed he'd understood people and their emotions. She showed him every day there was more. More emotion, more love, more life. When he sought her out, he'd had no idea how important she would become to him. Since she'd crashed into his life, she'd opened up his world.

From out of nowhere, the words that wouldn't come earlier were right on the tip of his tongue waiting to be said. He spoke even through the searing heat as he joined their bodies. "When I met you, I'd been alone for so long, I thought that's how it would always be. But now, here you are. Essential. Indispensable. Vital to me. You are the air I breathe. You are my heart and my soul. You are the best part of me. I love you."

He sank into her, then out. "I love you." And again. "I love you." And again.

His name was a gasp on her lips then, "I love you too, Tom." He thrust firm and deep, as deeply as he could go, until there was no him or her, only the two of them together, moving as one, hearts as one. Pleasure overwhelmed them both and there were no more words, only action until simultaneous release rushed through them.

****

After their unforgettable wedding night, they honeymooned in Greece. During the day, they swam in the Aegean and at night, they made love. There was no talk of work or the coming battle. Instead, they rejuvenated and recharged themselves while focusing on pure pleasure and cementing their new bond as husband and wife. It was the most perfect month of both their lives.

But in this life even perfect comes to an end sooner or later and they both knew they would have to go back to the real world at some point.

"This has been paradise," Thomas stated as they walked along the beach one golden afternoon.

"Yes, it has," she replied without looking at him. Instead, she kept her gaze focused on the sea, the setting sun and the horizon. "We have to leave soon though, don't we?"

He nodded. "We are more than ready for the next phase, so yes. It's time to go home."

She gave him a long, lingering kiss then said, "I'll go pack."

PART TWO: FORTIFICATION

Chapter Six

"So, here it is. Home," Thomas announced. After a drive of an hour and a half from Heathrow airport, they rounded a bend into a clearing and the car rolled to a stop as they came out of the trees. Thomas gestured to the large Elizabethan mansion, although he scarcely needed to since the massive structure dominated the landscape. It was old, with towers and turrets and too many windows for her to count, more like a castle than anything else. "Welcome to Avery Manor, soon to be home of the Avery Institute."

"Wow." That one word was all Jessilyn could manage, because once again, she was floored. After she picked her jaw up off the car mat, she turned to look at him. "You weren't kidding about the size of this place or its grandeur. I feel like I've been dropped onto the set of Downton Abbey."

"Actually, they did use the manor and the grounds for a few of the exterior shots. Mum was thrilled," he said with an absentminded glance over the grounds in question as he hit the gas and the car sped to the end of the drive.

This comment rendered her quite speechless until they arrived at the front entrance. A young man waited on the steps, ready to usher them in and Jessilyn saw it was the butler, Styles. After the two men exchanged affectionate greetings, she followed Thomas inside. As they crossed the threshold, Jessilyn tried to look everywhere at once while appearing not to look everywhere at once. Thomas smiled and showed her around.

"The estate as a whole, including the outbuildings, grounds etc., is in good shape, but will need some renovation and repurposing to make it viable as a school."

"You grew up here? With all this beauty? Amazing."

"I did, very happily." His smile held a touch of nostalgia unless she was much mistaken. "My parents were great and so was this place."

"Where are they? I take it they don't live here?"

He shook his head. "Dad died eight years ago. Mum's at their villa in the south of France. The climate there suits her, but she also spends a good part of the year here."

Doing her best not to gawk at the Vermeer painting on the wall, the object d'art in the sitting room, the antique furniture and Aubusson carpets throughout, she took it all in without any untoward ohhs or ahhs until they stopped before a set of double doors.

"I think this might end up being your favorite room in the whole house," he told her as he opened the entrance with a flourish.

Jessilyn gasped. The room was larger than some small-town branch libraries she had seen and looked to have a far better collection of books even at first glance. She stopped in the middle of the space and executed a complete 360-degree turn in order to take in every bit of it.

"Wow," she whispered again. For such an educated woman, one who prided herself on her gift with words, it humbled her to realize 'wow' was the best she could do.

"It is wonderful, isn't it? Feel free to read any book you like."

She wandered around the space glancing over the shelves. "Are you sure? Some of these look very old and expensive. Jesus, is that a first edition Pride and Prejudice?" She gasped again and was drawn toward the precious book, but kept her hands to herself even though she itched to touch it.

Thomas bent close and examined the spine. "It is." He removed it from the shelf and held it out to her. "Please, enjoy it with my compliments."

When she hesitated, he brushed his hand over her cheek. "What's mine is yours, wife."

A slow smile spread across her entire face. "Really?"

An answering smile curved his lips. "Really."

"Well, thank you, husband."

She took the book then ran a finger over the cover and thumbed through the pages with a careful reverence.

Thomas took one last look around. "Come on. There's more to see and the sooner you've seen all of it the sooner I can show you our bedroom. It is quite lovely, there is a four-poster bed made of oak by my grandfather and the most comfortable mattress you've ever slept on. The bedding is forest green and cream. The room itself is spacious and opens onto the terrace. Like many of the larger rooms, it has its own fireplace. I think you will love it. I know I will love sharing it with you."

In sync with him as ever, she let him escort her to the next grand room.

****

As Dorothy Gale said, 'There's no place like home' and Thomas was in complete agreement. To be back in Britain on his home ground, in the place that formed the seat of his family and the heart of his power was intoxicating. This was the place he felt strongest and most grounded. Over the past several years, although he had learned to live without it, he had not realized how much he missed his home, not until his return. So that evening while Jessilyn settled in, he took the time to wallow in the feeling and indulged himself with a walk around the grounds despite the many tasks demanding his attention.

He had not meant to wander as far as the forest, but found himself amongst the trees without conscious thought. It did not occur to him to question the impulse. Instead, he let his feet take him where they would. Still less did he question where the power he could feel in the depths of the earth would draw him. It could only be the stone circle.

The place was a short ten minute walk from his door. In the clearing, twelve standing stones stood in a perfect sphere and were the source of his power, a fact he had been aware of since boyhood.

The sense of the dark forces rising, that instinct compelling him home, was a thousand times stronger now he was in the circle. Well then, he considered, maybe he ought to make his own presence known. Decision made, he walked to stand in the center. With all that was in him, he let his power rise to connect with what was there in the land beneath his feet and under the sky. The response to his greeting was welcome from the forces of light, those in nature and in those ancestors that came before him. He let the strength and power of it flow through him then he said the spell he had long prepared for this moment.

I come to seek my birthright.

The forces of evil I come to fight.

I come to meet my fate.

Know forces of light I join with you now.

Know forces of dark I am here.

Never will I bow nor cringe in fear.

I will stand for the light no matter my plight

and send you back to the dark away from sight.

In one thousand years, times three,

Never will you know one so powerful as me.

As I will so mote it be.

Every inch of him blazed with his power, a bright clear blue. Light burst forth from the center of the circle and poured into him, fused itself to him and melded its power with his. As the magic of the circle faded, for the first time in a long time, he felt entirely himself and, moreover, he was ready to meet his fate whatever it might be. He was come home.

****

Water sluiced off his well-muscled body as Elias Charles Winfield III got out of the Olympic sized pool attached to his villa in the south of France then sat in a comfortable deck chair. It was his parents' villa, but whatever. It was his alone to enjoy right now and he would make the most of it. The bright sun warmed his skin and even the stone under his feet, so unlike the all but perpetual clouds and fog of England, and he soaked it up.

He figured he had about another forty-eight hours before his parents came looking for, then found him. He'd passed his A-levels in chemistry, modern and classical languages, history and biology and his parents ought to be grateful. While he'd been tossed out of more schools than he could count, his marks had always been good and his mind sharper than most. It was his behavior that was the problem, as his father reminded him. Repeatedly.

So, having graduated at last, he decided he deserved a vacation. After ditching his parents as soon as the commencement ceremony was over, he'd bought a first class plane ticket to Dijon and hadn't looked back. Knowing full well his father would have to return to work and his mother would set her lips in a line of stern disapproval but say nothing, he had no regrets. It had been almost two weeks now, however, and if he wasn't on a plane home by tomorrow when his father contacted him, there would be hell to pay. He sighed. Home, ughh. That place of rules and expectations, but not love, never that, nor even simple kindness. Unfortunately, he didn't have much choice about going back, at least not yet. Since he was eighteen now and mere days away from being granted access to the first portion of his trust fund, things would change and soon. Before much longer, no one would have a say in his life, least of all his father or mother. Shortly he would be free to do whatever he wanted, thank God.

Tomorrow was soon enough to start that intriguing process. Today, however, he'd left an amazing woman still sleeping in his bed upstairs. French, older enough than himself to be interesting, yet still young enough to be beautiful (i.e. early forties), Amelie was gloriously uninhibited with lots of dazzling, thick, wavy dark hair and a firm, toned body. A few wet strands of his own blond hair fell into his blue eyes and he brushed them back. With a sigh, he rose in one languid motion, and left to rejoin her.

****

Twenty-four hours later, Elias was back in his suite at home. He unpacked a few basic necessities leaving the rest for the servants to do then in his usual indolent way, he checked his e-mail. Among the reams of spam, one caught his attention. From a place called the Avery Institute, the subject line promised 'a unique educational opportunity'. Curious, he clicked on it despite the risk to his computer and read.

Dear Mr. Elias Winfield,

You have been selected to receive this offer of a unique educational opportunity due to the events that occurred on 12 September 2028. Please come join select others with your particular skill set to explore the exclusive, one-of-a-kind instruction and highly secure environment we can provide at the Avery Institute. We hope to see you at our open house on 10 June 2030 at 9:00 to 17 June at 17:00. If you have any questions, please contact me via the information below. Looking forward to making your acquaintance.

Sincerely,

Thomas Avery, PhD., president

The Avery Institute

Far beyond curious now, Elias noted the contact information provided and considered the very generous offer and what it might mean.

The reference to that day in September almost two years ago was most troubling. He was very well aware of what had happened on that day, what he had almost done. The mention of it could not be a coincidence. He sure as hell didn't believe in them anyway. Which meant either there had been a witness or he was being watched. Anger and fear rolled through him in equal measure as he reflected on that disturbing fact.

Undertaken on impulse, the encounter had gone bad very quickly. He'd almost killed the girl he'd met in a bar in Chelsea that night and had not learned her name until later from the papers. When she refused to have sex with him, rage took over and he'd beat her nearly to death before he'd realized what was happening. Luckily, he had been able to adjust her memory so she remembered nothing. He'd been freaked out, but he'd managed to think clearly enough to do that before getting the hell out and away. Since they had not left the bar together and there had been no witness to their altercation, all that could ever be proved was he had spoken with her briefly in a public place. At the time that had been enough to keep him safe.

He hadn't covered his tracks as well as he believed he had if this Avery institute knew enough to refer to it. On the other hand, they had not reported him to the authorities or mentioned any specifics, so he might be safe. But could he afford to take that chance? No, definitely not.

Besides, it sounded captivating, especially the part about 'join select others with your particular skill set'. That pre-supposed there were others like him, something he never would have believed possible much less had ever encountered. There were stories, going back centuries of course, but he had never believed them. It seemed for once in his life he was wrong. That being the case, perhaps he should at least find out more about the Avery Institute. Still, it was a risk and Elias knew it. It could be a trap. Yet somehow, he could not quite convince himself it was. There was no way to be sure. It might be what it purported to be, a school. In which case, he would have some decisions to make. He had intended to go to Oxford, but if the Avery Institute was everything he supposed it to be, he might change his plans.

Well, one step at a time, he advised himself and gathered information.

****

Dominic Foster tried not to panic as he looked down at his I-pad. What had he been thinking? He'd used his magic to help a dying little girl and thought he'd kept it secret. Nothing was secret and he ought to have known better. On that terrible night last year, he hadn't been able to save her, but he had relieved her pain and even now he did not regret it. But here was this e-mail from the Avery Institute making a reference to the event. Was it a threat or was it his salvation? How the hell should he know? And if it was his salvation, what was he supposed to do about it? Just as important, what did he want to do about it? Should he give up his medical career for the magic in his blood, always assuming that was a real possibility?

His pager beeped and he put the question aside in order to concentrate on the latest trauma coming into London's Jenkins Street Hospital. He was a consultant there and as he waited, he brushed his dark as midnight hair back from his face with an unconscious gesture. He set his strong chin, targeted the ambulance bay with his well-set green eyes and focused.

At end of shift, when he had a moment to breathe, the matter resurfaced. His good friend, Jack, walked into the locker room moments later, coming off shift as well.

They exchanged greetings then Dominic decided to ask for the advice he needed. The two of them had been close since starting at

University and his friend always had his head on straight. He could not ask anyone better.

"So, Jack, I have this opportunity."

"What kind of opportunity? I hope to hell we aren't talking criminal because you know that sort of thing never ends well," Jack said, half joking.

Dominic gave an emphatic shake of his head. "No, nothing like that. It's an educational opportunity."

Jack pulled a fresh shirt over his head then gave Dominic his full attention. "You're thinking of leaving the program? For one at a rival University or hospital? I never figured you'd –"

"This new program isn't medical. It's in a different field." When his friend opened his mouth to ask a question, Dominic held up a hand and interrupted again. "I know your next question is going to be what field, but I'd rather not say if it's all the same to you."

Jack rubbed a hand over his chin. "First, I'm not sure how well I can answer if I don't know all the facts. I mean how do I know this field suits you? Second, now I'm back to being worried. Are you sure this is on the up and up?"

He shrugged. "As sure as I can be. It isn't criminal, but it could be dangerous. It is something I've always been interested in exploring and now I have the chance. The prospect dropped into my lap a few days ago. Until now, I never even thought it was possible to do it, but I found out it is and I'm trying to decide whether to go for it. I'm torn because, giving up medicine? I don't even know if I can. I might as well try giving up breathing. On the other hand, this... this calls to me in a way nothing else ever has or ever will."

"Sounds like you've made your choice, man. Go for it if it's what you want." Jack rose and clapped him on the shoulder. "I'll miss your pretty face around here, but..."

When his friend was almost out the door, Dominic called out, "Jack?"

Jack turned back to face him. "Yeah?"

"Thanks."

Jack sent him a crooked grin and murmured, "Sure." A second later, he was gone, leaving Dominic alone with his thoughts.

****

"Gran," Katherine Mary O'Reilly, Kate to her friends and family, called. "Gran look at this."

Nineteen-year-old Kate rose from her favorite armchair in what her Gran called the sitting room and walked into the kitchen. The homey scents of her grandmother's baking and strong coffee filled the air. She poured herself a cup in a thick blue mug and smiled a little, knowing her grandmother had made the brew for her, since Maureen O'Reilly preferred tea. She held out her tablet for her Gran to peruse then sat at the scarred oak table for ten crafted by her great-great-grandfather over a century before. On the screen was an e-mail from a place called the Avery Institute.

Dear Ms. O'Riley,

You have been selected to receive this offer of a unique educational opportunity due to the events that have occurred throughout your life. We are aware of your own ability as well as your family history and would be honored by your presence. Please come join select others with your particular skill set to explore the exclusive, one-of-a-kind instruction and highly secure environment we can provide at the Avery

Institute. We hope to see you at our open house on 10 June 2030 at 9:00 to 17 June at 17:00. To set up your interview and if you have any questions, please contact me via the information below. Looking forward to making your acquaintance.

Sincerely,

President Thomas Avery, PhD.

The Avery Institute

She waited with rising impatience as her Gran read then demanded, "Well, what do you make of it? Could it be real? Is it a hoax do you think?"

Maureen O'Reilly looked up as Kate spoke. A small, slim woman with auburn hair with tiny hints of gray, and bright green eyes filled with life and sparkle, she was quite spry, that was the only word for it, for her seventy-five years. After scanning the document once more, she pursed her lips. "Well, it could be, but I can't be sure. If you're interested, why don't you check it out?"

Kate blinked. "But it's in Kent. In England."

Maureen rolled her eyes at her granddaughter. "I know where Kent is."

"But if I got accepted there it would mean leaving Ireland and living miles away in another country. I don't want to leave you," she stammered.

Maureen set the kettle she was putting on for tea on the stove then turned back to Kate. "Sit down, girl."

Kate obeyed by reflex.

"You haven't been happy this past year, not since you graduated, and don't try to tell me otherwise."

Kate sighed, unable to dispute the fact, but wished she had been able to hide it better.

"Ireland is in your blood and I have no doubt you will come back, but right now this place is too small for you and you need to see other countries, meet other people, breathe some other air. The Avery Institute ought to be perfect it seems to me."

Both longing and fear rushed through Kate. To encounter others like her, to hone her skill was beyond tempting. Even the idea of parting from her dearest Gran could not kill the longing she felt.

Her grandmother must have seen it because her expression was understanding and sympathetic. Maureen took her hand. "I'll still be here when you get back. I'm not going anywhere."

"But, Gran I can't leave you."

"Oh pish, children, and even more so grandchildren, are meant to fly. Also, I think this place was meant for you."

"Gran, I…"

When Kate was still unable to find the words to protest, Maureen went on, her voice growing a bit stern. "Kate, do you want to go to this school? Don't you lie to me now or to yourself."

For one stunning moment, Kate imagined all the possibilities. "Yes, I do."

"Well, that's settled then," Maureen patted Kate's hand then rose as the kettle let out a whistle.

Kate's lips curved in a slow smile. "All right." With a tap, she opened her e-mail to reply.

****

It took several hours for Elias to discover all he could. For a start, although recently founded, the Institute did indeed exist and

Thomas Avery was in fact a well-respected scientist from a good family. Given all he had already confirmed, did he wish to make contact? Elias decided he did. Letting others know who and what he was, well, that was a terrible risk, but he was willing to take it if it meant meeting others like him and being able to hone his power. In the normal course of things, he was not one to take risks, even calculated ones and, if he was honest with himself, he could admit having anything to do with the Avery Institute was a significant risk. Demanding to meet the president of the Institute for a private interview was downright crazy. But that was what he would do. While he had not made a final decision regarding whether to attend, he was dead certain he wanted to know more and a personal call was the best way to accomplish his goal.

To that end, he did not waste time. Once Elias made a decision, he acted on it. He picked up his cell and dialed the contact number provided in the e-mail.

His call was answered after two rings by a cheerful, American accented voice saying, "You've reached the Avery Institute, how may I help you?"

"I would like to speak to Dr. Avery please."

"I'm sorry; Dr. Avery isn't available at the moment. I can take a message for him and he will get back to you as soon as possible."

"Okay, please tell him my name is Elias Winfield. I am a potential student and I would like to meet with him before the open house."

"I'm sorry, sir, but that goes against procedure. You can meet Dr. Avery at the open house. That is what it is for after all." The voice was still cheerful, but now invested with steel.

"Well, then I won't be attending the Avery Institute. Please explain to the good doctor what I am doesn't grow on trees. If he wants me to even consider attending, he will need to contact me with the time and place for a meet. Before the open house." He placed deliberate emphasis on the before.

After a slight pause, the administrative assistant said in a cooler tone, "I'll give him the message. What's your contact information?"

He rattled off his details and ended the call more than satisfied, confident Dr. Avery would contact him and soon.

****

Thomas made himself comfortable in what used to be his father's study. Dark oak paneling covered the walls and there was a very large hearth at one end. On the left, French doors led to the terrace beyond, which overlooked the park and gardens in the distance. When making the room his own, he changed very little, going so far as to replace the worn rug that had been new in his grandfather's time and add a computer to the surface of his father's desk.

Thomas sorted through his messages and found what he expected until he read a message from one of his prospective students, Elias Winfield.

"Jessilyn, did this boy really demand a meeting prior to open house?"

Jessilyn nodded. "Even after I told him it was against policy. He was rather rude and arrogant about it as well."

"Any other impressions?"

"He sounded very confident in himself, his own ability and the belief that the talent he is able to offer us would be irresistible no matter what."

"Well, he may not be quite right about that, but he is pretty damn close. What do you think? Should we break our own protocols and meet with him?"

"I think it sets a dangerous precedent. It also shifts the balance of power in his favor which is not a good idea at all."

"True but… we need him. We need every person with magical blood we can find so I am not inclined to let him get away. He's got balls, I'll give him that, and that's something I admire. I think I want to meet him for myself. And there's no reason why we can't make sure he knows who's in charge when I do. We can make sure that balance of power tips right back in our favor. That sort of thing is best done in person. So…"

"I'll call him and set up a meet on one condition."

Thomas gestured for her to go ahead.

"That I go with you."

"Jessilyn, I am the most powerful wizard in the world, I am Merlin's heir. I can handle myself."

She gave him a look, but refrained from commenting on his arrogance. Instead, she said only, "I know you can, but there is something about this kid. I don't want you going alone."

Now Thomas's gaze and his wits sharpened. "You think he's dangerous?"

"Yes. I don't know whether he's dangerous to you, himself, others or a combination, but he is dangerous. I am sure of it."

He considered for a long moment then nodded. "All right. I trust your instincts. So, are you up for a little road trip?"

His grin was as charming and infectious as he could make it and he was rewarded when she smiled back. "Absolutely. I'll make the arrangements."

****

In Jessilyn's opinion, it was best to conduct the interview in a public place. With security as her primary concern and Thomas's personal safety uppermost in her mind, she insisted on the point. Truth to tell, Thomas did not put up much of a fight on the issue. In fact, he saw no reason to. He had no wish to be ambushed then injured or killed by some kid he had underestimated. So, they met in an out of the way English pub halfway between Elias's estate and Thomas's.

He and Jessilyn made certain to arrive first. They settled themselves at a table in the back with a view of the entrance. The pub itself was charming, traditional bordering on rustic. With the large quantity of dark wood, bench seating covered in red leather and a vast number of various ales, it could have been any pub in England and Thomas felt quite at home.

Which was fortunate, since Elias kept them waiting. He arrived a full forty-five minutes later than scheduled. Since they had arrived forty-five minutes early, they had been cooling their heels a full hour and a half by the time Elias walked through the door.

He arrived wearing expensive shades and even more expensive clothes. Although they were casual in style, Thomas had no trouble recognizing tailored pieces when he saw them since he wore the same sort of luxurious garments himself. The young man glanced around, searching, and at last spotted them. Without hesitation, he approached their table.

"Dr. Thomas Avery?"

Thomas nodded. "Elias Winfield?"

Elias nodded in his turn then removed his sunglasses to peer at Jessilyn. A smile full of lazy charm spread over his face as he looked her over from head to toe and gave her the benefit of his assessing gaze, one a lion might give a particularly delectable gazelle. "And you are?"

"Dr. Jessilyn Matthews, vice-president of the Avery Institute and Dr. Avery's wife," Jessilyn replied.

Thomas was pleased to note that, although she offered her hand for Elias to shake, her tone was cool, bordering on discouraging and definitely uncompromising. It was her professional tone, the one she used with him when they first met then off and on during their initial weeks together.

Thomas got right to the point. "So, you insisted on seeing us before the open house. Why?"

"I don't trust things I can't see and feel and touch with my own hands," Elias explained. "And you presume a great deal Dr. Avery. I needed to see you in person before I could be sure I could trust you."

"And? What's the verdict? Can you trust us now?" While Thomas well understood the impulse for self-preservation, he couldn't help but be mildly insulted, not so much at the boy's words, which were reasonable enough, but by his overall manner. Elias Winfield gave every appearance of being an arrogant, entitled ass. It remained to be seen whether he had any legitimate reason for his arrogance.

Elias shrugged. "Perhaps. Tell me more about the Institute."

Thomas stifled a sigh, but complied. He gave a more detailed picture of the Avery Institute with Jessilyn chiming in from time to time. At last he ended with, "Do you have any more questions for me?"

"Plenty, but the first is this: why did you agree to this meeting?"

"Two reasons, one, I figured since you had the balls to make a demand like this, I wanted to meet you and see for myself. Two, I wanted to make very sure you were quite aware of the balance of power here. That sort of thing is best done in person."

"The balance of power?" Elias's tone was innocent, but his face carried the merest suggestion of a sneer.

"You have something special, yes, granted. Please do not make the mistake of thinking that fact puts you in control or that you are the only one with unique abilities. I decide who attends my school. I make the rules. Believe me when I tell you I am powerful enough to enforce them." With his mind, Thomas called the air, creating invisible bonds to strap Elias to his seat. He held Elias immobile for perhaps thirty seconds, just long enough to make his point, then released him.

"Now, since we've come all this way, why don't you show us what you can do?"

****

"Here? Now?" It was an effort for Elias to keep the surprise from his face and voice, but he thought he managed it. His heart started to pound in his chest, but there wasn't much he could do about that. Even the mere idea of doing magic under ordinary people's noses appealed to him.

Dr. Avery nodded. "I've placed a barrier around us. It encompasses the entire pub. We can see out, but no one can see in or hear us."

"In that case." With no further hesitation, Elias made all the lights blink on and off as if he were flipping a switch.

When Thomas and Jessilyn remained distinctly unimpressed, he offered them a full-fledged smirk. "Child's play for those like us I know, but I couldn't resist."

"Stop playing games and show us what you've got unless you don't have any true ability at all," Jessilyn demanded.

The taunt found its mark and had him stiffening in spite of himself. With one angry jerk of a hand, liquor bottles smashed one after the other, contents spilling all over the bar. With a hard push of his other hand through the air, the alcohol burst into flame. Jessilyn jumped half out of her seat in panic, but Thomas held her back with a hand on her forearm.

With a murmured word and a far more subtle gesture, Thomas extinguished the flames before the whole pub could be engulfed.

"I think you've made your point, don't you?"

It wasn't phrased as a question, but Elias answered it anyway. "That was only the beginning. I have more if you're interested." This time the wind whistled through the place as if they were outdoors. It started slowly, but then grew to the force of a hurricane.

"Enough!" Thomas roared. With one strong, decisive gesture, Thomas calmed the wind.

After one heartbeat of deafening silence, Jessilyn cleared her throat and broke the awkward stillness. "Well, you have plenty of raw talent. Even so, if you want to attend the Avery institute, you'll have to learn to control that temper of yours."

"Like hell. I don't have to do anything I don't want to do. Not anymore," Elias spat the words, unable to conceal the venom within.

"Maybe not, but nevertheless, if you want a place at the Institute, that's non-negotiable," Thomas stated. The set of the older man's jaw was uncompromising and reminded Elias far too much of his father. "Barring that, we'd love to have you." He rose in clear dismissal and Jessilyn followed suit.

As she gathered her things, she beamed her bright professional smile at Elias. "We do hope we've answered all of your questions and hope you will seriously consider studying at the Avery Institute."

Elias sat in shock as Dr. Avery and Dr. Matthews got up and walked out as calm as you please. Then shock turned to fury. No one but no one walked out on him. Decision made, then. He would attend the Avery Institute and while there, he would meet others like him and do exactly as he pleased. Once he had learned everything he could, he would destroy it.

Chapter Seven

Their next meeting with a perspective student took place for a far different reason and Jessilyn hoped it would yield a far more positive result. It was important to her every effort was made to convince Hannah Barnes to attend The Avery institute. In certain unique cases, a greater effort to recruit was made and Hannah was a prime example. The girl was still so young, at age fifteen, and so vulnerable. After surviving a great deal of trauma, more than any other potential mage they had yet to discover, the girl merited a chance at a quieter, more serene life along with an excellent magical education. After everything she had been through, the girl deserved at least that much; Jessilyn believed this wholeheartedly. Convincing Hannah and her mother was another matter, but Jessilyn was determined to do that. If necessary, she would make it her mission to do so. Since the initial contact via e-mail and telephone had produced a negative result, an in person meeting was the next step.

To that end, she and Thomas knocked on Tracy Barnes's door. The woman who opened it was in her early forties according to her birth certificate, but she appeared older by almost a decade.

"Ms. Tracy Barnes?" Jessilyn asked.

"Yes, I'm Ms. Barnes. May I help you?"

Tracy put on a polite, if brittle, smile, but Jessilyn could see the fear scurrying around behind her eyes almost like a living thing. To put the woman at ease, she hastened to reassure her. "We aren't police or reporters. We are from a place called The Avery Institute and all we want is to help. If we could see Hannah?"

In an instant, the polite veneer vanished. Tracy stepped forward a pace so she stood on the threshold, half in, half out of the doorway. Lowering her voice, she demanded in a fierce whisper, "Do you have any idea how many people have wanted to 'see' Hannah since the fire? Too many to count. And do you want to know how many actually wanted to help? None! I won't put my daughter through that again, not one more time." She took a deep breath, seemed to regain a modicum of calm, then continued, "Now, I'm done talking to you two, whoever you are."

When she stepped back and started to close the door, Jessilyn braced a hand against it to hold it open. "Ms. Barnes, please, this is different I promise you. We are starting a school for children like Hannah and we want to offer her a place there."

"A school? You can't be serious." Notwithstanding her scoffing tone, Jessilyn could tell the older woman was intrigued. With a look, Jessilyn let Thomas know to take over.

"I assure you we are. It's called The Avery Institute, as we said. You didn't receive our letter?"

"No. Hannah may have it."

"Well, then, let me tell you a little bit about the Institute. It's in Kent, England and –"

Holding up a hand, Tracy interrupted. "Wait, this school is in Kent? In England?" She shook her head and laughed when Thomas nodded. "So, let me get this straight, you want me to let you take my underage daughter half way across the world, to another country no less? You want me to let my minor child go off to another continent with total strangers? That's not going to happen. I appreciate the offer, but no thank you. Now, get off my property before I call the police."

"Ms. Barnes, wait. Please –"

Tracy paid Thomas no attention. Instead, she turned and started to shut the door.

"No, Mom, stop." A girl's voice sprang from the dim interior of the house.

"Hannah, go get ready for school," her mother ordered in a sharp tone.

Disobeying this command, Hannah came into full view, wearing a school uniform and looking somewhat younger than her fifteen years, in contrast to her mother's ravaged appearance. She turned her attention to Thomas and Jessilyn. "Did you say something about a school?"

Thomas nodded. "Yes, I did. Dr. Matthews and I would like to speak to you and your mother about it. If we could come in, Ms. Barnes, please?"

Tracy looked at them for a moment then studied her daughter's wary but hopeful expression. Finally, she gave a resigned sigh, opened the door fully and ushered them inside. "Fine, come in. But make it quick, Hannah has to be at school and I have work."

She escorted them into a homey kitchen that wasn't above a little clutter. To Jessilyn, it looked lived in and comfortable.

Tracy gestured to them to seat themselves at the breakfast bar and they did. In a few brief sentences, Thomas explained the function and purpose of The Avery Institute. Hannah listened with fixed attention, making herself a bowl of cereal, which remained untouched while Thomas described the Institute. Her solemn eyes remained trained on his while she took in every detail.

Once he had wound down, Jessilyn asked, "Do you have any questions, Hannah? What about you, Ms. Barnes?"

"One," Hannah said in a soft, serious voice.

"What's that?"

"When can I start?"

Tracy groaned. "No, Hannah, we need to discuss this. I am not at all sure this is a good idea. I'm also not prepared to let you go to school so far away. You are only fifteen years old."

"I know, but can't you see this is an opportunity? I could meet others like me and maybe even learn to control my powers."

Jessilyn could hear, all but feel, the earnest longing in the girl's voice and hoped Tracy would listen to it.

"Is this really what you want?" Tracy asked.

"It is. At the very least, it couldn't hurt to go take a look at the place, right?"

Tracy glanced from her daughter to the two strangers in her kitchen. "I suppose not. Let me see what arrangements I can make."

The girl offered her mother a sweet, gentle smile, rose, and hugged her. If Jessilyn had been Hannah's mother, she would never have been able to resist that smile.

Tracy kissed the top of Hannah's head then stepped away. "It's time you headed to school. Get your stuff. We leave in five minutes." She shooed her daughter out of the kitchen.

Once Hannah was out of earshot, Tracy turned to them. Her expression was as hard as stone. "My daughter wants this so I will check you out. If you are who and what you say you are, then we will come for a visit in a few weeks at the end of the school year." Her jaw tightened. "My child is the most important thing in my life. If you hurt her in any way, trust me when I tell you, I will make you regret it even if it is the last thing I do on this earth."

"We understand, Ms. Barnes," Jessilyn replied. Thomas murmured his agreement and they left.

Once out on the pavement, she asked, "Do you think they'll come?"

Thomas said, "I do. Like Tracy said, her daughter wants this." He shrugged. "Well, come on, we've got a plane to catch."

****

"What the hell is this?"

In response to his father's bellow, Elias stifled a sigh as he dealt with the most recent crisis. Thaddeus held up a large packet and Elias recognized right away that it was an information package from the Avery Institute. He didn't even have to see the letterhead. A wild elation filled him which he had a hard time concealing. It was essential he do so, however, since any show of emotion in front of his father was tantamount to a show of weakness. Bearing that in mind, he took a calming breath and got control of himself.

Thaddeus reached into the already open package, extracted a sheet of paper and read. "'We are pleased to inform you of your provisional acceptance into The Avery Institute.' You aren't going to the Avery Institute, you are going to Oxford like I did, like your grandfather did, like your great-grandfather did and so on back."

Fury engulfed Elias more than it ever had in his life. His father was dictating to him. Again. All at once, he broke, but instead of the rage he expected, utter calm settled over him. No, he thought, I am *not* going to Oxford.

He turned on his heel without another word and headed up the stairs to pack.

His father took the steps two at a time, so Thaddeus soon caught up and grabbed Elias by the arm. "No son of mine is going to attend some upstart university like this Avery Institute. You'll go to Oxford."

Elias said nothing.

"What's so special about this place anyway?" His father asked as he tried to answer his own question by flipping through the papers and scanning them as he trudged up.

Elias hesitated at the top of the staircase. "It's a place for… people like me. It's somewhere for people with abilities like mine."

His father's face paled then turned a very unattractive puce. It was the first time in ten years or more that Elias had mentioned what he was aloud and the shock did not agree with his father at all. "Oh, no you are most definitely not going there. I am your father and you will do as I say. You'll go to Oxford, experience the privileges others wish they could enjoy and that's the end of it."

"No," he stated.

"What?! What do you mean no? You'll do as I tell you, boy."

"No," he repeated. This time he punctuated the word with magic. Green light burst from the palm of his outstretched hand and hit Thaddeus square in the chest. His father flew back into the thin air above the stairs then hit the floor at the bottom with a terrible, bone-cracking thud. He lay crumpled, his neck at an unnatural angle, broken.

For the longest time, Elias did not move. He didn't even breathe. The shock of using so much of his magic so unexpectedly, combined with the result, held him immobile.

The grandfather clock chiming the hour broke him out of his reverie. The first rational thought he had was of wondering how to cover things up. As if on cue, his mother's voice called his name. His head spun and he did not answer right away. He couldn't. This turned out to be a mistake, as Meredith kept calling her son's name, her voice as well as her footsteps coming closer and closer.

Within seconds, her screams rang in his ears. She raced to his father and dropped to her knees beside him. Her yells turned to wails as she cradled Thaddeus's head in her lap, treating him with far more tenderness in death than she ever had in life.

Her incoherent shrieks soon transformed into cries for help. And that's when she looked up to see Elias at the top of the stairs. With his father dead at the bottom.

In spite of her shock, Elias knew Meredith Winfield was a woman with an iron will, great intelligence and little sentiment. All of these characteristics stood her in good stead now. All he had to do was look in her eyes to see she was able grasp what happened with one glance. One look into her son's stunned, emotionless face and she knew.

"What did you do, Elias?"

The words came out in a low fierce whisper, which nevertheless reached him clearly enough. The blame in her eyes brought him out of dazed shock, at least enough to speak. "It was an accident. We were arguing and …" His voice trailed off at the look of furious disbelief on his mother's face.

"An accident?"

She didn't believe him. His own mother did not believe him; it was as plain as the nose on her face. Despair rolled through him at the knowledge. If his own mother did not believe him, what chance did he have to convince anyone else? The same black, blinding rage overtook him again. He'd be damned if he'd go to prison. He would not go to prison. He would not!

Elias nodded. "One you stumbled upon unexpectedly. The shock was too much for you." He felt quite calm now and knew what he had to do. He began a slow, inexorable walk down the stairs.

Meredith stilled as terror coursed through her, but for a moment only. Seconds later her jaw was set. No pushover, she pulled herself together, laid Thaddeus's body down and got to her feet.

"You are crazy if you think you will get away with this, son. You murdered your father and you will be going to prison. You are dead to me." She scrabbled in her purse for her cell phone.

With one simple twitch of a finger, he flung the phone aside and it smashed against the opposite wall. He shook his head. "No, Mother, I am going to get away with it because it is you who will be dead to me and not in the metaphorical sense."

For the first time, fear showed in her eyes, replacing her arrogant expression and Elias reveled in it. Three steps from the bottom of the staircase now, he continued toward her.

Seeing rage in his every move and murder in his every aspect, she gasped, "You wouldn't. Elias, you wouldn't. I'm your mother."

He gave her no response, only kept moving forward.

Animal instinct had her backing away and whimpering, "Please."

Elias ignored her. Instead, he backed her into a wall then put a hand to her head. Magic coursed through his fingers and straight into her brain. If her death was painful, at least it was quick.

****

By the time Elias pulled up to the gate of the Avery Institute a week later for the extended open house and testing period he was calm. His hands were steady on the wheel and he was unruffled and composed. The aneurism he had given his father after the man's fall down the stairs and the heart attack he had subsequently given his mother looked like natural causes and shock respectively. He'd cleaned the scene thoroughly and he had nothing to worry about. He'd been questioned and cleared of any suspicion by the police within hours. For the next several days he spent time making the funeral arrangements and dealing with all the other practicalities, things like closing up the house, receiving his inheritance and going through his father's many business interests and investments and deciding what to do.

Now, through the dark lenses of his ray-ban sunglasses, he studied the grand house as he sped up the drive toward it. It was time to decide whether this would be the best place to begin his new life. The Avery Institute looked like a rather nice place to spend any amount of time in his opinion, even if he opted not to make things permanent in the end. Best of all he was free. As he braked and the car rolled to a stop, he took a deep breath and savored the knowledge that for the first time, he had a choice.

****

Hannah could not believe she was at the Avery Institute. Over the past weeks, the battles she and her mother had had over it had been many and epic, but Hannah had won out in the end. Mostly, Hannah figured, because her mother was at her wits end regarding her daughter and, even more, her daughter's powers.

"C'mon, Mom. I have to register. It looks they are almost ready to get started. I don't want to miss anything."

Obediently, Tracy followed Hannah to the registration table.

"Name dear?" the lady behind the desk asked when Hannah stepped forward.

"Hannah Barnes."

The woman consulted a list, checked off Hannah's name then held out an 8 ½ X 11 envelope filled with papers and a sticker bearing the legend The Avery Institute on it. "Here is your welcome packet." Hannah took it. "Write your name on a name tag and make yourself comfortable. We'll be starting in few minutes."

Hannah smiled, did as instructed, and then settled to wait.

****

Kate could not believe she was at the Avery Institute. What was even more amazing was the sheer number of others with gifts. There were at least a hundred potential students in the great hall, if she had to make a guess. She had not ever believed she was alone, her heritage put paid to that notion, but she had assumed talents like hers were rarer in the wider world. She had been wrong. To find even this many like her was astonishing and she tried her best not to gape.

Suddenly a voice filled the room without the benefit of a microphone and Kate all but jumped out of her skin she was so startled.

"May I have your attention please?"

Once her racing heart slowed a bit, Kate looked about for the source of the sound and saw it originated from a dark-haired man in his mid-thirties. He possessed an aura of power she had only ever seen in her Gran, a fact which impressed her.

"I am Dr. Thomas Avery and I am happy to welcome you to the Avery Institute." He gestured the pretty woman beside him forward. "This is Dr. Jessilyn Matthews, my wife and vice-president."

"We are delighted all of you have chosen to join us," she said. The woman gave a wave and a nod then stepped back.

"Over the next several days you will be put through some very rigorous testing. There are various ways power manifests and we have stations set up for each. We want you to show us what you can do," Thomas began.

"We encourage you to try all of the stations, as you may have an aptitude you are not aware of. If, on the other hand, there is a known talent you would like to share, by all means, show us," added Jessilyn.

Kate's own greatest ability was telepathy followed by divination, both of which she was willing and eager to share. Right away, she found herself wondering whether she might have other skills she was not aware of and she longed to know what surprises her body and mind might have in store for her. She also found herself curious as to what the capabilities of the others might be. Heartbeat elevated, she tried to listen as Dr. Avery continued.

"This week is also a time for you to get to know us and what we are about. Tour our facility, enjoy our library, and socialize with other potential students like yourself. Decide if you want to study here. We do hope you will choose to attend. For now, please register, relax and enjoy. When you are ready, feel free to find your assigned quarters."

Kate had every intention of obeying. Unable to restrain a little squeal of excitement, she headed over to the registration table.

****

Elias could not believe he was at the Avery institute. Even after he'd read the e-mail and spoken to Dr.'s Avery and Matthews, he'd still half expected to be on the beach in St. Tropez not in the cold of England. Yet the price of the miserable climate was worth paying. For the first time, he could be himself. With a pleasant jolt, he realized he could do magic whenever he wanted. He did not have to keep it secret and no one would stop him. Smiling genuinely for the first time in years or maybe ever, from where he stood in the middle of his bedroom, he raised a hand and dimmed all the lights in his suite.

As soon as he opened himself even that little way, he felt... something. Something dark and dangerous and, as far as he could tell, pure evil. It was like nothing he had ever sensed before, at least not anywhere other than in himself. Tentatively he stretched out with his mind and felt a surge, like it, whatever it was, had been waiting for him. Oh, yes, he thought, he was going to like it here.

****

Dominic could not believe he was at the Avery institute. He'd done it. He'd gone crazy, given up a promising medical career and moved to bloody Kent. He took a deep breath and tried to compose himself. After all, what was done was done. There was no turning back now and he could not find it in himself to regret it.

Turning in a slow circle, he looked around at his accommodations and found them a damn sight better than the on-call room at the hospital where he had spent most of his time. The place was the size of a small flat with its own living area, kitchen, bedroom and bath. Everything was done in an elegant, modern style, which still fit well with the ancient feel and gracious atmosphere of the castle.

Everything from the furniture to the light fixtures was the best money could buy. A huge four-poster bed made of heavy oak took up most of the bedroom. A wardrobe, which appeared to be made of the same material, stood in one corner. His rooms opened on to a terrace of gray flagstones with an impressive view of the grounds. The living room contained a 40-inch television mounted on the wall. A modern essential much appreciated. Over the mantel of the large fireplace a very expensive painting of a forest path hung. A comfortable settee covered in well-worn green brocade with occasional tables at each end completed the furnishings. The wood-paneled floor gave way to beige tile in the tiny but modern kitchen. A bistro-sized table for two was arranged in the dining area. The luxurious bath sported white tile, a pedestal sink he suspected was newly installed and a claw foot tub, which might have been there for decades.

"I could live here," he decided as he unpacked.

****

"You will be tested in six categories: spells, potions, telepathy, healing, divination, and finally pure magic." Thomas Avery announced the next morning.

All the students were assembled in what had once been the grand ballroom of the house which had been transformed into a testing area. It's smooth hardwood floor along with windows which reached the ceiling and spanned the length of the room, made for a massive space full of air and light. The spot was ideal for its new purpose.

As Dr. Avery explained the examination procedure, Kate found herself fascinated by the process, although she was also a bundle of nerves. She had a fair idea of her own abilities, but what if she choked and became unable to demonstrate them? Well, she would have to make sure she didn't that was all. Letting her grandmother and her family down was not an option.

Thinking of her grandmother made her smile. She could hear her voice as if the older woman were standing beside her. 'Stop fretting, Katie, and do your best. Do that and you will make me proud no matter the outcome.'

Feeling a thousand times better and more confident, she focused in on Dr. Avery's words.

"When I say begin, each of you will choose whichever station you wish to start with then continue to the next and the next until you have completed all the stations. Results will be delivered to you in two days' time. If you pass, you will also receive a class schedule determined by your level of skill as well as your personal preferences."

Thomas paused a moment, creating a nice effect, then gestured to the stations. "Begin."

Kate let the others, so anxious and eager, rush forward. For a time, she stood debating between magic and telepathy. Her telepathic ability was prodigious, but her magical gifts were even greater. With a mental shrug, she began with telepathy because she had to start somewhere.

Kate was not the first to arrive at the telepathy area, but soon it was her turn. In a few quick words, the proctor explained the procedure. The telepathy station consisted of a simple table with little on it. The proctor sat with a stack of oversized cards behind a barrier made of simple corkboard and the student sat facing him on the other side. Unable to see, the student was to guess each card the proctor held. Kate acknowledged the simple instructions then began.

At first, the mental picture was fuzzy, nothing more than a blurry, blank white wall, then as she focused on the person behind the barrier, the image cleared. She saw the card with the symbol on it, as well as a view of the room from a different perspective. In fact, she could even see the proctor behind the barrier, a woman of perhaps thirty with long brown hair and green eyes wearing a white peasant blouse and a long, flowy blue cotton skirt with white flowers. Detail after detail piled up minute by minute. Taking a deep breath, she focused on the card the proctor was looking at.

"The card has three wavy lines."

"Thank you. Next card."

This time it took ten seconds for her to get a clear picture. "A star."

This went on for quite some time until Kate had gone through the same procedure with one hundred different cards.

The proctor rose from her seat and announced. "Your test is completed. You'll get the results in a few days."

Kate nodded, continued to the next testing station and did not look back. She had done her best and no one could ask for more than that.

****

Elias was of two minds about tests. There was one part of him that never liked being tested, not ever. It was his innate arrogance, he supposed. Another part of him, however, was deeply competitive and welcomed the chance to trounce any others taking the exam with him.

Which way he felt at any given moment depended on his mood, his liking for the test material and the worthiness of his opponents.

Elias strode to the telepathy station without a second's hesitation. Once there he wondered whether he had made a mistake. The things asked of the participants were ridiculously easy, simple things Elias had been doing since he was twelve. He almost turned and walked away, but then he thought better of it. Why not make an impression? Why not blow everyone else away with his skill? No reason he could think of not to.

When his turn came he did a few of the simple tricks then demanded, "Got anything more difficult? Because this is way too easy."

The proctor who stuck his head out from behind the barrier looked surprised, but unoffended. "Such as?"

"Such as in your former life you worked at your parents' pub using your magic to charm the patrons into buying more drinks and the pretty girls into your bed. You attended university on scholarship wanting to get the hell out of the sleepy village where you spent your whole life. Then you heard about this place. You dropped everything to come here."

"That's right."

The man blinked then sense returned to his eyes. A moment later a shield fell into place preventing Elias from going any deeper. "That will be quite enough. Your skill is obvious. You can move along to the next station."

The proctor clenched his jaw in clear disapproval. Unconcerned, Elias shrugged then headed to take the next test.

****

Dominic relaxed a little when Dr. Avery announced they could choose where to begin. For him, that was a no brainer. Without question, healing was his gift. As he approached, he heard an unmistakable sound of pain. Once he got closer, he realized the noise originated from a tiny kitten. The scrawny little creature was asleep with its eyes tight shut, but even while resting it was mewing from severe discomfort.

"We have sedated this little guy since we don't want him to be in pain. It's your job to diagnose then cure him," Dr. Avery explained.

Student after student tried and failed until Dominic began to feel a bit nervous.

Dr. Avery consulted his clipboard. "Dominic Foster, your turn."

Dominic took the kitten in one hand, the other he passed over the tiny body. It was difficult to pinpoint the source of the trouble and he had a moment of sheer panic. What if he somehow could not figure it out? Cold sweat broke out between his shoulder blades and rolled down his back. After allowing himself one moment of fear, he gritted his teeth and set the feeling aside. He was trained in emergency medicine and, what was more, he had often used his magic to enhance his diagnostic skill. Surely, he could help this little creature.

As if on cue, the animal let out a distressed meow and a corresponding wave of pity moved through him at the sound. He concentrated as hard as he could and at last sensed the problem. A tumor was lodged in the cat's belly. Without further consideration, he stretched out with his magic to heal. Soft blue light fell on the kitten, which stirred but did not fully wake. The tumor was deep and very aggressive and it was some time before Dominic was satisfied it was entirely gone. By the end, he was drained, but pleased with a job well done.

"He had a tumor in his stomach. I've healed him," Dominic announced at last.

Dr. Avery, a skilled healer himself, placed a hand over the kitten and scanned him. "There is no trace of the tumor. I'm very impressed. Cancer is very difficult to detect and get rid of even in animals."

At this point, the kitten yawned, stretched and opened its bright golden eyes to stare up at Dominic. A small smile played around the corners of his mouth as he stroked the kitten from the top of its head to the tip of its tail. The cat let out a soft but unmistakable purr.

"Excellent work."

Dominic nodded in Dr. Avery's direction, acknowledging the compliment, then moved on to the next station.

****

They might as well begin as they meant to go on, Thomas decided several days later. So, telling his students/army about Baylor and his dark forces and that they would be fighting them sooner rather than later was critical. He was more than a little nervous and still wondered whether he ought to have told them from the very beginning, before he'd sent out even one letter to prospective students of the Institute. On the other hand, many students (or more likely their parents) would have dismissed the Institute out of hand had they known of the danger and then the students would never have known what they would be missing. In the interest of full disclosure, however, and so each student could make a fully informed choice, it was time to tell them all of it.

With a school full of magical people, chances were good some might well sense the dark forces without even having to be told. Some might already be getting close to the truth and soon enough someone would figure it all out. The weeklong open house would end and classes would officially begin on Monday. Those who opted to leave would need to make arrangements. The time was now. The entire college took the evening meal together in the great hall on Saturday and Thomas decided that was the place and time to announce it.

He clinked his glass with his fork to get everyone's attention.

"I would like to formally welcome you all to the Avery Institute. You are here because of your great talent and unique abilities. As you know, classes begin Monday, but before they do, there are things you need to know and decisions each of you will have to make."

He paused for a moment to collect himself then began. "Dark forces are rising. Every thousand years they gather their strength to try to take over the world. Only forces of light and good can stop them. This is the true reason I brought all of you here."

Troubled murmurs filled the room. Thomas let the sound roll over him and play out for a moment then held up a hand for silence. "All I have already told you is true. I just didn't tell you everything. I wanted each of you to see this place, to know it before coming to a decision. Like I want you to know about the dark forces before making a final choice."

"What are these dark forces?" one brave young girl piped up.

"They are known in every culture and by many names, but their ruler was called Baylor by the ancient Irish. Simply put, Baylor is pure, distilled evil and he rules all dark demons. He and his demons must be stopped."

"But why is this happening now? Why us?" another student demanded.

"In my long life, I have discovered many things, but only two guiding principles. There is and must be balance in everything and that love is greater than any other force in the world. There is dark and there is light. $E=Mc2$. There is matter and there is energy. There is no one without the other. With the forces of dark and light, it is the same. Light magic has ruled this world for centuries, but the dark must have its chance. That is the only way to maintain the balance. Its chance has come."

"If you're the most powerful magician in the world then why do you need us?" Elias voiced the question in what Thomas considered his usual rather arrogant fashion.

"I am the last direct descendent of Merlin, so it is up to me to beat Baylor and his demons back, but not alone. I need all of you. I need as much help as I can get. Merlin worked alone and he was able to subdue the dark forces, but Camelot was destroyed and Arthur died. I don't want to take any chances."

"I understand this is a lot to take in. Take whatever time you need to process then decide. If you choose to leave, your tuition will be refunded in full as well as any other fees you might already have paid and you will always be welcome to return. If, however, you choose to stay, understand you will be learning, but in the end, you will be fighting too."

The murmurs died away as the students each considered the seriousness of the question.

After some minutes one young man, Dominic Thomas thought he was called, rose to his feet. "Before I came here, I was pre-med. So, in a way I'm used to fighting. I'll stay."

Then a very pretty redhead called Kate stood. "I'm not going anywhere. I love this place. I love this world and I am willing to use what I am to defend it. I know it's what my Gran would want."

Soon most of the students were standing and Thomas breathed a sigh of relief even as his gut clenched. These young people were willing to stay and fight no matter what that might mean. No matter the cost, they made the decision to protect and defend. It was his job, moreover, it was his responsibility, to make sure that cost was not too high. He hoped against hope he was up to the task.

****

Elias could not believe it. Dr.'s Avery and Matthews knew. They knew about the dark forces he'd been sensing for days, since his arrival in fact. He was not at all sure how he felt about that. Up until now, the dark forces had been solely his, or so he'd believed. Now everyone knew about it. In a very real way that made things that much harder. Yet, on the other hand, it might be easier too. Now he could ask questions and maybe get some answers all without arousing undue suspicion. Either way he had been looking for something all his life and this might be it. Baylor was calling to him and he would answer.

So, step one would be to find out everything he could by exhausting all the resources of the extensive Avery library. He'd had a solid plan, but now there was also a brand new source of information to consider, Dr. Jessilyn Matthews. It would be a shame not to make use of her. Hell, he thought, it might even be fun. All things considered, he would be staying for the foreseeable future. He wasn't going anywhere.

Chapter Eight

When Dominic entered the room on the first day of classes, he discovered three others were in the Advanced Telepathy course, a rather mousey girl of no more than fifteen, a boy of eighteen and another girl of perhaps nineteen who was the most gorgeous woman Dominic had ever laid eyes on. Her long red hair cascaded down her back making him itch to run his hands through it. She was tall and lanky with the porcelain skin common to many red heads. Although she was speaking to the younger girl, she must have felt his gaze on her because she turned her own large, attractive blue eyes on him for one brief, searing second then she returned her gaze to the front of the room in a careful sort of way.

He took a deep breath and made a valiant effort not to drool or otherwise embarrass himself. He did his utmost not to let her or anyone else know what he was feeling, as desire, or to be blunt, rampant lust, ran through his veins and straight to his groin. Trying his level best not to show any outward signs, he chose a seat across the aisle and to the right of the woman and then turned his attention back to the professor, who turned out to be Dr. Avery, as the man headed to the front of the classroom.

****

Elias was not the first to arrive at the Advanced Telepathy class. Two girls were already seated and chatting in a comfortable way. One was very young, an awkward looking fifteen at a guess. The other… The other was the most stunning woman he had ever seen in his life. She was tall, slender with magnificent red hair. But it was her eyes that drew him. There was something about her eyes. Her voice was also tantalizing. It was Irish accented, warm and sweet as honey. He wanted her and he decided right then and there that he would have her. To hell with the fact that he didn't even know her name. He could bloody well find out in his own good time. For the moment, however, he would sit back and observe. Whoever she was, he had no doubt he could take her whenever he wanted her. Since in other aspects of his life, time was of the essence, other priorities had to come first, like beginning his new existence. Reminding himself of that, he found a seat and prepared to listen to the lecture.

****

Kate sensed eyes on her and shifted in order to discover whose. It turned out to be a man not much older than she was, with eyes as green as the hills of her home in Ireland. For one instant, she could not look away. His gaze, his very presence was too powerful, too magnetic. Then she forced herself to stare blindly at something, anything, else. The podium in the front of the room seemed as good a choice as any. Continuing her previous conversation also struck her as a good idea. It might be a good way to preserve the illusion of normalcy. She also hoped switching her focus would help her to behave like something other than an imbecile. Although she was no longer taking in a word of what was being said, it was the best she could do.

While Dr. Avery re-introduced himself and gave a brief description of the course, she pulled herself together. Lucky thing too, because there were to be introductions all around. Each person had to give his or her name, age and where he or she lived. Hannah she had already met. She discovered the rather arrogant young man in the corner was named Elias and the man who had so unnerved and fascinated her with his stare was called Dominic. A nice name she could not help but reflect before she crushed the wayward thought.

Preliminaries completed, Dr. Avery glanced around the room at his students and began the lecture. "The first thing you need to understand is that telepathy is like sex. It is intimate, often messy and should never be done without the other person's express permission."

Kate felt her cheeks heat, but kept her attention on Dr. Avery. In her peripheral vision, she noted Hannah was red-faced as an apple and stared fixedly at her hands clasped primly on her desk. In Elias's bored eyes, she detected a flare of interest he did not bother to conceal. She wondered about Dominic's reaction, she could not help it. The temptation to glance over to see for herself all but overwhelmed her, but she resisted.

Dr. Avery's voice continued to reach her, but from a great distance. "Over the next weeks, we will begin with some simple exercises. We will also make an extensive study of the ethics involved here. All of us will be getting to know each other very well. This may be too uncomfortable for some of you. If at any time all of this becomes too intimate, all you have to do is say. There are many other areas of study you may choose to concentrate on instead."

With no warning, she felt Dominic's gaze on her again (already she recognized it as his). She decided on the spot that if he could look at her then she could look at him, and so she did. It was the same as before, only more intense. Perhaps because this time, she didn't look away; she didn't want to.

"Okay. So, first a definition of telepathy." Dr. Avery turned to the white board and began to write, but Kate did not notice or take in a word of the lecture.

****

The Science in Magic course was required for all students. What a load of utter bullshit, Elias thought as he headed toward the assigned classroom with the greatest reluctance several days later. Magic was and that was all, and could never be completely explained, so why try? In fact, such a thing should not ever be attempted in his opinion. To do so was to destroy its mystique and that was something Elias could not abide, because mystique was useful and had its place. So, while he would have enjoyed studying the subject on his own, up to a point, he was very much against others being offered the same opportunity, even if they were considered the elite.

To tell the truth, the one reason he showed up at all was because the teacher was the delectable Dr. Matthews. She was the sort of woman he would not mind, in fact would downright enjoy, having in his bed (i.e. older, intelligent, classy, gorgeous) and he intended to use the lecture as a means to that end. Keeping that in mind, as soon as she entered he forced himself to be attentive and to project a positive vibe he did not feel. He comforted himself with the idea that there might be a bit of fun to be had once this tedious lecture was over and tried his best to pay attention.

After the farce that was his Science in Magic class ended, Elias slipped out behind the conservatory for a smoke. He figured he deserved one for sitting through the whole wretched lecture and not killing anyone. To his surprise, the place was not deserted. Another student was there. The guy, who was half-way through his cigarette, nodded but said nothing as Elias joined him.

When his lighter refused to ignite, he tossed it into a bush with a curse, then turned to his companion. "Got a light?"

"Sure."

As Elias lit up the guy drew a deep drag then offered, "I'm Troy."

"Elias."

Troy exhaled on a cloud of smoke and a sigh. "That's better. I had to get out of there. That science class is completely useless."

Elias handed Troy back his lighter. "I agree."

"It takes all I've got not get up and walk out."

"It takes all I've got not to tell Dr. Matthews exactly what I think of it."

Troy guffawed. "Now that I'd like to see."

Elias shrugged. "Stick around a bit longer and you might."

Troy took one last puff on his cigarette, tossed it to the ground then crushed it out under his boot. "I look forward to it, mate. Later."

"Later."

Troy walked a few steps then turned back. "Want to head down the pub for a beer tonight? Maybe pick up a couple of girls, have a few laughs?"

Elias considered. The class had been deadly dull and he could use a few laughs and more than a few drinks. As for girls, well, he could always use one (or more) of them. "Sure. Why the hell not?"

"Well all right, meet me in the entrance hall at ten?" Elias nodded and Troy lifted a hand in salute. "Cheers mate."

****

What passed for a club in the small village of Braxton did not impress Elias in the least. It boasted dim lighting, a d.j. playing out of date American hits from the mid-nineties, and flooring of dull gray none too clean linoleum. Since it was the only game in town, it did do a brisk business, however. The slim pickings it contained consisted of forgettable local girls who barely impinged on his consciousness and inferior liquor which impressed him even less. Still, he reasoned, it was better than nothing. He bought two shots of the best vodka available and surveyed his choices.

He downed his drink in one then motioned to the barkeep and ordered another round for himself and Troy while he considered. His attention did not fall on the best-looking girl there, but close. She was, of course, not the least attractive woman in the place, nowhere near it.

He had to think of his pride after all. Thick, dark hair, straight as a pin, fell in a long line down her back. Her pretty face had good bone structure as a foundation topped with big, gorgeous blue eyes. Her body curved in all the right places. Overall, she was the most striking woman in the club. As he watched, a friend joined her. Fair where her companion was dark, the other girl was almost as stunning. Perfect for Troy.

He got Troy's attention with a nudge.

"Yeah?"

Elias tilted his head in the direction of the table his prey currently occupied. "What do you think? Want to have a go?"

Troy scoffed. "Who wouldn't? Girls like that are way out of my league in case you didn't know."

Elias studied the other man. Troy was over six feet but 140 lbs soaking wet, red haired and freckled. He wasn't what Elias would term handsome but he was far from ugly. He was, to put it simply, average and Elias privately agreed. Alone, Troy would have had no chance with the two girls. A wicked grin stole over his features. "Not anymore. I want the girl with the dark hair. You okay with the other?"

Troy stole a quick glance at the pretty blonde. "Are you serious?"

"Yeah." Elias tossed back the last of his drink. "Are you in or not? If you're not, I'll take them both."

For a split second, Troy's jaw slackened with shock, but he soon recovered. "Hell yes I'm in."

Without further comment, Elias approached the table, Troy following close behind.

****

The first weeks at the Avery Institute were a revelation for Kate. Wanting to learn everything she could, she soaked up all new information like a sponge. It was exciting, yet peaceful. Able to be who she was with no restraint was amazing and soon she was happier than she had ever been. About two weeks into the term, however, things changed. In the corridor after class, she watched as the jerk from her Advanced Telepathy lecture, Elias, leaned into Hannah, crowding her and intimidating her. Several others looked on and jeered, encouraging him.

He stroked his fingers down Hannah's cheek and she knocked his hand away. "Stop it," the girl ordered.

Elias didn't of course. Instead, he caught her wrist and gripped tightly enough to make her wince.

Before her conscious mind told her feet to move, Kate was already striding in their direction. She halted three feet away and stood firm. "She said stop."

Although he did not stir an inch, Kate sensed Elias's focus shift toward her. "Did she? What if I don't want to stop?"

"Too bad."

Elias chuckled. Then, to Kate's intense relief, he left Hannah where she was. Kate's stomach sank, however, when he turned his full attention to her. "And who is going to make me stop? You?"

"Yes." Without another word or any warning, she used her magic. Rose-colored flame shot from her fingertips and forced Elias back several steps then knocked him on his ass a second later. Still, his reflexes were quick as lightning and he brought up his own defenses as he got to his feet in one swift, fluid motion.

His green fire was more than a match for her flame and soon she was sweating with the effort of keeping upright. Inch-by-inch, he backed her into the wall at the opposite side of the corridor.

"You are very strong. I like that. On the other hand, you did interrupt me and then had the gall to knock me on my excellent, if I do say so myself, ass. Not very nice."

Pinned against the wall now, she struggled and groaned, but got nowhere.

"You're a fighter, I see, and I want you on my side."

"Go to hell!"

Far from being displeased, he was delighted, if the hard light in his eyes was anything to go by. "Definitely a fighter. But, you need to be taught a lesson first." His jaw firmed and his expression was solid as well-honed steel. "No one is as strong as I am and no one tells me what I can and can't do."

She hadn't believed it possible, but he took his power up another notch and Kate had to grind her teeth together to keep from screaming. She was determined not to give him the satisfaction.

"I won't be going to hell, by the way. I'll be staying right here. Are you sure you don't want to join me, Kate?"

"Oh, yeah, I'm sure all right."

He shrugged then very slowly, very deliberately, let her go. "Have it your way. For now. I hope, for your own sake, you come around." Without another look or gesture, he gathered up those attached to him and left.

Kate replayed her confrontation with Elias and shivered. The most frightening part, she admitted to herself, was when he had walked away from her. She was thoroughly beaten, yet he let her go. Obviously quite sure he could recapture her at any time, he had let her be, like a cat content for the moment with its current prey, but still on the watch for future quarry. As if he could do whatever he liked to her whenever he liked. Moreover, she wasn't the only one he felt that way about. Otherwise, she wouldn't be in this mess in the first place. Sooner or later, something would have to be done about him; she could feel it in her bones.

Glad to see the back of him for the time being, she took a few shaky breaths then steadier, she called, "Hannah, are you all right?"

"I think so," the girl replied. "What about you?"

A little dazed from the blast of magic and the previous clash, Hannah struggled to her feet, but when Kate tried to join her, she noted idly that her vision was going black and decided moving was a bad idea. With little choice, she dropped back down to the floor in an ungraceful heap.

****

As Dominic walked through the corridors, he saw several other students loitering. Loitering wasn't all they were doing, however. They were, in fact, accosting a girl. A younger man with a shock of blond hair seemed to be the leader of the group and Dominic realized they had met in his Advanced Telepathy class. Elias appeared to be taunting the girl he, Dominic, had noticed before. Today Kate's wild red hair hung in a thick braid down her back and judging by the bright pink in her cheeks, and even more by the look in her eyes, she appeared to be angry. She gestured to Hannah. Had the whole thing started when Kate stepped in to help the younger girl? He suspected as much, but had no time to think any more about it, as all hell broke loose. Using her magic, Kate kept Elias from harming Hannah, but then Elias fought back with amazing results. Dominic's mouth dropped open in awed shock as she used her magic on Elias. The scene played out so fast he barely had time to think, let alone react.

Until Elias had Kate pinned. Once that happened, his feet moved of their own accord. As he got close enough to hear Elias's voice, he kept moving and never broke his stride. He was closing in on the group and making no attempt to conceal his approach. Luck was with him; everyone's attention was focused on the drama unfolding in front of them.

"I won't be going to hell, by the way. I'll be staying right here. Are you sure you don't want to join me, Kate?"

"Oh, yeah, I'm sure all right."

For one terrible instant, he wondered whether Elias was going to try to either kill her or kiss her. Either action would have been irrevocable and would have required his immediate intervention to prevent, but to Dominic's astonishment, Elias let Kate go.

"Have it your way. For now. I hope, for your own sake, you come around."

Then Elias was gone and while Dominic wanted to follow, he had more important priorities at the moment. He completed his headlong rush over and inspected Kate for injuries. She jerked away as he checked her for concussion.

"I'm fine. Check on Hannah. She needs help."

Ignoring the order, he held her head still in a gentle but firm hold while he checked her pupils with a little pocket light he kept on his key chain. "Pupils are equal and reactive. You've got a slight concussion, but I think you will be okay."

He probed the knot forming on the back of her head. "Ouch," she yelped and ducked away to avoid his searching fingers. "Who do you think you are, a doctor?"

"I was pre-med before I decided to come here. You'll do. I'll check Hannah."

"Yes, good. She's over there." For the second time, Kate tried to rise, but a wave of dizziness had her swaying and landing back on the cold, rough flagstone floor. A warm, strong hand on her shoulder held her in place when she made a third attempt.

"Stay here." He made the words a command not a request. Sensing that, she did as she was told.

Some minutes passed before he returned. "Aside from a bruise or two on her back from when Elias slammed her into the lockers, she's fine," he informed her, certain she would want to know right away.

Her chest rose and fell with a deep, unsteady breath. "Well, that's a relief."

"Too right you are," he agreed. "You know, for a minute there, I wasn't sure what he was going to do. I'm Dominic Foster by the way."

"Kate O'Reilly. I recognize you from Advanced Telepathy class. Thanks for the help."

"No problem. Look, I don't think you need to go to the infirmary." In fact, he was quite sure she did not need the infirmary. One of his particular talents was being able to diagnose and medically assess using his powers, so he was certain a slight concussion was the worst of it. "But," he continued, "you will need someone to watch you tonight and wake you every two hours."

Before he could volunteer for the task, Hannah spoke up. "I'll do it. You got hurt because of me, after all."

Damn it, Dominic thought but didn't say. He wouldn't have minded spending more time with the beautiful Kate, who was also apparently a bad-ass defender of the innocent.

"Hannah, you are not responsible. Elias is. But, I'd be grateful for the help."

"Good."

As Kate started to struggle to her feet once more, he held out a hand to help her. "Take it slow," he told her. Then to Hannah he said, "Wake her every two hours," He turned his attention back to Kate. "And if you have any vomiting or blurred vision get to the infirmary pronto."

"I will," Kate promised. "There's no sense in playing around with a head injury. Thanks for the medical assistance," she said in a formal tone.

"You're welcome. I wish I could've gotten to you a minute sooner. If I had, I might have kept you from needing it."

She cleared her throat. "You did plenty. I won't forget it."

With that, Kate turned away and she and Hannah headed out.

****

Dominic headed to Dr. Avery's office at 9 a.m. as instructed, more than a little curious as to why he had been summoned there. Classes had been going on for a few weeks, not enough time to settle in much less get into any trouble, not that he ever did. As he sat in the small waiting area wracking his brains for possible reasons, to say he felt inquisitive didn't cover the half of it.

He arrived ten minutes early, but he did not have to wait long to be called in. Soon enough the office's inner door opened and Dr. Avery appeared.

"Ah, Dominic Foster. Thank you for coming."

Dominic rose and took Dr. Avery's offered hand. The professor's handshake was firm but not crushing and his palms were calloused and warm. Dominic's own handshake was much the same, he realized, and this reassured him somehow. "Sure. You said you wanted to see me so, here I am."

Dr. Avery gestured for him to sit in one of the visitor's chairs and Dominic lowered himself on to the padded leather.

"I took a look at your records. When reviewing your background, I discovered you were in the third year of your MBBS courses at Imperial College in London and doing an internship at Jenkins Hospital."

Dominic nodded. "That's right."

"It seems you gave up a promising medical career to study here at the Avery Institute. I must say I am honored."

"I am the one who's honored. I don't think of it as giving up my medical career, just putting it on hold while I explore a new, exciting field of study, magic."

"How would you like to do both?"

"Excuse me?" How would he like it? It was all Dominic could do not to sit up and cock his ears like an eager puppy. Already he loved the Institute and he knew he made the right choice coming here, but he missed medicine like he would have missed a lost limb. The prospect of being able to do both was beyond tempting.

"I'd like to set up a small emergency room/triage center and a clinic here on the grounds. We have several medical doctors on staff. You could assist them, learn and do a good bit of the day-to-day administrative work. Would you be interested?"

Dominic stammered something vaguely affirmative.

Thomas wasn't finished. "Dominic, I have never seen such raw talent for healing before. I think that if you combined that with both a magical education and training in traditional medicine, you could be amazing. What do you say?"

Dominic found his voice. "I say, I'm very interested and want to learn more. What do you have in mind?"

"It would mean you could still continue your medical career, if at a slightly slower pace. It would also mean carrying more of an academic load. Because, concurrently, you would be taught the basic principles of magical healing. Personally, I think you can handle it, if I didn't I wouldn't have asked you, but what do you think?"

Dominic considered for a very long moment. Once again, his mind raced with the possibilities. In truth, he had never been so tempted by anything in his life and he realized he did not have the strength to resist. He gave in without another thought.

"I think we would have to tailor my hours and my course load to avoid burn out, but if we can manage to do that then… Yeah, I'm in."

"Terrific! I'll schedule a meeting with all the M.D.'s on staff and we can start organizing this thing."

Dominic blinked then nodded, still a bit bemused. Career wise he was being given a chance for everything he ever wanted. It was that easy. Slowly, irresistibly, his lips curved.

Chapter Nine

"Today we are going to learn about various areas of the brain, specifically the areas utilized during magic," Jessilyn began as the class settled.

That was it. Elias had had enough. In fact, he'd had more than enough. Weeks and weeks of explanation and scientific fact had been drilled into him. Shag-able or not, he was done with Dr. Matthews and the Science in Magic course. He put his hand up.

After a moment, Jessilyn acknowledged him. "I'll take questions a bit later, Elias. So, when –"

Well, he'd be damned if he'd let her dismiss him. This time he did not bother to put up his hand before he spoke. "Sorry, I'm wondering why the hell we have to learn all this. We are supposed to be studying magic. Not science."

The room went still and silent. Every student watched to see what their professor's reaction would be to such an incendiary comment. They were not disappointed. "There are many reasons which we can discuss during my office hours, not during class."

"I'd like to discuss it now. Magic is mysterious and powerful. In fact, it's arguably the greatest mystery of all time and you are trying to disprove that. Much of its power comes from that mystery. Destroy that and, in essence, you take away our power. In the end, what you are doing might even be worse than that; you might be giving it away. Because if you can study something then you might eventually be able to duplicate it. If you have your way, Dr. Matthews, in the future power won't be a birthright, but something everyone has access to. Or it might even become a commodity. You are opening the door to all of that."

"You pose very interesting questions, Elias, ones I do want to address, but, as I said, not here and not now."

"When then? I question whether you have considered these issues enough. Or at all, frankly."

Dr. Matthews was very pretty, even when her face flushed an angry red as it was doing now, Elias noted. Her voice when she replied was still quite calm, however. "In fact, Dr. Avery and I have considered all of these issues at length. Think of what we will learn about the human mind. Think of how we will be able to better teach children to control their abilities once we know how they work."

She was, Elias was amused to see, getting into the spirit of the thing and becoming quite enthusiastic although she had not wanted to discuss the subject in the first place. She jabbered on for several minutes about all the positive applications the study of magic from the scientific perspective could have.

At last, she wound down with, "After much deliberation, Dr. Avery and I determined studying the mysteries of magic from a scientific perspective would benefit us all."

Elias laughed. "Really? If I were sleeping with you I'd agree to whatever you asked as well."

A ripple of shock flowed through the room. Jessilyn's face paled and her expression changed to one of cold fury. "Okay, Elias, that's it. Go to Dr. Avery's office now. I will join you both at the end of class and we'll discuss what comments are and are not appropriate when speaking to your professor."

At first, he didn't move a muscle. He was afraid if he did, he might do something he could not take back. It would be so easy. He could use his magic to snap her neck and within seconds, she'd be dead. For one sweet moment, he imagined it, but then he forced himself to reconsider. To murder her here and now would mean fifteen witnesses. He would never get away with it, damn it. Besides, being caged... well that wasn't on.

"Now, Elias!" she snapped.

He counted to ten, then twenty, then thirty before he was confident he had himself under control. Calm enough, or at least calmer, he rose from his seat and walked out without another word.

As he headed to Dr. Avery's office, Elias was not looking forward to being disciplined over the incident and he considered leaving, not just the classroom, but the school itself. Then something stopped him. Somehow, he couldn't get around the feeling deep in his gut that his life, even his fate, was here and he'd be damned if he'd let anyone alter that. The course of his life was his to set. So, he let out a string of virulent curses for several minutes as he continued walking in the direction of Dr. Avery's office.

He gave the door a light tap then heard Dr. Avery's voice. "Come."

Dr. Avery gestured to the comfortable guest chairs in front of his desk to indicate to Elias he should sit. He did.

"So, I hear there was a problem today in the Science in Magic class."

Elias said nothing.

Avery held Elias's gaze, but he too said nothing, at least not at first. After a time, Avery stated, "Understand this, if you ever insult Dr. Matthews the way you did today again, you will be expelled. In fact, you will be lucky if that is all that happens to you." He studied Elias a moment more before remarking, "I'm a civilized man, Elias, but don't test me. Not on this."

For one charged instant, Elias sensed Avery's reined power and indomitable will then the impression subsided. Even so, he was left feeling uneasy.

"As to this particular incident, the insult to Dr. Matthews and all the rest of it, I have a few directives. First and foremost, you will personally apologize to Dr. Matthews. Elias, it had better be sincere.

Next, you will learn better manners in the future by observing Dominic, Dr. Matthews and I, and by working alongside us here in this office and the clinic. You will also learn a bit of humility by serving lunch to your fellow students. And finally, you will research magic and science and write a fifty-page paper on how science can be used to benefit magic and those who practice it, and vice versa. You will research how the two disciplines can and should co-exist. You will do all this for a month with the paper being due to Dr. Matthews at the end of that time. Then, if no further similar incidents have occurred, we'll see," Thomas decreed.

"No," Elias said.

Avery's eyebrows winged up. "No?"

"No."

Avery's jaw tightened, but his voice was calm when he spoke again. "Am I to understand you no longer wish to study at the Avery Institute?"

"Not at all. I do find this particular course of study unnecessary, maybe even dangerous. So, I do not wish to continue it."

"Dangerous? In my view, it's hardly that. You may feel free to disagree, but you will do so with respect. In any case, the course is required, so if you still want to study here you will complete the course and you will do everything demanded of you. You will do everything we have discussed today without complaint. Otherwise, you will have to leave. It's up to you."

Unable to say no, yet unwilling to say yes, Elias maintained a stubborn silence.

Seeming to recognize the corner he had backed Elias into, Avery nodded then said, "Let me know what you decide. Now, if there's nothing else, you ought to get back to class."

Burning with suppressed rage, Elias did as he was told. It seemed he had little choice.

He'd opened the door to leave when Dr. Avery added, "If you intend to continue your studies, I'll expect you back here this afternoon at four p.m. sharp. Be prompt."

For Elias, the words barely registered. He had hoped things would be different here, but he was as caged here as he was in the non-magical world. Not only caged, but also humiliated. Well, he was done with that. Murdering his father and mother had damn well brought that part of his life to an end. So, while he might be enraged, he would not let that draw him into making a mistake. For now, he would follow orders and research. He would deliver an excellent paper on science and magic, all the while focusing on what truly mattered to him: the history of magic, its origins and his own. In addition, he would find out more about this Baylor and these dark forces they were supposed to fight. That was where he would start.

****

Over the next weeks, the Avery Institute's library became his second home. He spent his every free hour there and soon learned wizards kept meticulous records, just as non-mages also did. Everything from births, to marriages, to deaths was accounted for. Even, he discovered, criminal records going back hundreds of years. This was only somewhat surprising to him. In spite of the risk if said records were ever found by non-magical people, they had been kept for posterity for close to a millennium.

What was shocking? Seeing his mother's surname, Benedict, in connection with various crimes. Not once or even twice, but multiple times over the centuries, he saw as he flipped through the pages of an old tome listing perpetrators, crimes and punishments throughout

Western Europe. At least once a generation, he calculated, from 1000 A.D. to 1789 A.D, various ancestors of his had committed numerous atrocities. Looking over the list almost made him understand the need for the Inquisition and later the witch trials in America.

1789 he mused. At which point, the records stopped. Already he had noticed fewer and fewer birth records leading up to this period. Still, that could not account for the sudden and immediate absence of records after that time. Many were slaughtered during the Inquisition, more during the Salem witch trials in 1692 and 1693 and still more during the chaos of the French revolution, of course, and yet... Could there have been some other reason for the disappearance of so many? Did the survivors go into hiding? If so, and he thought it likely, then there would be traditional human records from this point, right? Sensing their grip on power was lessening in a steadily more modern, secular, educated world, did they decide to give that part of their existence up and continue working in the shadows? Again, he thought it likely.

With a new avenue to pursue, he started to search for birth and baptismal records. Luck, or perhaps even Baylor himself, was with him because he found what he was looking for after a few hours. Constance

Benedict, born 1701, presumed dead, 1723. Constance had been raised in a convent in Burgundy, France after her parents died. According to convent records, she proved a most recalcitrant pupil. In 1716, she was flogged for the sin of fornication which she committed with the young man who brought in food to the convent. He was dismissed from his employment with the convent, tarred and feathered by the townsfolk and replaced with a far older, less susceptible man. As for Constance, she was given the lash to chastise her unruly spirit then kept a virtual prisoner, confined to her tiny room.

He next found mention of her in 1722. In the autumn of that year, a pregnant Constance was discovered, 'practicing the dark arts and consorting with the devil.' A lengthy trial was held and in May of 1723 she was convicted of same. On the eve of her execution, however, the convent burned to the ground. There were no survivors, but the origin of the blaze appeared to be the cell in which she was held.

Although she was presumed dead, a woman claiming to be her daughter, Marguerite Benedict, caused great havoc in the upper echelons of Parisian society some twenty years later. Marguerite's journal, an excellent find, described her adventures in her own words. Constance having been pregnant at the time of her supposed death, if she had survived it was conceivable a daughter might have been born. That the girl was by all accounts the very picture of her mother justified this supposition.

According to the journal written by the lady herself and corroborated by other more objective sources, Marguerite spent much of her life in the decedent salons of eighteenth century Paris. She offered… unique services of all types and descriptions. By age 36, she ran the most exclusive, discreet, high-class brothel in all of France called Amour. But in truth, Amour was a cover for a great coven of witches, doing dark magic for their own gain and to the detriment of the kingdom of France. In 1785 before the terror began, a premonition of the chaos to come and the death of her child and grandchild caused her to send her son, Francois, age 42, by all accounts a decent fellow, and her grandson, Louis, age 18, a dissipated, immoral wretch, to England while she remained to take advantage of the chaos. In 1791, she met her death at the hands of Madame la Guillotine when she was betrayed by a member of her own coven who was frightened of Madame Benedict's worst excesses.

Louis Benedict and his father arrived in England and took possession of a grand estate purchased by Marguerite some years before. A mere month after their arrival, Francois suffered a fatal fall from the highest turret. The incident was ruled an accident by the local magistrate, leaving young Louis in charge of the estate. The same estate he, Elias, had called home since birth.

By this point, Elias's head spun with so many facts and such wild speculation he had to pause. There was more, so much more, but he needed a moment to take it all in. He took a deep breath and tried to clear his mind. He came from a long line of dark wizards, or so it appeared. Perhaps this was why he never felt connected to anyone or anything. Perhaps this was why he was able to murder his own parents in cold blood and with little regret.

In that moment, he realized he would do the same again if he could. That they kept all of this from him didn't only gall, it filled him with a murderous rage. As a Benedict, his mother at least must have known. The irrational fear coupled with a noticeable lack of surprise in her face when he had killed her made far more sense now. Hot, black fury rolled through him then cooled once he grasped nothing had changed. He had come here to find his place and by God, he had found it in the shadow of his ancestors. Satisfaction surged inside of him at the thought and, calmer, he settled himself to discover everything there was to find about his bloodline and the dark forces ruling it.

****

After some weeks of researching his family history, Elias decided he had enough to be getting on with and turned his attention to the dark forces. It did not take long to discover Baylor was rising as Avery had said. Not only that, he would manifest himself in the very woods surrounding the estate. But Elias wanted to learn more and in spite of this confirmation, he did not trust Thomas Avery as a source of information. He had to see it all for himself, preferably in black and white.

Luck was with him again. After much searching, he found a direct, well-documented connection between his ancestors and Baylor. What an exciting discovery. That the incident involved both was quite a bonus. When he unearthed a full and complete account of his great-uncle William Benedict's encounter with Baylor and his dark forces, the blessing of the dark god was with him. The dark forces were at their height every thousand years, yes, but there were other times that were turning points. There were times when the dark was stronger and almost powerful enough to overcome the light. William discovered such a time was approaching and so in 1939 he supported the Nazi's and hoped to use his own talents to call Baylor and his forces and press them into service. Most unfortunately, things had not worked out. William called the dark forces, but was consumed by them.

What a pity, Elias mused. He could have learned so much from this man, his great-uncle.

"So, this is where you've been. I've been trying to call you."

Troy's voice coming from close behind him startled Elias, but determined not to show it, a slight tightening of the mouth was all he allowed himself.

"What the hell are you researching that's so important?" Troy made a grab for The History of Baylor in Britain and Ireland from 1000 A.D. to 1500 A.D. but Elias snapped the book shut, almost catching Troy's fingers, then turned it face down.

He wasn't fast enough, however, because Troy said, "Baylor and his dark demons from hell? Really?"

"Yeah, every villain has an origin story, right? I'm sure it's the same for Baylor. What I've found out so far is fascinating."

Troy gave him a sharp look. "Fascinating huh? It's more than that for you. You have something in mind. What is it?"

Elias let his lips curve. "I'm not sure yet, but when I am you'll be the first to know." He turned back to his work. "Now bugger off so I can get on."

"Fine. Drinks tonight?"

Elias shook his head. "Not tonight. Tomorrow maybe. Now sod off."

Troy made a very rude gesture, but headed toward the exit leaving Elias to his work.

****

It was time to tap other resources for answers, for further information as well as confirmation. To that end, Elias entered Jessilyn's office and waited for her final class of the day to be over and her office hours to begin. He made himself at home in her space which included a desk of maple and a sleek, ergonomically correct chair. Atop the desk sat up-to-date office equipment and a mass of pink roses in a delicate crystal vase. It was, like her, elegant yet comfortable.

He did not have to wait long for her, as moments later the door opened. "Elias, what are you doing here?" Jessilyn asked by way of greeting as she entered and saw him.

He hoped finding him in her office was as unnerving and unexpected as he intended.

Elias rose, falling back into the old-fashioned courtesy he'd been taught by his murdered father. "I have questions I wondered if you could answer."

She fixed him with a wary look. "Questions about?"

"Baylor and his dark forces, what else?"

"There is nothing more I can tell you at this point. We know very little."

He let his skepticism show. "I've only been here a matter of weeks and I've already been able to find out quite a lot. You and Dr. Avery must know more than you are saying." She opened her mouth, probably to deny any knowledge, but before she could speak, he held up a hand to stop her. He put on his most humble demeanor for her now. "I know we didn't see eye to eye at first, but I hope I proved these last few weeks that I can change. Or at least that I can take direction. The truth is I regret what I said to you in class that day and there is no one I admire more than you. You have an amazing mind and I know you could help me understand. There are things you know. I'd love it if you shared whatever you know with me." Now he gave her his most charming smile. In addition, he let his desire, not only for the information, but also for her, show. That he wanted her in his bed could not have been plainer.

It was remarkable how unimpressed she was and her lips stayed in a firm tight line. "As I said, we know very little right now. So many mythologies interconnect and gods and monsters go by so many names. That said, to share unsubstantiated theory would be unethical of me, and that's not to mention the fact that you are a student. To share any information like this with a young man, even as talented a man as you, who is under twenty-one, would be very unprincipled and even if I could, I wouldn't."

All his charm oozed out of him, disappearing as if it had never been, leaving rage in its place. Going with the feeling, he reached across the desk and grasped her by her upper arm to hold her in place.

"Nevertheless, I am telling you I want to know. I have a lot less scruples than you and I will have no compunction about using everything at my disposal to find answers."

She didn't even flinch and he had to admire that. "Well, that's up to you, isn't it?"

"It is. Now, do you want to be a part of the problem or the solution?"

Instead of looking terrified as he had expected, she considered the question. "Hmmm, am I part of the problem or the solution? I mean it all depends on your point of view. I repeat, what you already know is all I can tell you. Now, get to class, Elias."

An all too familiar, embarrassing heat rose high on his cheekbones. The humiliation of being dismissed like a five-year-old child too young to play with the grown-ups burned. "This isn't over, Jessilyn." Unable to help himself, he used her given name in a deliberate effort to convey his contempt.

Again, she remained unmoved and waited until he started toward his next class before rising and shutting the door behind him.

****

Elias was impatient. What was more, he was bored. Troy shot Elias a sidelong glance as they walked through the small village headed back to the Institute, a look Elias ignored. What should have been a most satisfactory evening of drinking, drugs, partying and sex had, at least for Elias, fallen flat. Nights like the one he had just experienced were all very well in their way, but were beginning to wear thin. In short, he wanted more. All he could think of, all he could focus on, was his connection to Baylor, his heritage, and most of all reclaiming his birthright. His heart hadn't been in the usual entertainments at all. That Troy had noticed was made plain a moment later when he asked, "Something on your mind, boss?"

Elias hesitated. Was this the right time or was it too soon? Should he reveal his half-formed plans at all? If so, how much should he trust his current companions with? Should he wait and say nothing whatsoever? These questions circled around in his head until at last he made a decision. He might as well start as he meant to go on. He might as well take the leap now as well as later and let his most trusted people know at least some part of what he intended.

He refocused on Troy. "What we've been doing, it's child's play compared to what I want to do, what we could do together," Elias began.

Two heads turned and conversation died away. "What do you mean?" Gilman asked into the silence.

Gilman had never been the brightest bulb in the box, but he made up for it with sheer ferocity, so Elias decided to answer.

Troy beat him to it. "He means the leader of the dark forces, Baylor. Don't you?"

Elias studied Troy's shrewd expression and determined the truth, or at least some portion of it, was best. "Yes. I believe we can use them."

"Use how?" Gilman demanded.

"Any way we want, to do anything we want." The thought alone made Elias's blood heat. When he studied the others, it didn't take telepathy to see they felt the same. They looked at each other a moment then all three grinned.

Pure anticipation covered Troy's features. "Right then, what do we have to do?"

"I've been studying and I have a few ideas," Elias admitted.

Ever succinct, Gilman barked, "When?"

Eager to begin, Elias considered for a moment. "Let's say tomorrow night. Meet me in the entrance hall at 8 o'clock."

The other two nodded, as keen to get started as he.

"Until then, say nothing to anyone, and I mean that. The only way this is going to work is if we operate in absolute secrecy, at least for now." There would be time enough to gather followers, ones full of unswerving loyalty and well vetted.

"Got it," Troy replied.

Gilman gave an affirmative grunt.

"All right, see you tomorrow then."

****

Contrary to Jessilyn's wishes in the matter, Thomas called Elias to his office again. The previous afternoon he'd been about to enter Jessilyn's office when he heard Elias's voice coming through the crack of the open door and decided to listen. He figured he heard much of their discussion and so when sounds of Elias readying to leave reached him, he ducked behind a pillar in a dark corner to avoid discovery. He'd had no wish to meet the boy right at that moment and he needed to check on

Jessilyn. Now, however, it was time to show his teeth a bit. He was the most powerful wizard alive and a direct descendent of Merlin, after all. This boy needed to be reminded of that.

Elias entered and Thomas gestured the younger man to sit.

"I hear you have been doing research on Baylor."

Elias's face flushed a dull red. Good, Thomas thought, the boy realized now he had been caught out.

"You also questioned Dr. Matthews and when she would not tell you what you wanted to know, you threatened her."

Elias started to speak, but Thomas held up a hand. "Don't try to deny it. I heard your conversation yesterday afternoon." Thomas used his magic to deliver a hard punch to the face. Elias head jerked back with it. "That is for threatening my wife."

Elias ground his teeth so hard the sound carried, but at last he said, "And if I did? You have no authority to stop me."

Thomas let out a laugh that had very little to do with humor. "No authority? If anyone has the authority, the means and the skill to stop you, it's me. You know who and what I am."

Now it was Elias's turn to laugh. "Do you think any of that matters? It sure as hell doesn't to me."

"It matters to me and one day it will to you too. For now, understand this: you will stay away from Dr. Matthews and anything having to do with the dark forces."

Elias exploded, "Can you blame me? I came here to discover who I am and so I have. But I never expected to find I am supposed to take part in some battle I know very little about. You expect me, you expect all of us, to be soldiers yet you tell us nothing!"

"I have told you all you need to know at this juncture. When the time is right –"

"When the time is right?! Like hell. You implied I don't know who and what you are. Well, it is clear you don't know who I am either. My ancestry contains some of the greatest dark wizards down the ages and I have power of my own, by God. I did not come here to be told what to do. I sure as hell didn't come here to be a soldier in your bloody army. I came here to embrace who and what I am."

"Even if that means embracing the dark?"

"Yes."

Thomas stilled for a long moment. "I see my instincts were right. I started this school to develop a means to fight Baylor and his dark forces, not to encourage others to embrace him. One more incident like this and you will be expelled, not only that, imprisoned. You will stay away from the dark forces because you cannot handle the proximity. If you don't, it won't be a mere matter of expulsion. I will come for you and I will stop you. No matter what it takes."

Elias showed his teeth in a ferocious grin. "Really? Somehow I'm not so sure of that." He rose. "You once told me not to test you. Don't you test me. Not on this. Not on anything. I won't be dictated to. If you can stop me, try it. Please, I'm begging you. But I don't think you can."

"Well, I suppose we'll see then, won't we? You have one more chance, just one. Now go." After a pause, Thomas added, "Elias, I will be watching you."

Fighting the impulse to use his magic every step of the way, Elias did as he was told. At least for the moment. His slow, deliberate strides lasted until he was out on the grounds then he let loose with a burst of power strong enough to turn several rather large trees into burning sticks of kindling.

He would not be dictated to. Not ever again. Even through his absolute rage, that one decision reverberated through Elias's mind as he strode through the grounds. That was something Dr. Thomas Avery would have to learn. Going with that theme, it was time to make a more concerted effort to teach the good doctor that lesson. A decisive move was called for. As luck would have it, he already had one in mind. In fact, he had it planned down to the very last detail and ready to go as soon as he gave the word. Pulling the trigger on that would be a real pleasure, he decided, and he went to do so.

Chapter Ten

Weeks passed and even though Dominic was swamped with work, he could not get the beautiful Kate O'Reilly out of his head. Joining her in Advanced Telepathy class was the highlight of his day. When he was partnered with her to do simple ESP exercises, he was over the moon, but he did his best not to let it show. In short order, he discovered she was powerful. That she loved to laugh was obvious to anyone acquainted with her. In addition, her intellect was formidable. Even observing her from a distance, he was able to determine these things. The more he learned the more he wanted to know.

His busy days notwithstanding, whenever he had a spare moment, his mind inevitably dwelled on her. Even after weeks, he couldn't seem to stop it. He wanted to ask her out to dinner or for coffee, or to bed, whichever she wanted, whatever he could get her to agree to.

He'd probably do best to start with coffee, but that didn't keep him from wanting more.

With his schedule, he had no business dating anyone, or so he tried to tell himself. He managed to convince himself of this until the morning she walked into the clinic. The tiny waiting area was furnished with a few plastic chairs arranged in groupings of twos and threes around a scarred coffee table holding out of date magazines. Kate bypassed these and headed straight to him.

Right away, her limp was apparent. "Kate, are you okay? Let's get you to an exam room." As he guided her down the hall from the small office to the even smaller but better equipped exam room, he asked, "What happened?"

"I was walking in the woods and I turned my ankle. There was a small hole I didn't see and I stepped right into it. Stupid."

"Hey, it happens. I'll take a look then we'll go from there okay?"

"Okay, sounds good."

With a few gentle tugs, he removed her hiking boot then her sock, trying not to notice how soft her skin was. "Well, there's no bruising. I'll just… " He took her foot in both hands, rested it on his thigh then he focused his power on her ankle, seeing through skin to muscle, tendon and bone. The scan he gave her ankle was a thorough, careful one, checking every last cell. He was unwilling to let even the most minor injury slip past him.

"Good news. It's not broken only strained. I can fix it easily. That is if you want me to."

For a few seconds her gaze remained on his but unfocused. Almost as if... Dominic shook off the thought. She was in pain; she was *not* entertaining some doctor-patient fantasy. He cleared his throat. "Kate?"

She blinked and came back to earth. "Oh! Sorry. Yes, please, anything you can do."

Concentrating his power, he soothed muscle, eased strained tendons. Kate shivered almost imperceptibly then sighed.

"Better?"

A slow smile curved her lips. "Yes.

"Good."

"You are amazing, Doctor."

"It's not doctor yet, but thank you. Try to put your full weight on it."

She lowered her feet to the floor and for an instant she stood firm, then without warning, she wobbled. By reflex, he caught her by both upper arms to hold her steady. The action brought them mere inches apart, so close he could feel the heat of her skin and smell the sweet flowery scent of her hair. With her eyes clear and steady on his, all at once he was drowning in them.

He steadied himself enough to ask, "Are you okay? Is there pain?"

She lowered her lids then shook her head. "No, my equilibrium must have been a little off that's all."

Say something, anything, ask her out, even if it's just for coffee, his mind screamed, but he couldn't manage to get his mouth to form the words. Possibly because he was too busy looking at her lips and imagining all sorts of things to do with them, kissing them to begin with.

He cleared his throat again. If he didn't stop that shit, she would think he had some kind of rare throat disease. "Good. Well, you should take it easy for a few hours. Then as long as you don't have any further pain, you can resume normal activities, okay?"

"Wonderful. Thank you so much."

"The nurse will be in with a prescription for some ibuprofen and you'll be all set. You take care."

"I will. Thanks."

He got himself out the door, down the hall and around the corner before he stopped to thump his head none too gently against the wall. "Resume normal activities? Take care? Ugh. Really smooth, Dominic," he muttered to himself. It wasn't as if he'd never asked a woman out before. He could charm women when he wanted to, which, he admitted, wasn't often, but he could and had. Yet somehow this woman had him tied in knots and feeling like he was sixteen again, making a fumbling attempt to ask the prettiest girl in school to prom. He shook his head then gave it one more solid bang for good measure. Okay, so he lost this opportunity. Since going back in time wasn't an option, he would be ready to take advantage if another presented itself. Better yet, he would make his own. To be blunt, he would damn well grow a pair. Feeling marginally better, he rubbed his now aching forehead and attended to his next patient.

****

Sleep was a stranger to Kate that night, not because of any residual pain from her injured ankle, but from an inability to get the man who healed it out of her mind. Dominic, she mused, his eyes seeing straight into her, seeking out and eradicating every bit of pain, his strong, gentle hands on her skin. She'd wanted more. She'd wanted him to kiss her right then and there and for one heart-stopping instant she had thought he might, but the moment passed. So now she was lying awake unable to sleep from thinking about him.

Rolling onto her back, she stared up at the ceiling and sighed. She was dreaming, all but fantasizing. That one electric second non-withstanding, he was way out of her league. He would never give her a chance. She turned nineteen a month ago and she was in her first year of college. He was twenty-three and busy with med-school/healing tutorials and from everything she had heard as well as observed herself, he was focused on that to the exclusion of all else.

Still, there had been that moment. How could she forget it? For that one small space of time, he had truly seen her. Seen her and wanted, she knew it. For once, she had wanted right back. Men had looked at her with desire before, had looked at her that way since she was fourteen, but until now her responses had ranged from friendly affection to annoyance to disgusted rage depending on the man and how he expressed his admiration. With this man? Her response was nothing like what had gone before. It was something visceral and hot, something that originated deep inside of her.

It was something she had to get under control. First, because she had no desire at all to humiliate herself. She might be young and inexperienced, but she was not foolish enough to believe that one moment meant Dominic would pursue any kind of relationship with her. Second, because she needed to focus on her own studies. Studying at the Avery Institute was the opportunity of a lifetime and she'd be damned if she wouldn't take advantage of every second of it.

Putting these considerations at the forefront of her mind, she composed herself for sleep.

****

Opportunity didn't just knock, it metaphorically pounded on Dominic's door mere days later in telepathy class.

"Ladies and gentlemen, if you could settle please." Dr. Avery's voice carried through the room demanding everyone's attention and silence fell.

"Excellent. Today we are going to take a major leap. We have now completed the most basic exercises. All of you can complete a light scan of another person's mind. Now, I am going to ask you to go deeper."

After letting that sink in, Dr. Avery called out every student's name, pointing out who each person would be partnered with. When Dominic's name was paired with Kate's, he experienced a surge of triumph and anticipation as he hurried to her side.

They exchanged greetings, then, for lack of anything more original or imaginative to say, Dominic asked, "How's the ankle?"

"It's fine. Great in fact. Thank you so much for your help the other day. I appreciate it."

"It's no trouble," he assured her. He tapped a pen on the desk in a nervous gesture he could not help. "So, are you ready for this new exercise?"

She looked away and her gaze darted about the room for several moments before returning to his. "Yeah, I suppose."

He dared to place his hand over hers. "Don't worry. We'll get through this together."

Turning her palm over, she gripped his then gave him a firm nod.

When Dr. Avery spoke again, they turned their attention back to the front of the classroom. "Take both of your partner's hands and do not let go until the exercise is complete."

Dominic took hold of Kate's other hand as instructed and waited.

"I want one of you to delve into the other's memories," Dr. Avery continued. "Not short term this time, long term. Memories from two years ago will do for this first run. Remember, you will have to sift through the short term memory first in order to access the long term. Decide which of you will do this first. Later, we will switch."

A cursory look at his other classmates had Dominic stopping short. "One second." After a word with Hannah, he was back at Kate's side a moment later.

"Ladies choice," Dominic told her before she could ask him to decide.

"Er… I think I'd like to scan you."

Dominic swallowed hard then nodded. He wanted this on a deep, primal level. That did not mean he wasn't skittish. Who wouldn't be at the prospect of such close intimacy? He took a deep breath, squared his shoulders then calmed his mind. As the tension faded, he cast his mind back. What had he been doing two years ago?

Before he could answer that question, every iota of his tension rushed back as he felt her in his mind. All his memories of two years ago flew straight out of his head and he was left with the sense of her, like a flame, pure and bright, in his brain. She was irresistible and he was so drawn to her he was very much afraid he was the moth. He could not back away.

Then her voice reached his ears, strong, reassuring, and exquisite. "It's all right. It's me. Relax."

He obeyed as best he could, but the task was difficult and it was some minutes before he was calm enough for her to proceed. At last, however, his body and mind surrendered.

For God knows how long, he drifted on a warm, comfortable ocean with her voice a soft murmur in his ear. After some undetermined amount of time, she said, "You are in a hall with an endless number of doors on both sides. Behind each is a memory. I want you to open one from two years ago. Can you do that for me, Dominic?"

He inclined his head then replied, "Yes."

****

That one word, 'yes', coming from him, set Kate's pulse racing, no matter the context. Stop that, she told herself. Now was not the time; she had to stay focused.

In her mind's eye, she paced along beside him down the hall until he stopped in front of a door. Painted forest green, it had a large brass knocker. He reached for the door handle but made no move to open the door.

"Go ahead," she encouraged.

He opened the door and she was thrown into the chaos of an emergency room. She was so deep into his mind that what she was seeing felt real, not like a memory at all. It was all so vivid and strong that she was immediately and completely drawn in.

"What have we got?" Dominic shouted as he and several other doctors? Interns? Med students? She had no idea whether they were in their second year of medical school like he was, but whoever they were, they raced through the doors rolling a gurney carrying a girl of perhaps seven or eight years old. Her pretty, golden hair spread across the gurney but blood dripped from her mouth down her chin and covered her chest.

Dominic bent over the child, ready to shine a light into her eyes, but froze in shock. "It's Carrie Frost." All the color drained from his face and he went still. For a second, she believed he might faint, but instead his jaw firmed and he blazed into action.

In a few swift motions, he checked Carrie's eyes. "Pupils equal and reactive. Where's her mother?"

"En route," another intern told him. "She was at school when she collapsed and started spitting up blood. They called 999 then Corrinne."

"Good. Right, let's get her intubated and see if we can't keep her alive until her mother gets here at the very least."

"Her right lung has collapsed and her left is well on its way," an EMT reported.

"Jesus," Dominic muttered. He didn't waste his breath on any more prayers, but raced down the short corridor to the nearest exam area.

****

Then he was back. Panting and sweating, but back. The first thing Dominic saw was the quiet blue of Kate's eyes. He latched onto them like the lifeline they were and took deep, slow breaths until he felt grounded in the present.

"Who was she?"

"Carrie Frost."

"No, I mean who was she to you?"

How could he explain how much this one little girl had meant to him? "Carrie was this sweet little ray of sunshine who ended up in the emergency room one day with her mother. Cystic fibrosis. This kid, she didn't let anything get her down. Seven years old and all she wanted was to make her mom happy and get well."

"What happened to her?"

"She was in and out of our emergency room for a year, weaker each time. The memory you saw? That was the last time."

She squeezed his hand. "I'm so sorry, Dominic."

"I tried to cure her. Even though I was hiding who I was, and with good reason, I tried to heal her, but I couldn't. I wasn't strong enough, not to heal a chronic disease like that. In the end, all I was able to do was ease her pain and let her go."

Tears spilled down her cheeks. "Oh, Dominic."

"I couldn't make her lungs work, but I could tell her nerve endings to stop registering the pain. That was all I could do for that little girl so I did it. I helped her to let go." He raised a hand to his face and found wetness from tears he had not even realized he was shedding.

"She was so lucky to have you." She still had hold of his other hand and she gave it a comforting squeeze.

"Thank you." After a moment, he continued, "It's the most painful memory of my life, but I want to remember her. Carrie deserves to be remembered."

"You'll tell me more about her? So I can remember her too, through you?"

Her voice was gentle and he nodded.

"Good." She smiled and he gripped her hands in response.

Filling his lungs with a deep, cleansing breath, he wiped his face with a surreptitious swipe of his hand, and, blinking several times in quick succession, composed himself.

Clearing a throat gone hoarse, he said, "Your turn."

"Are you sure you are up for this?"

Her brow knitted in concern and he had the sudden urge to kiss those lines away but instead he said, "Definitely. It'll be a relief to explore someone else's memories."

****

Kate was not at all sure she was ready, but she prepared herself anyway. They went through the whole routine again only this time she could feel him inside of her mind, like the strong solid presence of the sea at her back, with waves of inevitable warmth it would be so easy to immerse herself in. Resisting that temptation, she stayed on the shore and listened to his voice as he guided her to the same image of the hallway with its innumerable doors.

"So, Kate, two years ago. Find a memory and open the door."

Kate opened the door, but two years wasn't long enough ago as it turned out. She was twelve years old, tall and lanky with it. It was not until her Gran appeared at her side and Kate heard her voice that she realized she had stumbled onto possibly the most important memory of her life. No, not stumbled on, it had called to her and she'd been compelled to answer.

In her Gran's kitchen, she stood before the familiar, if cold, hearth.

"So, give it a try. Power runs strong in our family. That means we can call to the elements with no trouble."

"And control them?" the little girl she had been asked.

Janet shook her head. "No, to work with them, to connect with them, to ask and be answered if you're lucky." Janet gave a brisk tug on her granddaughter's braid. "Fire is the first power we gain and the last we lose and it is time for you to see what you can do."

"But what if I can't do anything?"

"Then it's time we find that out as well, but I doubt that will happen." Janet stepped back so Kate could have a clear field. "Remember what I taught you. Focus. Then call."

Kate did as instructed. In her mind's eye, she envisioned fire, a single candle flame, a cheerful spark against the night. In her heart, she asked the fire to come to her and do no harm. For a long moment, nothing answered and she feared the worst. Then heat streaked down her arm and out through her palm. With a whoosh, a blaze roared to life in the empty hearth. Kate's eyes widened then she laughed with the pure joy of it. "I did it! Gran, I did it!"

"You did! That's wonderful!" A moment later, she was enveloped in a fierce embrace, full of pride and affection.

In all her life, no one had ever made her feel as safe and loved as her grandmother did. Now, however, for the first time she'd been given wings. Such a beautiful gift. Such power and such love. Even at twelve,

Kate knew enough to appreciate every bit of it. Her eyes stung with tears.

Then she was back in the present, sitting across from Dominic.

His eyes were suspiciously bright. "That was a lovely memory. Thank you for sharing it with me."

She sniffed a little. "It's from much longer ago than two years. Sorry about that."

Dominic gave a firm shake of his head. "Don't be sorry. This exercise has been a true pleasure."

"For me too." Kate said the words before considering them, then realized they were true. As they locked eyes, she wondered how on earth she was going to manage to maintain her focus when moment by moment her fascination with him increased. Drawn to him more by the second, she exerted her considerable will and broke the contact even though losing the intimate connection was the last thing she wanted. It was, however, a good thing all in all, as Dr. Avery was signaling the end of the experiment.

****

Elias came close to letting out a groan when Kate was paired with Dominic. His desire to get into Kate's mind was a visceral thing, almost as strong as his yearning to possess her body. When he ended up with Hannah instead, however, doing the exercise all of a sudden did not seem like quite such a chore.

Hannah on the other hand went from pale to white as a corpse. Her step back was involuntary, instinctive and he had to quell a reactive shiver. There was something about fear, wasn't there? About knowing he had that power over others. Still, he hid a satisfied smile when her chin firmed and her back straightened. Good, he thought, much as her abject fear appealed, he was also in the mood for a good fight.

"Hannah."

Her response to his terse greeting was a stiff nod.

"Well, I'll start, shall I?" Elias let his lips curve.

Then, as happened far too often, his fun was spoiled. Dominic glanced over, saw whom Hannah was partnered with and asked, "Sure you wouldn't rather partner with me, darling?" His tone was so gentle and affectionate it made Elias nauseous.

Hannah gave Dominic a grateful glance, but shook her head. "No, that's all right, you are already partnered with Kate. I'll be fine."

This interplay was observed by Dr. Avery and he hurried over. "Hannah, I think this exercise might be a bit too simple for you. If you would partner up with me please. Elias, Ben needs a partner."

A far too familiar fury surged and every muscle of his body clinched with the effort of holding it back then containing it. After a great deal of exertion, he tamped it down, imagining all the things he would do to the good doctor when he had the chance. Moderately more in control, he completed the exercise, terrifying the witless Ben and doing his best not to let boredom crush him until at last the tedious lesson was over.

****

The night was cool and crisp as Kate walked through the woods. Fallen leaves crunched under her feet and the air smelled of wood smoke from the chimney of the caretaker's cottage at the edge of the trees. She breathed it in and smiled. Deep in the heart of the English countryside as they were, with no city lights, the stars were easy to see even with the moon high in the sky. On an evening like this, she felt like the druid her ancestors had been and she loved the sensation.

She was well into the depths of the forest and approaching a clearing when voices broke the silence, disturbing her solitude. As she moved closer, she was hit with a wave of what could only be described as evil. Her every muscle clenched tight against it and all of her instincts told her to run, but she did not. Instead, she kept moving forward and soon reached the edge of a meadow. At its center were nine standing stones set in a precise circle. Her natural inquisitiveness, combined with some premonition deep within her, held her where she was in spite of another wave of fear telling her to flee.

From her vantage point on the edge of the tree line, she could see the goings on around her without making her presence known and the light of the full moon was more than bright enough for her to make out the figures gathered around the stones. One she knew very well appeared to be the leader. It was Elias. There were four others there also and their attention seemed to be riveted on him. There were times when Elias could charm blood from a stone; she had seen him in action more than once over the past few weeks. If he were in the right mood, he could convince almost anyone to do almost anything. It was obvious he was in such a mood right now. The way he looked at each person, as if they were the one thing that mattered in the whole world, was beyond compelling and his smile always seemed to be for the intended recipient alone. Using his considerable allure, he worked the small crowd.

After giving personal attention to everyone present, he gestured around him to each of the stones in the circle. Next, he paced to the center, dropped the black robe he wore, then stood, motionless and naked, his arms held out wide. A sharp intake of breath at the stunning sight of his smooth, well-muscled body might have given her away, but they were all too intent on what they were doing to hear her. When a blush rushed into her cheeks, she refocused her mind and brought her eyes back to his face. After a moment, he spoke in a loud, clear voice pitched to carry into the trees and so she understood his words with no difficulty.

"I call to you, oh king of darkness, Baylor. I am your willing vessel. Use me however you wish."

A great rumbling started, deep in the bowels of the earth. The sound caused such profound, primal fear in Kate she could barely breathe much less move. The rumbling transformed to a roar and a cyclone of whirling black smoke carrying the stench of pure evil and ancient death rose up from the center of the circle. Elias stood right beneath it and it engulfed him. He cried out and the sound was an unmistakable mixture of pleasure and pain. The cyclone forced his limbs apart until he was spread-eagle then lifted him several feet off the ground, but he remained in place otherwise, steady in the center of the circle. The smoke entered his open mouth then Elias's veins lit up as if molten lava had been poured into them. Perhaps it had. His eyes burst open and instead of the striking gray she was used to, they burned like hot coals in his head. He shrieked again, longer and louder, and this time Kate could hear a definite note of triumph in his voice.

Then, as quickly as it had begun, it was over. The cyclone swirled back into the ground which swallowed it greedily up. After what seemed like ages, the influx of smoke diminished and what remained dissipated into the open air. For one more heartbeat Elias's veins burned even brighter than before, then the light faded and he collapsed to the forest floor, landing hard on his hands and knees.

Putting a shaking hand to her mouth and praying to God the contents of her stomach would stay right where it was, at least until she could get the hell away, Kate stumbled back then ran, her step as quick and as quiet as she could make it and with no clear idea of her direction. She had no desire to see anything more. All she knew was the blind instinct to get away.

After what seemed like hours, but was in fact mere minutes, she saw the lights of the Avery estate. Tears prickled on her lashes, her relief was so overwhelming. Those lights meant safety. She realized her mind, paralyzed with terror for the last quarter of an hour, must be working again when it occurred to her this was not strictly true. Elias, once he recovered, would return and as soon as that happened, safe was the last thing she or anyone else would be.

Well, she had to tell someone what she had seen, but who? For some reason only one name came to mind, Dominic. Perhaps because he had protected her and Hannah from Elias before or maybe because she'd been inside of his mind, even if for a brief time, he struck her as rock-solid and she knew, without having any real idea of how or why she knew it, that she could trust him with her life. Lucky for her, since that was what she intended to do.

Chapter Eleven

Another tidal wave of relief hit her when Dominic opened the door to his apartment regardless of the lateness of the hour. It was clear he had been asleep, however, because he answered the door wearing forest green boxers, a befuddled, groggy expression and nothing else. With an abrupt jolt, desire replaced her fright. The sight of Dominic's heavily muscled body was an enjoyable distraction even though she could not fully appreciate it given her current state of mind.

"Kate?"

"Hi, Dominic, I am sorry to bother you so late, but could I come in? Something's happened and I need your help."

Looking far more awake than he had even seconds before, he ushered her inside. He studied her for a moment and noted the leaves in her tangled hair as well as the dirt on her jeans. "What the hell happened to you? You look like you've been running through the woods. Are you all right?"

She took a deep breath, nodded. "I am now I'm here."

"Good." His gaze rested on her face for the briefest instant then he closed the door behind her. "Let me get a shirt on and I'll make us some coffee, yeah?"

"Yeah, that sounds great," she called to him. Since he was already halfway to his bedroom, she pulled out a stool and sat down at his charming breakfast bar to wait.

Seconds later, he reappeared wearing a plain white t-shirt. As he made the promised coffee in his little kitchenette, he asked, "So, what happened?"

In a few succinct sentences, she told him. While she did, he said little, but asked a few pointed questions from time to time to clarify this or that point. When she finished, he sat back and ran his hands through his sleep-tousled hair.

"That slimy, little punk. I knew something was off with him from the second we met and of course, I've never forgotten what he tried to do to you and Hannah that day. From what you've told me, there isn't anything more we can do tonight. We should arrange to see Dr. Avery and Dr. Matthews tomorrow though."

She rose to pace. "That's not what I want to do."

"Kate, this is serious. We have to report it," he insisted in a stern tone.

She shook her head. "You misunderstand. Reporting Elias isn't enough. I want to kill him with my bare hands."

His expression altered from severe to faintly shocked. "Oh, well…"

"Yeah, oh. He is playing with the dark force. No, he's not only playing with it, he's inviting it in for the love of Pete. Not to mention, he scared me half-to-death tonight and not for the first time. Worst of all, he is putting everyone here in serious danger. And I'll tell you one thing, I won't have it!"

He rose and stopped her in mid-pace by the simple expedient of grasping her by the shoulders. "Okay, I understand the impulse, believe me, but try to calm down."

Even distracted as she was by the feel of his hands on her, she was nowhere near ready or willing to comply. "Calm down! Calm down! I –"

"Look, we can't kill him, as much as he deserves it and as much as we might want to. First, because it's wrong, but there's another even more important reason we can't. We can't because we have no idea what he's unleashed. Until we do, he has to stay alive."

"What? Of course we do. It's Baylor and his minions."

"Yes, more than likely, but we can't be sure, not until we consult the experts. I have the feeling Dr. Avery, if he is an expert on anything, is an expert on this."

Kate clenched her teeth and let out a frustrated sound. "Damn it. You're right. So, we report it."

Dominic nodded. "First thing in the morning."

When she started to protest, he interrupted. "Kate, it is almost 2 a.m., I doubt anything more will happen tonight. It can wait a few hours. We're going to have a hard enough time getting the good doctors to believe us about Elias's involvement in all of this anyway. The last thing we need is to wake them up in the middle of the night."

She sighed then muttered, "Don't you ever get tired of being right?" He grinned in response. "Fine, but I… I don't want to go back to my room tonight."

"You can stay here. I'll take the couch and I have a very comfortable bed you can sleep in."

She smiled for the first time in what seemed like forever. "That sounds great. I'll take the couch though. I don't want to put you out any more than I have to."

"Fair enough. I've got some extra bedding. Give me a sec and we'll get you all set up."

****

Dominic turned out to be invaluable. He set up an appointment with Dr.'s Avery and Matthews in between classes that very morning. Kate tried to control the nervous flutter in her stomach with little success. Would they believe her? Dominic had been easy to convince, but then, he was Dominic. Already, she was more than aware of how unique an individual he was. She had no idea how easy it would be to persuade others of what she had seen if she could at all.

"Good morning."

Kate smiled in response to this brief, if pleasant enough, greeting. "Good morning, Dr. Avery, Dr. Matthews Thank you for seeing us on such short notice."

Avery replied, "It's no problem. My door is always open and Dominic made it clear it was urgent."

Kate nodded. "It is." She took a deep breath and described the events of the previous evening. It only took a few minutes to get Dr. Avery and Dr. Matthews up to speed. She kept her words concise and her voice level. From time to time Dominic added his insights.

When she was done, Thomas sighed. "I understand all you said and I believe you, but now is not the time to take action, not yet. If we act too soon it could be disastrous. For now, until the time comes, I need to focus on figuring out how to defeat Baylor." He looked thoughtful for a moment, then continued, "Still, if we can learn through Elias how Baylor plans to use him, points to us. If we can find out anything about Baylor's plans as a whole, so much the better."

"So, you'll need to keep a close watch on him?" Kate asked. Her mind began whirling with ideas.

"Yes, until the Winter Solstice at least. I have the feeling things will be over one way or another by then."

"I can do that." In fact, she was now quite determined to do so.

Thomas glanced at her in surprise. "It's not so much a matter of can you, as should you. You and Elias have already had an altercation in case you forgot."

Jessilyn spoke up. "I don't think this is a good idea at all. I have had my own run-ins with him. The boy is very dangerous."

"He is," Kate agreed. "He is also a dirty, filthy traitor and he has to be stopped. I believe I can stop him, what's more, I think maybe I can save him. Besides, I wouldn't leave my worst enemy at the mercy of the dark forces, even if that's what he wants and has chosen. Even if I can't rescue him from himself, I want to do what I can to keep others safe. I'll be scared down to the bone, but I can do it."

Thomas and Jessilyn shared a look, then Jessilyn shrugged as if to say, 'it's up to you.' "All right. But promise me you will check in with us often and call for help right away if you get in over your head," Thomas ordered.

Up to this point, Dominic had said little, but now he turned to Thomas and Jessilyn and made his opinion known. "Are you insane? You can't let her do this."

Her temper, always quick, was already flowing through her. "Excuse me, no one *lets* me do anything."

Her anger rose even higher when he ignored her and spoke to Thomas and Jessilyn. "She's not anywhere close to twenty-one and she has no experience or training with this sort of thing. Putting her in this kind of danger is not acceptable."

Thomas turned a bland look on Kate, who they were discussing after all. "If I tell you you can't do this, you'll go and do it anyway, am I right?"

She held Doninic's gaze for one long moment, then and only then did she transfer her gaze back to Thomas. "You're damned right I will."

"Christ woman, this isn't a game!" Dominic exploded.

"You think I don't know that?!" Kate roared back.

In their fury, Kate and Dominic took several involuntary steps closer to each other and Jessilyn stepped between the two of them.

"Calm down, both of you," she said in a sharp, commanding tone Kate found very impressive. Dr. Matthews wasn't a professor and high-powered scientist for nothing. "I think I might have a solution."

When she was sure she had everyone's full attention, Jessilyn continued. "In intelligence agencies, agents, or spies if you like, always have a handler. Someone who sticks close, communicates missions and objectives, relays orders, assesses the fitness of the agent and extracts them if necessary. Dominic could act as Kate's handler."

Thomas looked bemused. "What?"

"Why not?" Jessilyn continued, getting into the spirit of the thing. "We are seeking intelligence after all."

"I don't need a handler," Kate protested.

Dominic interrupted. "I'll do it. Oh, and FYI a handler is exactly what you need."

Kate could feel her cheeks heat and knew her whole face was red with anger, the curse of her pale looks. "And I'm supposed to sit back and accept that? Not bloody likely."

Thomas held up a hand to forestall further argument. "Jess, that's a great idea. Kate, if you want to do this then Dominic will be your handler. He is already familiar with the situation and the fewer people involved the better."

Kate was torn. On the one hand, she wanted to stop Elias. On the other, answering to Dominic, or to anyone at all, was not her style.

Perhaps sensing her indecision and the reason for it, Dominic caught her eye. "I know I can't stop you. Hell, I don't really want to. I'll be honest, I wish anyone else aside from you was doing this because I don't want to see you hurt, but I promise you I believe in what you are doing. I can't stop you," he repeated, "but I can keep a close watch on you and do my best to protect you. What you are going to do is dangerous. You need someone out there on your side."

She narrowed suspicious eyes at him. "You won't get in my way." It was a statement not a question.

"Not unless you are in imminent danger."

That was the best she was going to get and although that answer was hardly satisfying, either way there was no help for it. "All right," she agreed.

Everyone else took a long and, she suspected, relieved breath as Thomas brought the meeting to a close.

****

As the door shut behind him and he strode down the hall, Dominic fumed. He was a healer. He was not a damned spy, nor was he even a handler. He sure as hell wasn't a soldier, but what else could he do? What other choice did he have when Kate, a woman he was already coming to care very deeply about, insisted on hurling herself into danger? As he strode down the hall, Kate erupted through Thomas's office door after him.

"Do you have any idea how to be a handler?" she demanded.

"No. Do you have any notion at all of how to be a spy?" he shot back.

"No." At that, she let out a burst of laughter, which sounded surprised, at least to his ears.

A little of his rage dissipated and his lips twitched in spite of himself although he managed not to smile. "I guess we've both got our work cut out for us then." He ran a hand through his hair and took a deep breath. "You want coffee?"

"God, yes," she replied in a fervent tone.

He laughed and they headed in the direction of his rooms.

****

"Well, I am not sure all that was advisable, even though it was my own idea," Jessilyn muttered once they were left alone in Thomas's office.

Thomas looked up sharply from staring at his knees. "Not advisable? If that's what you thought, you should have said."

"I may have been a little too enthusiastic," she admitted, her tone a bit rueful.

Thomas grunted, half amused, half irritated. "Had romantic ideas about creating a real-life James Bond or, more to the point, a Sidney Bristow or Lara Croft did you?"

"I guess."

Thomas could not help the swift smile that crossed his face, but he soon sobered. "It may not be advisable, but it is brilliant and, more than that, it is necessary. I need to focus on subduing Baylor himself. I can't do that alone. So, why not let Dominic and Kate deal with the next greatest threat? It is all interconnected anyway, right? And they seem capable enough."

A dubious expression crossed her face. "They do, but you'll step in if they get into any sort of bind or any trouble?"

"Of course. It's what I do; or one of the things at least. In the meantime, there are other matters I have to see to."

"Such as?"

"Such as taking Baylor's attention off you, Dominic, Kate and Elias and getting him focused on me. At some point, he will have to deal with me and I am going to make very sure he knows that."

Equal parts excitement and fear raced through Jessilyn. Thomas said nothing more; instead, he leaned back in his chair and shot her a fierce grin.

****

After the excitement of the previous evening, there came several nights of waiting. During those first two nights, Elias remained in his own rooms, as innocent as the day he was born. However, on the third evening, he left then met up with five others in the entrance hall on the ground floor. Four were those she recognized from the previous night along with one other who was new to the game from what Kate could tell. With as much stealth as she could muster, which, considering she was the first in her class to master the spell of invisibility, was a lot, she followed the group outdoors.

The closer they got to the stone circle, the worse she felt. Her heart pounded, sweat prickled on her skin despite the chill of the evening air and her breath came hard and fast as she walked. With a sickening feeling in her stomach she did her best to ignore, she watched the same scene play out as it had before. When at last it was over, she revealed herself.

Keeping it simple, she walked out of the trees and into the clearing with her hands at her sides in plain view. "That was very impressive."

Faster than she would ever have believed possible, she was surrounded by five men and one woman, all with their magic at the ready, if their palms filled with magical spheres of different hues were any indication. Each was masked and hooded except Elias, although it didn't matter since she knew who they were, of course, having seen them join Elias in the entrance hall and then not let them out of her sight since.

Elias walked toward her on legs that shook, yet that didn't detract from his aura of potent menace. "What the hell are you doing here, Kate?" he demanded.

"I watched you leave and I followed you. Then I saw... all this power. I've had a change of heart, like you hoped I would."

As Elias approached, his lifted eyebrows were the only indication of his great surprise. "Last time we spoke, you seemed rather vehemently opposed."

"I told you, I've had a –"

"Change of heart. Yes, you said. What if I don't believe you?" He raised a hand full of magic, red as flame and black at its center, and held it right over but not quite touching her heart. "What if I decide to kill you here and now to be sure or even because I think you would make a lovely sacrifice to the dark forces of Baylor?"

"You could do that or maybe I'm more valuable to you and Baylor alive." When she got no response, she added, "I want to help. I want to be a part of it all."

"You want to help?" She nodded and he continued, "Then keep your eyes and ears open and your mouth shut. If you say anything to anyone about what happened here tonight there will be serious consequences for you and everyone close to you. On the other hand, if you hear even a whisper that might mean the good doctors are on to us, come to me."

"That's it?"

"That's it for now. Once you've proven yourself, then you might be admitted into the inner circle. Then you will perhaps have the honor of being one of my dark apprentices. Be back here one week from tonight. For now, get gone and remember what I said."

He released her and she left at a brisk, but what she hoped was a dignified, walk. She be damned if she'd run from him ever again even though she hated turning her back on him and his group of maniacs even for a second.

****

In the early morning, Dominic set off to meet Kate in a deserted part of the estate. The place was vast and the entirety of the east wing was disused so it was easy enough to find an abandoned guest bedroom then arrange to meet. The place looked as though it had not been dusted for a least a decade and the furniture appeared to be from even further back. Late nineteenth century would be Dominic's guess. Faded and covered in years of dirt, if cleaned the furniture would still fetch a decent price. He could see that even with his untutored eye.

He had already been there for half an hour when Kate arrived. Seeing she was unharmed did a great deal to rid him of the tension he had been feeling since she had gone out the night before.

"You're all right?" He blurted out the words before he could stop himself. He needed her verbal reassurance as well as the physical evidence right in front of him.

"Yeah, it was intense, but I'm fine."

He let his gaze travel over her from head to toe one last time then met her gaze. "What did you learn?"

"I have names. He's gathering followers. He even has a name for them. He calls them his dark apprentices. I can also tell you Elias repeated the ritual, verbatim from start to finish and its effect increased exponentially. Other than that, not much."

"How did Elias react to you crashing the party?"

"He threatened me, of course." She ignored Dominic's curses. "But he didn't hurt me. He didn't touch one hair on my head. He knows

I am too valuable. I'm safe enough, at least while he believes I am on his side."

He drew his first free breath. "That's good. What's next? Do you have the time and place of another meeting?"

She nodded. "This coming Saturday, same bat time, same bat channel."

Dominic smiled but the expression was more acerbic than amused. "Very funny."

She beamed at him. "I thought so. Is there any reason I shouldn't go? This is the chance we've been waiting for and it's already falling in our lap."

"No, you are right. This is what we've been waiting for. You should go." He said the words with the greatest reluctance, but he forced himself to speak them.

Kate gave a brisk nod. "Good. Do you want to meet here Sunday morning after breakfast so I can tell you what I've learned?"

"Yeah. In fact, let's make that part of our standard operating procedure. Whenever you meet with him, you debrief with me within forty-eight hours. All right?"

"All right. Sounds good."

"Otherwise we shouldn't be seen together except in class," he added.

"Right."

He went over everything he had needed to discuss with her in his mind one more time to make sure he hadn't left anything out. He hadn't. He took a deep breath to steady himself then prepared to leave. "Well, I think that's it. See you Sunday.

She nodded again. "See you Sunday."

It was odd, but he had a very strong desire for the comfort of one brief instant of physical contact. To squeeze her hand and feel the corresponding pressure from her would have been enough. And that was bullshit. Nothing would ever be enough, not with her. Better to have nothing at all, or so he tried to convince himself as he walked away feeling bereft.

****

When Kate entered the dining hall for lunch the following day, she searched for and soon found Elias. When he noticed her, he gestured for her to join them. Simultaneously pleased at her progress and scared to death, she did.

After the usual hello's, she sat and ate. She suffered through the insouciant, cruel banter and her own impatience until she was half-way through her meal. Unable to wait any longer, when there was a break in the conversation, she asked, in as casual a way as possible, "So I have questions. The first one being, what the hell was all that last night?"

Glancing at her sharply, he said, "It's better if you don't ask questions."

"That's not how I roll. You ought to know that about me by now. You have to trust me sometime so why not now, right from the start?"

He shook his head. "Only once you've earned it."

She deliberated for a moment then took a risk. "Last night wasn't the first time I watched you and your little ritual, you know."

Elias's whole body tensed then his hand flashed out quick as lightning to grab her wrist. "What?"

Kate jerked out of his hold. "I saw you last Tuesday night. I haven't said anything to anyone. I've made no move to stop you. Done nothing. Told no one. Even though I haven't a clue what's going on. If that isn't proving myself, then I don't know what is. I think I've amply demonstrated my loyalty."

Elias chuckled. "Fair enough. I can't say I'm sorry you stumbled onto us. You'll be a valuable addition to my... collection."

Well, that word made Kate's blood run cold, but she did her best to be sure none of her revulsion showed.

"You still have a long way to go until I have complete confidence in you," Elias continued, "but I suppose I could tell you a few basic facts. The stone circle is an ancient epicenter of power both dark and light. The ancient leader of the dark forces is named Baylor, as you know. I called Baylor and his demons to me. I invited him to take me, but to be his vessel takes preparation and time. Opening myself completely right now would kill me. Even I am not that strong, but I will be. Instead of taking him in all at once in one greedy, fatal gulp, and believe me, I have been tempted, I open to him a little more each time. By the Winter Solstice, I should be ready."

"And what about the rest of us? What happens to us? All of us are strong, but we are nothing compared to you."

Elias smiled in a flattered, condescending way. "Oh, I wouldn't say that you are nothing. You have your own particular strength which is almost as great as mine and compliments my own well."

She rolled her eyes and let him see it. "Thank you."

He laughed then took a bite of beef. "The rest will be my servants, my dark apprentices. As I serve Baylor, so they will serve me." He looked her over from top to bottom, assessing her, and lingered first on her legs then her breasts and finished with her face. "But you, you I would have as my consort. Is that too antiquated a term?" He shrugged. "Even if it is, it fits. I want us to rule. I want you by my side always, in bed and out of it."

More than a little confused and unable to quite believe what he was telling her, she said the first words that entered her head. "But you just said you don't trust me. Now you are saying you want…"

He kept his steady gaze on her. "I want you to be mine in every way. It has nothing to do with trust."

Inside, Kate's whole body went rigid. He was trying to seduce her with the goal of possessing her. If she hadn't already known him for who he really was, he might have succeeded. He was that charming, intelligent and sexually magnetic. The mere thought chilled her to her bones. Displaying nothing of her reaction on her face, however, she said, tone light, "I'm not sure I'm cut out to be anyone's consort. I'm far too independent. Remember?"

He grimaced. "I do." His expression relaxed into a sudden grin, "Still, it'll be fun sparring with you, so long as you remember I always get what I want."

"So do I. That ought to make things interesting." She took a deep gulp of water then demanded. "What else do I have to do to prove myself?"

"Like I told you before, keep your mouth shut and your eyes open. Oh, and do what I tell you. If you can do that for a while, you'll not only be part of the team, but you can help me lead it."

Kate froze with her glass half way to her lips. "What?"

"You can be my second in command. When I said I wanted us to rule together I meant it. If you continue to demonstrate your loyalty, you can have everything."

She took another long swallow of her drink, finishing the glass. "I see. I'll take it under advisement."

Elias let out a roar of laughter then Kate turned the talk to other things.

****

Sunday evening Kate arrived at the appointed time and place to make her next report to find Dominic once again already waiting for her.

"Hi," she said.

"Hi," he said back.

His eyes slid over every inch of her as if checking her for injury. It disconcerted her to realize she liked his eyes on her, whatever the reason. Trying her best to shake off the feeling, she made herself as comfortable as possible on the hard floor of the guest chamber.

"You're not hurt?"

She shook her head and brought her knees up to her chin. "Oh, no, I'm fine."

"Good." He gave her a sharp nod and seemed to focus. "What can you tell me? What have you learned so far?"

"Elias wants to sleep with me," she blurted. That's what she decided to lead with? God, why couldn't she ever learn to think before opening her big mouth?

Dominic said nothing for several humming seconds. "I can't imagine a man alive who wouldn't want to sleep with you," he replied after some time. His tone was even, but not entirely cool. She could detect a distinct thread of underlying heat. Yet underlying appeared to be the operative word since his expression remained quite calm as he asked, "What ahem… precipitated this discussion?"

"I asked him what would happen to the rest of his little entourage when he became Baylor's greatest servant and blah, blah, blah and he said the others would serve him while he served Baylor. I, on the other hand, would be his consort. And yes, he used that word." Dominic swore in a rather creative fashion and she couldn't help a sardonic grin in response. "My thoughts exactly."

"How many times do I have to tell you, this isn't a damn game, Kate," he informed her in a fierce whisper.

"I know that," she snapped back. "Nobody knows that better than me."

He assessed her. "Fair enough. What else did you learn? Anything not of a carnal nature?"

She chuckled then gave him the particulars, everything she could remember, which, as it turned out, was quite a lot.

"The first thing I think I should tell you is, he's entirely serious. He intends to join with Baylor and the dark forces. One good thing though, time is, at least for now, on our side."

"Huh? What makes you say that?"

"He can't take in Baylor and his demons all at once. If he did, he would die. According to him, it has to happen by degrees. In the end, of course, the process will kill him, but Baylor wants to use him first. I got that much even though I tried my best not to open myself."

Dominic sent her a sharp glance. "You sure you're okay?"

"Positive. I've got a handle on it, at least for now. I hope by the time things get difficult we'll have enough to stop him."

Dominic nodded then asked, "Anything else?"

Kate shook her head. "Not that I can recall."

"When do you see him again?"

His phrasing surprised her, but she let it pass. "His little group of minions will meet again in a few days. Time and place to be determined twenty-four hours ahead of time via text on burner phones he handed out to us. It would be more convenient of course to use telepathy, but then that might alert Dr. Avery or one of the other professors. This way there is no magical trail of any kind. He's being very careful."

"Okay." Dominic digested that then peered at her. "Your head for detail is quite impressive. I'll report to Thomas and you contact me with the time and place of that next meet so we can set up our own."

"Right." She smiled at him, gave him a jaunty salute then left him to his own devices.

Chapter Twelve

There Kate was with Elias again. Hannah was more than a little stunned, very angry and, if she was honest with herself, hurt. For once Hannah believed she had found a friend in Kate, or at least someone to look up to. Like a big sister. She hadn't minded playing the role of annoying little sister at all since she could hang around with Kate. But now? She barely saw the older girl anymore much less spoke to her since Kate was now spending most of her time with Elias and his complement of creeps and there was no way Hannah was getting anywhere near them. The betrayal she felt was perhaps a bit out of proportion, she and Kate had enjoyed no more than half-a-dozen conversations after all, but Hannah could not help feeling it all the same.

For once, Elias and his group moved along quickly after telepathy class and Kate stayed behind. As soon as they were out of sight, Kate headed over.

"Hi, how are you doing, Hannah?"

Hannah said nothing. She did not even look at Kate, instead, she continued to grab the things she needed out of her locker.

"Are you okay?"

"Like you care," she muttered just loud enough for Kate to hear.

Kate had the nerve to look upset even a little shaken. "What? Of course I care."

"Really? Why are hanging out with those jerks then?"

Kate had the grace to look abashed, but said only, "I promise it isn't what it looks like –"

"Then what is it like?"

Kate winced visibly. "I can't tell you, but I swear –"

"You know what? Save it. I don't want to hear any more crummy excuses. You are like everyone else and it's time we both accepted that."

Hannah slammed her locker shut with a clang and left Kate standing there with her mouth open. She had her own projects now and that is what she would focus on. She would forget all about Kate.

****

Two weeks passed and they were no farther forward, but Kate considered the fact that she was still alive a victory in and of itself. Being unsuspected and undiscovered were also good things. As she waited for Dominic to arrive, (for once she had gotten to their meeting place before him) she soaked in the quiet beauty of the clearing. Located on the opposite side of the forest from the circle, the place was a favorite of hers and they met there at her request.

"Well, this is a nice spot." Dominic made the comment as he lowered himself to sit on the large boulder beside her.

Kate glanced over at him. "It is, isn't it? I like coming here; it reminds me of home, the quiet burble of the stream, all the green, even in autumn. It's so peaceful."

He shifted and cleared his throat. "So?"

Taking that as her cue, in a few brisk words she updated him on Elias and recent developments. Since there was little new to report, it didn't take long. Once done, she let out a long sigh of relief.

"Well then, how are you?"

Bemused, she looked his way. "Sorry?"

"How are you?" He faced her and gave her his full attention. "I don't mean physically. The main reason I am here, that I insisted on being here, is to make sure you are doing okay."

Her mind sharpened and she studied his face. "And to get me out if I'm not."

He nodded. "If necessary. So tell me, how are you coping?"

"I'm fine."

"Bullshit."

She let out a half-laugh, unable to help it, even as she ran a hand through her red hair, which she wore loose today.

"Look, think of me as a clearing house for all those feelings you have to tamp down when you are with Elias. You can vent if you are angry. You can tell me if you're scared. If you're disgusted or tempted or any damn thing at all you can tell me. I want to help you process whatever feelings you are having so they don't consume you and eat you up inside or worse, spew out at the worst possible time."

"When I'm with Elias you mean."

He nodded a second time. "Use me. Otherwise I'm not doing what I am here to do."

She had to move, so she rose and paced around the tiny clearing. "When I'm in it, when I'm with him, I'm okay mostly. I pretend I'm back on the stage." His eyebrows rose in question and she explained, "I was a lead actress in the community theater in my village and I almost studied acting in Dublin." She took a deep breath then returned to the topic at hand. "When I'm not with him I try not to think about the things I've seen him do. I put it all out of my mind. I won't say it isn't hard, but the worst part is worrying about getting caught. *That* keeps me up at night I can tell you. Weird, right?"

This time Dominic shook his head. "Not at all. That kind of reaction seems pretty normal to me."

She hesitated a moment, then decision made, she sat next to him again. "If ever I'm not, normal that is, you'll tell me?"

"I'd be happy too." He offered her a teasing grin and she rolled her eyes, but found she had to hold back a grin of her own.

Dominic pondered for a moment. "You do bring up a good point. This has all happened so bloody fast I never even considered it, but we need to have an exit strategy, a way of getting you out fast if it all falls apart."

"Too right you are. If there's anything I have learned in the past few weeks, it's that Elias is very dangerous and his lackeys only a little less so. It also concerns me that he seems to be collecting more and more of them every day. It's a very disturbing trend. Given all of that, and since I don't have a death wish, an exit strategy sounds like a great idea."

"Leave it to me. I'll come up with something." His tone was decisive as well as reassuring and she took comfort from it.

He rose and she did likewise. "Where and when next week?" he asked.

"How about 11 a.m., this Sunday in the east wing? It's deserted at that time of the morning."

"Sounds good. By then I'll have the things we discussed worked out."

She had almost gained the edge of the clearing when his voice reached her. "Kate?" She stopped, but didn't turn around. "If you need me, call me anytime, day or night."

"That offer means a lot. Thanks."

Feeling an all too brief sense of well-being and safety, she headed through the trees and back to the estate.

****

Sunday morning was cold and dreary and so was the corridor in the east wing, but Dominic barely noticed as he waited for Kate to arrive. Soon enough her distinctive footsteps echoed through the hall, the firm tap of her heels on the flagstones unmistakable.

They exchanged greetings then he gathered his thoughts and began. "So, we talked about an exit strategy last time we met and I'd like to try something," Dominic said.

"Such as?"

He chose his words with care. "Do you trust me?"

She shrugged. "As much as I trust anyone, I suppose. Why? What do you have in mind?"

Her tone was in fact deeply distrustful and if the situation hadn't been so serious he would have smiled. "Something that is going to require a great deal of trust. So, do you trust me?"

For one instant, she met his gaze and his whole being went unsteady. "I'm beginning to."

Sensing this was as far as she was willing to go, (and why not since they had known each other a matter of one month, two weeks and three days. Not that he was keeping track.) he told her his plans. "I think we should use telepathy." Her shocked face told him what she thought of that idea, so before she could speak he clarified, "Only in an emergency."

At the moment, she was incapable of speech, so he hurried on. "I know it is a very intimate prospect, but hear me out. This way, I'd know right off if you were in danger. I would leave myself open and unblocked during the times you meet with Elias and his cohorts. If the circumstances call for it, you send out a warning signal and I will be there in a flash. I can teleport to you within seconds."

"Hmm, I see." Her face and tone gave nothing away now and he wondered what she was thinking. He was sorely tempted to read her mind and find out, but he resisted the impulse.

"I realize it's a bit extreme, but it's the best way I know of to protect you."

"And we'd only use it in an extreme situation? Life or death?"

"That's right," he confirmed.

She considered logistics then said, "We'd have to test it to make sure it worked, as well as for range and you're right, we would have to trust each other implicitly."

He nodded. "And respect each other too. We'd have to go far deeper into each other's minds than we ever have before. It wouldn't be like it is in class. The deeper you go the easier it is to stray too far into another person's mind, we both know that. We'd have to be careful." After a pause full of some undefinable tension, he asked, "Are you game?"

She gave a sharp nod of decision. "Yes. Let's test it now."

"What, now?! Right now?"

"I don't have anywhere to be do you? Besides, there's no time like the present and we might need to practice a while before we get it right."

Dominic's belly jittered, but he agreed. Moments later they were sitting on the floor facing each other, eyes closed. They calmed themselves using meditation as they had been taught then, taking a deep breath, he opened himself, while, he assumed, Kate did the same.

In a flash, he was aware of her on every level. A very annoying noise, like a fire alarm resounded through his brain. The color red washed over his vision and he got a sense of place. He could see the room from her perspective and had no trouble pinpointing her location.

"Are you receiving me, darlin'?" she asked.

"Yes, yes, Christ, could you turn down the volume?" Her laughter rippled out then the noise cut off, the red tinting his vision turned a beautiful ocean blue and he disconnected. It was this sort of thing that it was vital for him to avoid.

She blinked and opened her eyes. "Why'd you stop? It was working."

Rather than try to find the words to explain, he raised an eyebrow. Any words he found would be woefully inadequate to describe the risk they were both taking and the temptation that filled him to take it anyway.

"Oh." The one syllable held a wealth of comprehension and nothing more needed to be said.

Some time later, he stated, "It works. That's all we need to know."

"But shouldn't we try it over different distances? What if the connection weakens if we are too far apart?"

"Yes, we should, but not now. We know enough to be getting on with and anyway I'll stay close."

She nodded and rose. "All right then." He rose as well and walked her to the door. "Well, I'll see you in a few days."

"Yeah, see you then," Dominic replied.

****

After several more weeks, Kate began to adjust to her new normal, at least as far as it was possible to adjust to the situation she found herself in. Meetings with Elias and his minions were followed by debriefings with Dominic which kept her sane. This morning, however, Thomas, Jessilyn, she herself and Dominic were all assembled and the fact made her nervous. What if Elias got wind of it? Quite as important, why were they all gathering in Thomas's office? Dominic met Thomas here to give him regular status reports because, unlike her, Dominic, as medical personnel, had a legitimate reason to be here. Were they planning to pull her out? Her fists clenched. Let them try. She was not done yet, not by a long shot.

As she and Dominic entered, Thomas invited them to sit then got right to the point. "Kate, I need your assessment of Elias."

Taken aback, she asked the first question that came to mind. "What sort of assessment?"

"How powerful is he? How much of a risk is he? Can he be contained? Should he be?"

Kate blew out a breath. "All that then?"

Thomas nodded. "All that for a start." He placed his elbows on his desk then steepled his fingers. "We have Baylor and his dark forces to contend with and that is our main priority, but don't think it hasn't occurred to me Elias could be, probably is, almost as dangerous."

Kate digested that for a moment then took the questions in strict order of asking. "Is he powerful? Absolutely. Is he a risk? Definitely, but there's no way I can gauge how much of one except to say, a big one. Can he be contained? I doubt it. Should he be? Well, now, who decides that? Us? I want him stopped and I'm prepared to be the one to stop him. But I'm not sure I am comfortable being judge, jury and executioner, if that's what you're asking."

Jessilyn cut in. "No one's saying anything about execution."

"Well, judge and jury then."

Thomas held up a hand before Kate could say anything more. "Let's take this step-by-step. It seems to me, according to our collective, expert judgement, he is dangerous." No one argued so he went on. "I think what we need is a containment cell. If we don't use it to house Elias, chances are we will have to use it to house someone else sometime in the future. Jessilyn and I will continue to work on that. While that task is being accomplished, a justice system will be developed then put in place. Dominic, I would like you to work with me on that."

Dominic looked shocked then doubtful. "Are you sure? I'd be happy to help, but remember, I was pre-med not pre-law in my former life."

"True, but you have an unerring moral compass. I need men like you to help establish a brand-new justice system. For that matter, I need help developing the structure for a new society. Will you do it?"

"I'm not sure…"

"Dominic, Thomas is right," Kate put in. "He needs a certain sort of man to do a very hard job. You are the most honorable man I know. There's no one better."

Dominic squared his shoulders. "Of course. I will do my best."

Kate had often felt the emotion pride in her life, often in connection with others such as her grandmother, and she felt it again now. Dominic was an amazing man, one ready to take on any task that needed doing. They were all coming to rely on him. More importantly, she was coming to rely on him. Thomas was right in recognizing Dominic's attributes and if she felt a slight bit of apprehension he might be taking on too much, she let it be.

A sudden, unnerving supposition occurred to Kate. "Well, where does that leave me?"

"That leaves you right where you are, at least for now. We still need you in the field, gathering as much intelligence as you can, if you think can manage."

"Will Dominic still be my handler?"

She directed the question to Thomas, but Dominic replied. "Absolutely." His rock solid gaze steadied her as always, she squared her own shoulders then nodded. If Dominic could take on building a new society, she could safeguard it.

****

Time to move things forward, Kate decided some days later. If she was going to make a more detailed, proper assessment of Elias, she needed to know more about him. So, when they were walking alone through the woods and back to the Institute after completing the ritual yet again, she said, "Can I ask you a personal question?"

"Sure, as long as you understand I can and will tell you to sod off if I like instead of answering," replied Elias.

"Why are you doing all of this? It will kill you in the end."

He shook his head. "I'm not so sure about that. I'm strong and it needs me. Besides, it's offering me everything I want in exchange." He glanced over and saw her somber expression. "And now you're asking yourself what's wrong with me and what sort of twisted childhood I had, I can tell."

She gave him a sideways glance. "Did you? Have a horrible childhood, I mean?"

He shook his head. "No. There was no physical abuse or neglect. Instead, there was privilege, disregard and unreasonable demands for perfection."

Kate absorbed that for a moment. "I know it's a delicate question to ask of someone I only just met, but I did wonder."

"It's okay. You should know I do not want this because of anything that happened in my past."

Kate was not so sure of that, but decided it would be best not to comment. In the end, she was glad she held her silence because it meant Elias felt free to continue speaking.

"I want this because for the first time I will be free. I call the shots now. I decide what I will and will not do. Baylor and his dark forces are granting me untold power and that is not something I will ever give up."

Now *that* she believed without question and it frightened her more than a little. Hesitation made her pause, but after a time she asked, "So you are stronger then. I suspected it, but I wasn't altogether sure."

"Hell yes I'm stronger." He faced her with a wild, reckless expression. "Would you like a demonstration?"

Feeling a little wild herself, she went with impulse. "Very much."

In a strong clear voice, he stated, "Come wind, come water. Dance wind at my call. Water pour out for all. Let this forever be. As I will, so mote it be."

He lifted one hand and the wind rose with it. When he raised his other, rain fell in torrents but it never touched them. He allowed the spell to run its course for a few moments then when he lowered his hands, all was as it had been before, cloudy and calm.

Damn right his power had increased. At first words would not come, she was feeling something much too close to awe for that. Finally, however, she managed to speak. "Your command of the elements is impressive."

His smile was a perfect mixture of charming and arrogant. "Of course it is." He shot her a look full of challenge. "So is yours I hear. I showed you mine, so…"

Kate had to think fast. She had no intention of showing him her full strength, but on the other hand, she had to show him most of it or he would get suspicious. She would need to demonstrate a certain high level of magic for him and hope it was believable.

She murmured her own spell and let the power inside of her free through her outstretched hand. Moments later, fire burst forward from her palm then into the frigid air with a whoosh. She reveled in it as always and saw no reason to hide her reaction.

"Remarkable. Your power is extraordinary," he murmured.

"Thank you," she replied. Seconds later, she extinguished the flame.

Elias approached behind her with the grace of a panther, sleek, gorgeous and lethal. He did not touch her, but leaned into her so mere inches separated their skin. She was equal parts appalled and fascinated. She couldn't help it.

"Come to bed with me,"

The whisper reached her ears and she had to suppress a shiver. The words were a seductive command that terrified her because a small part of her wanted to obey.

When she said nothing in answer, he continued, "C'mon, why not? You need a good, strong, hard shag. You have since I've known you and god knows so do I."

Kate stiffened at the crude statement then swallowed against her now dry throat. "Maybe you're right, but I don't think that's what we should focus on right now. We should be focusing on Baylor."

A wicked grin spread across his face. "Oh, there's always time for a good shag."

With great care, she stepped forward and away from his hard, muscled body. Without looking at him she added, "We also shouldn't mix business with pleasure, at least not yet. I know it's a tired cliché but there you go."

Silence reigned except for the crunch of dry leaves under her feet as she started back toward the Institute. When she heard the sound of his footsteps, some of the tension in her body eased. As Elias sidled up beside her, he grimaced. "I suppose you are right. I don't like it though. I want you, but I swear I won't touch you, not until you beg me to."

As she set a brisk pace down the path, she tried to get her anger and fear under control. Even though she wanted to tell him to go F himself, she didn't. Even though she wanted to run, she didn't. Instead, all she said was, "Good."

****

Kate participated in the same ceremony over and over, and each time it was like a recurring nightmare she wondered if she would ever wake up from. The dark forces rose again and again and each time they woke stronger and it became harder and harder for her to resist. Elias reveled in the pleasure of it yet again, as he took in as much as he could, then completed the ritual. When the last of the dark force left him this time, however, he collapsed to the ground, unconscious. Cursing, she raced toward him, her mind blank with terror regardless of everything else.

When she reached him, her worst fears were confirmed. "He's not breathing," Vague memories of learning CPR rushed to the forefront of her mind and she acted on instinct, doing what she could to revive him while the others either looked on, paralyzed by shock, or ran. After what seemed like forever, he coughed, gasped and his eyes burst open. While he rolled onto his side then struggled into a sitting position, she leaned back drawing air into her own lungs. As she watched, he spluttered, coughed and tried to recover while she was helpless to do anything for him. Unable to aid him in any way, her control, hanging by a thread for ages, finally snapped and she punched him, hard, on the shoulder.

"Don't you think you've had enough? Jesus, I feel like I'm talking to a drunk, or better yet, an addict. If you don't stop this, you are going to die!" The words were harsh, but they were what he needed to hear, by God, so she not only said them, but also grabbed him by the shoulders and shook him for emphasis.

He jerked out of her hold and pushed her back. In fact, he shoved her aside so forcibly she toppled over and landed hard on her rear end.

Swearing, she fixed him with a glare then rose, dusting off her pants with sharp movements. "Grrr! For once in your life, Elias, would you stop being an ass!"

He said nothing. Instead, he dragged himself to a large boulder a few steps outside of the circle to sit.

"I know you can't see it right now, but this force, it will extinguish everything else, light and friendship and family and love. It will destroy it all. You are captivated by the darkness, but there's so much more to life than that!"

His eyes, when she peered into them, were as obscure as obsidian and as untamed as a stormy sea, with no rational sense in them. "Is there? Light, friendship, family, love. Kate, you are talking about things I've never had. Baylor is the one rock solid thing in my life. He's the one thing worth having."

"You're wrong. There's this." Then she did what she swore she'd never do. She kissed him.

Hands framing his face, Kate pulled back enough to beg in a whisper, "Elias, please don't keep on with this. Stop this before it kills you." She took it as a good sign when he said nothing, but held her gaze instead. "Why don't you let me take you home? To my bed? I know it's what you want."

Giving her no more than an instant's warning, he took her mouth and this time their kiss was without restraint. In spite of herself, she responded to the hot, forbidden temptation of it. A small spurt of triumph surged. She would save him no matter what it took. Hell, she would save them all. Then with no warning, it ended. He pulled back from her and his eyes, which had been molten, cooled and hardened.

"No!"

His voice was a guttural growl and fury leapt and flared in his face a second before he backhanded her. Her right cheekbone stung then throbbed, but the pain snapped her back to reality. Horror filled her as Elias raised a hand and the dark forces rose again. With only the two of them for it to focus on, it became harder and harder for Kate to withstand the assault. The force of it, to use a very bad pun, knocked her to her knees. She found she did not have the strength to rise and Elias loomed over her.

"You say you care and you want me to believe you? Then let it take you, Kate. We can serve it together as equals."

It was not a request. It was an order and Kate was well aware of it. Still… "I- I can't," she stammered.

"You can and you will or I swear I will kill you myself, right here, right now."

Looking into his eyes, eyes now empty of all emotion, she recognized she had no choice and got to her feet. She took a deep gulp of air and opened herself a mere fraction. The dark forces lost no time. They pushed and tore at her, trying to rip into her and take her fully. Yet, it was enthralling in the worst possible way, like knowing something was going to kill you and wanting it anyway. It took every ounce of self-control she had not to give in. With all of her will she thrust it back, held it at bay, but was sure she would not last long. She had to end it. She had to do it soon and it had to be accomplished without alienating Elias.

Mind reeling, she said the one thing he might believe since it was true enough. "I'm not strong enough. At least not yet. If I try to take any more, it'll kill me." As if to support her claim, the dark forces knocked her feet out from under her and she hit the ground hard.

For one long moment, he let the storm continue to rage then he spoke the incantation that subdued it.

He turned his cold, direct gaze on her. "Not as strong as you thought, are you?"

She swallowed against a dry, burning throat and shot him a crooked grin. "Not as strong as you. I want to be though. Will you help me?"

Holding out a hand, he hauled her upright in one rough motion before answering. "Maybe." He began walking away then turned back to her. "Oh, and Kate, so we're clear, the next time you offer yourself to me, I will take you up on it."

Then he strode away, leaving her there, battered and broken, with her soul shattered.

Chapter Thirteen

Where the hell was she? Dominic asked himself the question for possibly the thousandth time as he paced back and forth across his living room. When she missed their weekly meet, he hadn't been all that worried, not at first. Once or twice over the past few months she'd had to miss their meeting to keep from blowing her cover. However, in every instance, she had contacted him within twenty-four hours to reschedule. Not this time. Over the past few days he'd caught glimpses of her so he knew physically at least she was fine, but still… Now a full week had gone by and since dinner tonight she had been nowhere to be found. Reaching out for her telepathically had yielded no more than a blank wall of absence. Either she was too far away for him to touch her mind, or far more likely, she was blocking him. The fact did his temper no good and damn well did nothing to ease the fear gripping and clutching at his insides.

Unable to find her by magical means, he hunted for her in the traditional way. He discreetly checked her usual places, favorite and otherwise. Then he even took the risk of checking her rooms, but she was not there.

So, after hours of fruitless searching of the mansion, the grounds and even the woods, he was back in his own rooms. Unable to remain still, he paced and checked his phone yet again hoping to see a text or voice mail he'd somehow missed telling him she was safe. No such luck. Inwardly, he cursed. Smashing his phone would feel immensely satisfying but would accomplish nothing other than not being able to receive her call when she made it.

He wondered again whether it was time to alert Thomas and/or Jessilyn. If Kate turned out to be unharmed then they would worry for nothing. On the other hand, if something terrible had happened and he or they could have stopped it, he would never forgive himself. One more hour. He would give her one more hour to show her face. If she didn't, then Thomas and Jessilyn would have to be informed.

In one fiery instant, his mind lit up with the sense of her nearness. After one swift wave of relief all but drowned him, he forced himself to focus enough to pinpoint her precise location. She was opening the door to her own rooms. Raw fury counteracted all the fear he'd experienced in the last hours; it even offset his staggering relief. Without hesitation, Dominic strode out and made for her. He marched down the hall and knocked on Kate's door. When she did not open it after thirty seconds, he pounded on the panels loud enough to wake the entire wing. He didn't give a damn. He had to see with his own eyes she was all right. At last he heard her voice, that husky Irish brogue of hers, as she muttered curses.

As soon as she opened the door he demanded, "Why weren't you at our last meeting? Why haven't you contacted me since and where the hell have you been tonight?" As he spoke, he pushed his way inside.

For the first time, the state of her registered. He uttered more than a few curses of his own once he took a good look at her. She was, to use an American idiom, a hot mess. She was chilled, pale, soaked to the skin from being out earlier in the freak storm he'd seen from his window and mascara made black tracks down her face. There was also a bruise forming on her right cheekbone. A small cut sat dead center of it as well. The fear rushing through him froze into a toxic ball of murderous fury. "Elias did that, didn't he? That bastard. I am going to kill him. Where is he?"

"Don't be stupid, Dominic," she snapped. "If you blow my cover now after everything, I swear to God I will kill *you*."

"Go ahead and give it your best shot. It's over. I won't let him hurt you like this ever again."

"Like hell it's over."

"It is over and you will answer my questions. Now!"

She brought shaking hands up to her face and rubbed vigorously. She looked so bone tired he almost felt sorry for her then he remembered the hours of worry, not to say abject terror, she caused him and his jaw tightened. "Answer me."

"You know it's been a slow process, this preparation for Baylor to take him over. Elias believes and, after seeing the ritual numerous times, I agree, that it can't happen all at once. If it did, it would kill him. Well, he took another step tonight. I tried to stop him and this," she gestured to the bruise, "was the result."

Angry all over again, Dominic swore.

"He could have done much worse, believe me."

"Oh, I believe you. I also know there is more and you will tell me all of it but first, sit down and let me take care of that bruise."

She did not protest so he figured her cheek must ache like a son-of-a-bitch. Well, that at least he could deal with. On solid ground, he let his training, both medical and magical, take over. While he fetched the first aid kit from the bathroom, she did as he suggested and sat in a corner of her massive sofa. First, he cleaned the wound in the traditional way and when she winced, he did the same himself. Clenching his teeth, he completed the job then proceeded on to the magical. With a murmured spell and a gentle caress over her cheek, the bruise, already the color of a ripe plum, deepened then faded. Pain surged to flashpoint as he took her hurt into himself, then as it eased, he took a deep breath. Unable to help himself, he brushed a kiss over the spot where the bruise had been. She sighed in clear relief and he felt somewhat better.

"Now, what aren't you telling me?"

Before she spoke, she swallowed so hard he could see the movement of her throat. "I offered myself to him."

Shock prevented him from saying a single word for several seconds. "Dear God, why?" he managed at last.

"Why do you think? I was trying to get him to stop, to get him to want something else, anything else. It didn't work. He didn't take me up on it."

For the second time that night, relief all but floored him, but he would be damned if he'd let her see it. Composing himself, he turned back to face her and hoped to God his expression was non-committal. "No, I mean why didn't you try something else, anything else?"

She shrugged. "Nothing else worked and it is just sex after all. It's nothing much in the grand scheme of things. If letting Elias shag me saves him and countless others, why not? With so much at stake, what does it matter if I give him my body?"

An inarticulate sound of distress escaped him before he could stop it.

She heard it but did not acknowledge it; instead, she continued speaking. "People are dead and you are worried about me getting a little bruised or, God forbid, losing my virginity. Well, it's nothing worse than a bruise or two, they'll heal and it's only sex. So what if I haven't done it before? The point is, I won't let anyone else die. I swear that on my Gran's life and my bloody own as well. I don't care what it takes. What does it matter anymore what happens to me?"

For a moment, his vision wavered and had to shut his eyes to regain his equilibrium. Hearing her speak like that knocked the wind out of him and he all but swayed on his feet. "What happens to you matters. You matter." He took her by the shoulders and gave her a little shake. "You matter to me." And then, he kissed her.

For a long time, he couldn't stop. He lost contact with the whole world except her. He lost himself in the smell of pine in her hair, the warmth of her lips and the cold of her soft palms as she clasped his wrists to hold steady the hands he used to frame her face.

For one heartbeat, she was still, but then she responded in a major way. It was as if he were her one lifeline in a wild storm and she clung to him as if she would never let him go. With a gasp, she opened her mouth. With a groan, he did likewise and soon her tongue was caressing his. Hands, his and hers, were everywhere. His travelled through her hair, over her back then down to her perfect bum while hers stroked his chest.

He drew her against him and when an appreciative noise came from her throat, triumph raced down his veins. As she pressed even closer to him, desire surged then rushed over every inch of his skin and he let himself go. For once he let himself simply be the man he was, desire and all. Everything he wanted was his for the taking and he was not of a mind to let it or her go.

Then without warning, various images flashed through his brain at top speed. The two of them sitting by the lake laughing. Her pretty mouth forming the words of her verbal reports and finally the bruise on her cheek. With shocking swiftness, desire was swamped by memory and some other indefinable emotion he could not put a name to.

As he wrenched himself away from her, he wondered if he would ever get his breath back. Pulling away was the hardest thing he had ever done in his life, but he had to. He had to protect her, even from himself.

"God, I'm sorry."

"What? Why? What the hell for? That was wonder –"

If he heard the rest of that sentence, he would forget why he had to do what he was determined to do, so he interrupted her. "You aren't in any condition to make a major decision like this right now and I won't take advantage of you. I care about you too much to ever do that."

"Don't be daft. You aren't taking advantage of me. How can you if it's what I want? Please, stay."

More than anything in the world, he wanted to heed that plea and accept her invitation, but he gritted his teeth, shook his head, and stepped back from her. "You should rest. We'll talk in the morning."

Even from his new vantage point of several feet away, he could see her entire body stiffen. He turned to go, but as he shut her door behind him, he thought he heard her murmur. "You're damned right we will."

****

Kate woke to the sound of her door creaking open and the smell of (thank you, Jesus) coffee. Dominic set the little cardboard tray holding the two cups on the bedside table then sat down next to her.

She took the first glorious sip then another and, feeling moderately human again, she focused on him. When she did, her stomach lurched. She knew that look on his face far too well for there to be any mistake. They were going to have an argument; that is if she could even work up the strength to put up a fight.

Instead of his usual stubborn implacability, however, his voice, his whole manner in fact, was gentle, something she never could or would have anticipated. "You can't keep going like this."

A sudden, vivid memory of herself telling Elias the exact same thing flitted through her mind, but she ignored it. "I can and I will."

Now a flash of white-hot anger filled his eyes, surprising her even more. He was always so controlled; it was fascinating to watch him lose his composure even a little. "Damn it, Kate! Last night could've killed you!"

"But it didn't. We are so close now. Baylor and his army of demons is rising and Elias is starting to trust me. I think he might even be falling in love with me, if anything he feels can be called love. I can't walk away, not when we're almost there. So much more than only my life depends on it. You know that, Dominic."

"Yeah, I know that. Do you know what else I know? The longer you are with him, playing this game, and the closer you get to him, the more dangerous this all becomes for you in every way."

"You think I'm not strong enough to resist?"

He shook his head. "It isn't that. No, I think Elias, and even more the dark forces he is calling up, are very compelling and they are all focused on you. I think it would be hard for anyone not to become involved."

"No."

"No?"

"No, it will not happen. Do you want to know why?" Without waiting for an answer, she plunged on. "You. The one thing that keeps me centered and focused on what I am there to do, is you."

Dominic said nothing. Judging by his expression, she figured she had shocked him into utter silence. She took another sip of coffee and spoke in a careful, what she prayed was a casual, tone. "Besides, if you are worried he'll seduce me, he won't. Not in any sense of the word. Even if I slept with him, I could never be seduced by him. Not when I am in love with you." Startled to her core those words had actually come out of her mouth, she gasped. "Oh, Lord. Did I really say that? Out loud?"

Dominic stared at her and did not look away. "You did."

She took a deep breath to steady herself. "Okay, well, it's the truth and it's time I was brave enough to say it. In fact, I'll say it again. I love you."

Some emotion leapt in his eyes but it was quickly tamped down and all he said was, "You don't. It's okay though. You are confusing gratitude with love, that's all. And I know I didn't help matters by kissing you last night."

She snorted. "You sure as hell didn't, not if you want to put me off. Not that I minded kissing you in the least," she hastened to add.

He ignored that and rushed on. "Look, I've been with you through all of this. I've been your one safe place, but that isn't love."

For a moment, Kate was what could only be described as gob smacked. Then fury rose up in her like never before. "How dare you tell me how I feel! You think I don't know myself and you well enough to tell the difference between gratitude and love? That is beyond insulting." She slammed her half-full coffee cup down then paced back and forth from one end of the small room to the other. "You challenge me. You infuriate me. You are smart and fun and sexy as hell and yes, you make me feel very, very safe. I feel gratitude to you, of course, but I feel a hell of a lot more than that. And you think I don't know the difference, you imbecile?"

Need and panic warred in his eyes. "Kate, I didn't mean –"

"The hell you didn't! You are the one who is having trouble identifying feelings if you think what's between us has anything much to do with gratitude." With that, she grabbed him and didn't just press, but slammed her lips onto his.

This time it was he who, for one searing instant, did not move a muscle. Then his lips firmed, he shifted and devoured. She had intended to reignite the fire between them. What she hadn't known was that there already was one, not merely present and banked, but roaring inside of him. Add her own heat to the blaze, and it was explosive. Her heartrate zoomed up until it was racing at triple its normal speed. In a flash, his mouth crashed into hers and breath, lips and tongues mingled in a delightful tangle. With one jerk from his strong arms, she found herself flush against his well-muscled body.

Then, just as she started revel in his response, he stopped cold. Well, she'd be damned if she would give up that easily, not again. She did her level best to hold him to the kiss, while he did his best to bring it to a close. When he succeeded, she found breath enough to gasp, "Please. I've dreamed about this. I don't want it to end."

****

Dominic had to tear himself away from her mouth, from her body. At first, she wouldn't let him go, instead she followed his body with her own, and God, that alone made pulling away a thousand times harder. When he managed to get a little distance between them regardless of her vehement protests, he listened as she flat out stated her desire for him then fixed his gaze with hers. He found himself unable to look away and, what was more, he could not fight the rising tide of love and lust and desire inside him, not for one moment longer.

"In about five seconds, I don't think I'll be able say this, so... if you want me to stop tell me now." It had been a long time since he had been on speaking terms with any deity, but he prayed for the answer he not only wanted but needed to hear.

"I don't want you to ever stop," she said, answering his prayer without even knowing it.

"I know you stopped last night because you didn't want to take advantage of me. Well, like I told you then, you can't take advantage of someone who wants you. Let me be very clear, Dominic, I want you."

She backed away, only a little but even that felt like too much in his opinion. He was more than slightly mollified, however, when she grabbed the edge of her sleep tank and pulled it up and over her head. She wore nothing beneath it, of course. So there she stood, naked to the waist, skin glowing in the soft morning light. "So long as we've got that straight," she finished as she tossed the garment to the floor.

In a flash, he wrapped his arms around her and his body was against hers again. "Oh, we definitely do."

"Good."

Fine tremors ran all through him now and he wanted nothing more than to obey the dictates of his body and let his mind go, but there was one more thing. "I haven't ever done this before. Are you okay with that?"

Her eyes grew a little wide with a surprise he found flattering, as if his performance so far had not given the fact of his virginity away, for which he was profoundly grateful. He figured he must been doing something right. In any case, she didn't seem worried or disappointed and that was something.

Then she nodded. "Like I said, I haven't ever done this before either. Are you okay with that?"

He considered, tried to think past the passion haze clouding his brain and managed it enough to say, "Absolutely. It means we're in this together."

She nodded her agreement. "Like always."

Since they were, he reached out not with his body alone, but with his mind. Posing a question, asking… seeking entrance. After the briefest hesitation, she opened to him and in turn, he let her in.

Experimentally, he pressed his lips to the pulse at the inside of her wrist and it quickened. An instant later, a wave of pleasure swamped his mind. It was hers he realized. Hoping to achieve the same effect for herself, she placed a gentle kiss to the center of his palm. This time he felt his own physical pleasure from her touch first then, almost instantly, he sensed hers. Searching her eyes as well as her mind, he recognized she had experienced the same thing he had, some sort of sensual current running back and forth between them.

Right away he wanted to know what would happen if they kissed through the open link. Following the impulse, he took her mouth. The effect was electric, like closing a circuit. His pleasure merged with hers and hers with his over and over in a never-ending loop until there was no separating them.

On a gasp, she broke away and stared at him, blue eyes wide. He stared back, for once doing nothing to mask his desire. Without a word, she dragged him to her and gave herself up to the kiss and more. He broke it, but only to reach back and get his shirt off. Then he hauled her into his arms again, into the kiss, but now there was no barrier between her lush, creamy white breasts and his chest. As he kissed her again, he put his whole body into it by ravishing her mouth as well as stroking his upper body over hers then moving his hips and pressing his hard lower body into her soft one. Smooth, repetitive motions, stronger and with less time in between each, had their mutual pleasure soaring, but far too soon, he forced himself to a halt.

"What's wrong? Why did you stop?"

Her voice sounded breathless, nervous, confused and very aroused. He shut his eyes against the sheer temptation, took a deep breath. "Because if I hadn't this would all be over too bloody soon. And..."

"And?"

"I want to watch you when you come."

Her eyes widened even more then ignited.

Encouraged by her reaction, with hands a little unsteady but very determined, he loosened the tie of her pajama pants, slid them free of her hips then watched as they drifted down her legs to the carpet. For one moment, he stared, taking in the woman before him. "God, you are so beautiful, Kate."

"So are you. All this muscle." She ran a hand over his bicep as she strolled around his body. "And God your skin." Her fingertips skimmed over his pectoral then grazed his nipple and he bit his lip to hold back a gasp. "And not to mention." She glanced down and, notwithstanding her sophisticated demeanor, there was a flush on her cheeks. He was not small. Not to mention he was already hard and she looked a little anxious and very young.

"Don't worry. We'll fit together just fine," he reassured her.

Her fiery Irish temper overcame her trepidation enough for her to remark, "So you say, and how would you know since you are as new at this as I am?"

"I know." A firm kiss revealed better than any words how sure he was. "Trust me."

And she did, with no more hesitation. She let him do as he would.

Trapped in her eyes, he lowered to his knees. Simple cotton underwear came off, leaving him level with the soft hair between her legs. Gently, he placed her hand on his shoulder. She took the hint and used it for balance as she stepped out of her panties. Then he bent his head and licked. Shudders started from her toes and traveled up her body. As he continued to stroke her, he let his hands roam over every inch of her he could, like he owned her. And he let her do the same to him, God help him.

Working on pure instinct and guided by her thoughts and reactions, he did his best to arouse her with mouth alone, with lips and teeth and tongue. Then he experimented with his hands, rubbing a thumb over an already sensitive nipple and sliding the other over the sensitive place between her legs until she was gasping and moaning. When she reached the first peak, he groaned aloud in triumph. As her climax rolled through her and into him via their connection, it nearly triggered his own. He clung to sanity by his fingernails because he wasn't ready to let go, not yet. As promised, he watched as, on a wordless cry, she careened over the edge into sensual oblivion.

He held her for a long moment as her pleasure faded and she floated back to earth. Once she had, he lifted her off her unsteady legs and carried her to the bed. When mere moments later she whispered, "Your turn," his entire body went unyielding with desire. Suiting action to words, she put her hands on him. In seconds, his already firm prick went rock hard and he let out a heartfelt moan.

"Too many bloody clothes," he rasped, once he somewhat regained the ability to think. A few frantic tugs and he was as naked as she was.

"I want you so much."

He wasn't sure whether he spoke the words or if they only echoed through his mind. Either way, they were the absolute truth and she heard them. At last, he let his body down on hers, the full length of him against her, skin to skin. Lifting on one elbow, he ran a hand over her from shoulder to hip then inward to rest between her legs. She was warm and soft and ready for him and she moved slightly under his hand.

"Kate, are you sure?"

She didn't answer him in words. Never taking her gaze from his, she arched beneath him in one long, sinuous motion.

With a shaky breath, he shifted, took her hand in his and eased inside of her a little. She bit her lip, her entire concentration focused on the slow joining of their bodies. He thrust forward a few inches more. A second later he felt her tense and not in a good way, but she lifted a hand, cupped his cheek and when her body relaxed he kept going.

But she tensed again and he stopped again even though it was killing him on so many levels. His body clamored to plunge recklessly into hers, but his heart? His heart could never bear to see her in pain much less be the cause of it. So, he locked his every muscle and murmured, "Kate, do you want me to st –"

Before he could say any more she interrupted him. "Dominic Patrick Foster don't you dare stop now."

Her tone was fierce and commanding and not at all vulnerable so he took her at her word and in one strong, sure thrust, he was all the way inside of her. When he heard her sharp, pained intake of breath, he stilled to give her time to adjust. His body shook with the effort of holding back and those fine tremors, which had never stopped, were like little mini earthquakes now, but he was determined to give her all the time she needed.

After what seemed like forever, her hands began to run up and down his back. He wanted to stretch under her touch like a cat, but was afraid to move. Terrified his tenuous control would shatter, he held still. The last thing he ever wanted to do was hurt her.

Then, when he was at the limit of his endurance, he was only human and a virgin himself after all, the sound of her voice drifted into his ear. "Dominic, it's all right. I don't want you to hold back anymore. Make love to me please."

As her voice died away, he pulled back a bare inch then pressed in. When Kate did not tense up like she had before, he repeated the action. This time his was rewarded with a soft gasp and it sure as hell wasn't one of pain, thank the Lord.

"Sweet Mary mother of God. Do that again."

He did and the pleasure was so intense he thought he must have died and gone to heaven. It didn't stop there. Every touch and caress, every tiny motion increased their mutual pleasure. Then as he thrust down, she arched up, and he could not hold back a guttural moan. She let out another breathless cry, this one full of yearning and arousal. After that, she moved with him as if they had been lovers for years, as if their bodies had been specifically created to fit together and all the time their telepathic connection strengthened.

It was all skin against skin, and heated, sweaty movement as they discovered, in detail, how the other liked to be touched. In one abrupt motion, Kate's arms slipped down, skimmed over then got a tight grip on his ass. In response, he pressed even more deeply into her. The feel of her sent him reeling and he left all thought behind. There was nothing but sensation and her. Her heart, her soul, her body bound to his.

Right when he could feel another orgasm building for her, she whispered, "Come with me."

Obedient and more than ready, he did as she asked. He plunged into her body over and over, with deep, strong thrusts, caressing her everywhere he could, while at the very same time he surged into her mind. Her pleasure exponentially heightened his as it had all along. This time, however, he let himself go with it. He allowed himself to experience and enjoy it completely. In a heartbeat, they hit flashpoint and simultaneous release beckoned. As they crashed over the edge together, he said the words all his actions had indicated. Ones his heart, his very soul demanded. "I love you."

"I love you too."

They both knew the truth of it in their bones, on every level, and they rushed into passionate oblivion together.

****

Minutes or maybe hours later, lying with her wrapped in his arms, he couldn't help but ask, "It really doesn't matter to you that until tonight I'd never been with anyone before?"

"Of course not. It's sweet." He could tell she spoke the truth even though her eyes danced and teased him a bit.

"Sweet." Appalled, he said the word again. "Sweet?!" When she nodded, lips twitching, that was it. "I'll show you sweet."

He rolled her beneath him and proceeded to do things to her that could never, ever be described as sweet.

****

"I'm not going to ask you to marry me."

As dawn crept in, the words were a soft murmur against her ear, but she heard them all the same. Kate did her best to focus on something other than the wonderful things Dominic was doing to her body and answer, but all she could come up with was two breathless words. "You're not?"

Dominic shook his head. "Not yet. You are still in your bloody teens and I am barely out of mine. I'm not crazy. In a few years –"

That got her full attention. "Years?!"

He chuckled. "Yes, years. When we have both completed our education and are established. I want to finish medical school as well as my studies here. I want to be a healer and that will take time. Regardless, my heart is yours, now and always, and when the time is right we will make it official. Until then… That doesn't mean we won't be doing a hell of a lot of this." He moved against her in a way that made her shudder all the way to her toes.

"You are mine and I am yours. Nothing else matters," she whispered as she gave herself up to him.

****

They spent the rest of the weekend in her bed, but Dominic was well aware they would have to rejoin the real world at some point. On Monday morning, he woke her early so he could take her one final time. The encounter was heated, brief, mindless and intensely satisfying.

As they dressed, she put into words what he already knew. "If I disappear, if I stop attending Elias's little meetings, he will suspect something is wrong. He'll come after me." She hesitated, then admitted, "Not only that, I have to see this through."

His whole body tensed in negative reaction, but he ignored it. "I understand, but I want you to know I am going to stay a lot closer now. Where you go, I go."

Her pretty face, with its delicate cream complexion, paled to paper white. "What? You can't do that. What if Elias catches you? He'll gut you like a fish that's what. He already hates you; all he needs is a good excuse."

"I'll be careful."

"You'll be careful?" Her tone expressed the deepest doubt. One wild gesture then she pointed a finger at his chest. "No, you'll be dead."

"I will do my best to avoid that," he promised, tone dry. "You are the one who pointed out there is so much more at stake than your life or mine. Well, I won't let yours or anyone else's be sacrificed, not if I can help it."

When her jaw set in a stubborn line he was all too familiar with, he stiffened his spine and stated unequivocally, "It's that or this all ends right now. If you never believe anything else I say, believe I mean that."

She studied him for a long moment then, realizing he was not going to budge, sighed through clenched teeth. "Fine. I suppose there's nothing I can do to stop you, but if anything happens to you, I'll kill you myself." With that bit of illogic, she kissed him fiercely and left.

Chapter Fourteen

Baylor was rising, Thomas could feel it more and more each day and so he readied himself. More importantly, he prepared his students for the battle to come.

Since classes were, on the whole, a success, he put them at the back of his mind. A bit of tweaking was required here or there of course, but otherwise the lectures were going well. The majority of his students gave him their best efforts and there were several who were exemplary. Kate and Dominic vied for first in all their classes, of course, with Dominic leading in healing and Kate leading in telepathy, but with the two neck and neck in all the other subjects. Otherwise, Elias came in second in all but pure power; he and Dominic tied for first there. As for the rest, Hannah was a stand out in spells and potions. Dominic was also doing an amazing job with the clinic. Leaving aside the specter of the dark forces, things were going better than he had any right to expect.

There was, however, so much more going on in his world. Kate and Dominic and their spy game, as he liked to think of it, for one thing. Readying the students for the battle to come for another. After allowing the students to settle in for a couple of weeks, he began offering what he called battle training. The methods taught were, in the main defensive and, he prayed, effective. All students were trained in both magical and non-magical means of defense while some few learned more offensive tactics. From a purely moral stand point, he disliked even this small sign of aggression, but could not in good conscience take the chance of leaving his people without protection and every means, not only of defense, but victory.

His own personal preparations were also a priority. As Elias was readying himself to take in the dark forces, Thomas was schooling himself to take in the light. Equal and opposite forces represented by very different men, he mused. Not for the first time, he wondered which would triumph.

Being on his home turf was, of course, no small advantage. Born in the heart of England, no one knew or loved this land and its people better than he himself. Even so, the dark forces were strong. He had studied all his life. Against that, Elias had studied for mere months. He sighed, frustrated with his circular thought patterns. It was pointless to try to evaluate the odds of success from a logical or rational perspective, not when the heart could and would decide everything. The strength of his own heart and of all those who were his would determine the outcome. He believed that down to his very core. All he could do was act in whatever manner he deemed best and prepare. Hoarding his power, calming his mind as best he could and finding the answer to one last question was essential. To take Merlin's place and stand in as the most powerful magician, as the most powerful practitioner of the strongest white magic in the world, a sacrifice had to be made. Even now, he had an idea of what sort and the thought terrified him. He would not allow terror to control him, however. Instead, he would keep taking the steps one by one and confirm what he suspected. Then he would pray for the strength to deal with it.

****

When not teaching, Jessilyn devoted every spare moment to searching for scientific ways to combat Baylor. Redesigning then perfecting the dampening field was proving far more difficult than she anticipated. Exhaustion dragged at her, but she ignored it. Time was running out and she must not fail. The problem of developing a dampening field that would only control dark magic was the sticking point. It was the question she could not answer. It was the problem she could not seem to solve even with the help of the world's best scientists and magicians like Thomas. Still, she did not give up.

Each night, Jessilyn came home to Thomas after a long day. His support on every level, from emotional, to intellectual, to practical, gave her strength. She did her best to give him the same and hoped she succeeded.

Perhaps a new pair of eyes would help. Rubbing her hands over her face, she sighed. A new perspective on the problem would be useful, but who could offer that? An image of a shy young girl flashed through her mind. Maybe Hannah Barnes. The girl was brilliant at all branches of science and she was fast becoming an exceptional magician. The first term was half over, but what the hell. The more she considered the idea, the more she liked it. Without warning, her vision blurred from fatigue and she wondered what time it was. Late, she guessed. Or early, she discovered when she glanced at the clock. Time enough to ask for Hannah's help in the morning after some much needed rest.

As planned, Jessilyn approached Hannah after class. "If you could stay for a moment?"

Hannah nodded in her shy way and waited as the rest of the students filed out. Once they were alone, Jessilyn gestured for her to sit. "I'd like your help with something. I am working on a project and I think I could use your talents. I have heard you are good with spells and potions and I know you are great in science."

As usual, Hannah gave nothing away except a certain wariness, but Jessilyn could sense she was intrigued. "What sort of project?"

In a few brief words, Jessilyn gave Hannah an overview of the CDF. She spelled out its purpose, basic design, theory and the problems with function.

"So, you wondered if there might be a spell which could detect intent?" Hannah asked as she pushed her glasses up her nose.

"Precisely." Jessilyn smiled, pleased Hannah understood. "What is your opinion?"

"Well, I would have to do a lot more study. I am only just beginning to explore this new world of magic and there is so much about practicing I don't know yet. I would say it is a possibility and one I would love to explore."

Jessilyn beamed. "Excellent. If you could give me a bit of time in the lab after class and at the weekend, I would love to work with you on this."

Hannah's smile started in her eyes then spread over her entire face. "I would love that too."

"Excellent. I'll see you tomorrow then. Meet me in my office at four."

Hannah gave Jessilyn an eager nod of confirmation then left for her next lecture.

****

In many ways, keeping their relationship a secret was exciting at first, at least for Dominic. Watching Kate from afar was even more difficult than expected, however. Seeing her with Elias was, if he were brutally honest with himself, agony, but it had to be done. The fact that he lived in a perpetual state of heightened terror didn't matter. The constant worry Elias would hurt or even kill her right in front of him and he wouldn't be able to prevent it could not influence his decisions. Although nightmares of her being tortured, raped then murdered plagued his sleep every night, she had to go on with the charade. The game was not over yet. The dark forces had to be stopped along with Elias and his minions. Besides, if there were one thing he knew now about Kate, no one would keep her from doing what she set out to do, not even him.

So, he tried to focus on the positive and he lived for their private, stolen moments together. Moments filled with laughter, intelligent conversation, and, of course, amazing sex. He lived in a near constant state of arousal and his body craved hers. Every chance he got he made love to her and let her make love to him as well, until he couldn't imagine his life without her, couldn't imagine a woman so vibrant could ever cease to exist. He tried to think of that and nothing else as he waited for her to arrive for their usual meeting, but a particularly bad nightmare the evening before, as well as seeing Elias in Advanced Telepathy, made that almost impossible. Hell, he couldn't even manage to sit still and so he paced until he heard the sound of her footsteps.

Usually once she was in his presence and he could see she was physically unharmed, he was able shut down all the other thoughts and fears distracting him, but not today. Kate began her report and only the fact that her safety, even her life, might depend on it, kept Dominic even somewhat attentive. The effort it took was monumental and, for him, unprecedented. Never had he been so consumed with a woman before; of course, he'd never made love to one before either. Now he had, it stood to reason he, not to mention his body, would react differently.

Snapping fingers inches from his nose transported him back to reality.

"Dominic, are you even listening to me?" Kate demanded.

"Of course, I'm listening to you." When she narrowed her eyes at him, he insisted, "I am; I promise. I am a little preoccupied, though."

"Mmm hmm, I could tell. Most of the time, you are so focused and attentive during our meetings. What are you thinking about?"

Instead of answering her, he demanded, "Is your report finished?" She nodded. He hesitated, then asked, "Do you really want to know what I was thinking?"

She nodded once more and he took her hand and led her away. Seconds later, she questioned where they were going, but he didn't answer her. He couldn't since he was deafened and blinded by a vicious wave of lust. In the grips of an elemental force stronger than anything he'd ever experienced in his life, he led her down corridor after corridor. Operating on autopilot, he did his best to get them to his rooms without any one seeing them. He hoped to God he managed it.

In one swift, fluid motion, he ushered her inside, closed his door and pushed her back against it. Tantalizing and enticing them both, he leaned into her but did not touch her.

"This is what I was thinking about." His voice was so rough he had trouble recognizing it, but he didn't care. He was more than ready to stop talking. All he wanted to do was demonstrate by kissing her, so he did. He framed her face with his hands and parted her lips with his. When she moaned into his mouth, he pressed every inch of his hard, aching body to hers.

Long minutes later he broke away from the kiss to say, "And this," as he palmed then kneaded her breasts.

He found her nipples, circled them then brushed his thumbs over the tips. Her gasp was the sensual equivalent of a match to a flame. "And especially, this," he rumbled, as he moved evocatively against her.

He caught her gaze with his and asked, "What about you? Have you been thinking about this too?"

****

Kate was caught up in a sensual storm so strong she wondered if she might drown in it. His desire swept her away so hard and fast she had no time to form a coherent thought. After about five seconds of kissing him, she didn't give a damn.

She did not surface from her pleasure-drugged haze until he asked her a question.

"What about you? Have you been thinking about this too?"

Well, that was an easy one to answer. "God, yes." She grasped his neck and drew him down for another kiss.

"Thank Christ. Because I sure as hell can't stop thinking of you and wanting to do this." he stated, tone fervent.

This time he moved against her, stroking down her body and pressing his hardness into her. Even with the barrier of layers of clothing between them, it felt exquisite and she did not even try to bite back the moan rising inside of her. Panting, he jerked apart the halves of her button-down shirt sending little pearl discs flying. Her head fell back as he touched her and she let out a breathless laugh which turned into another moan. His lips quirked up for a heartbeat then he flipped open the front catch of her bra and she had the fleeting thought she was very glad she had put on that particular undergarment when dressing that morning.

Without taking his eyes off her, he reached down and unzipped her jeans. Then he slid his palms around to her lower back and slipped his strong hands between the waistband of the jeans she wore, her knickers and her backside. Using his thumbs, he skimmed pants and all down over her excellent ass all the way to her ankles, managing to turn the gesture into a caress. She lifted first one leg then the other and kicked the clothing the rest of the way off.

After one searing look, he fumbled with his own jeans and freed himself. Skin to naked skin now at least where it counted, below the waist, they both stilled. "Are you sure?"

The murmured words were like a caress and she shivered. Unable to speak, she nodded. It was enough and he surged into her.

The most accurate, brutally frank word used to describe what they were doing burst from him, (something she knew he never said aloud) then he suited words to action and Kate held on for dear life. To anchor herself, she raised her legs and wrapped them around his hips. The position opened her even more to his penetration and she bit her lower lip to keep from crying out. Then he was moving and the sensation was so all consuming, so exquisite she hadn't a hope in hell of stopping herself from… And then she was climaxing. As she savored that first incredible peak, she sensed his attention on her. She raised her heavy lids and he locked her gaze with his. Very deliberately, he thrust again, into her mind this time as well as her body, heightening the sensations tenfold. Managing to caress her inside and out, he sent lightning down her veins. He did it again, then again. With his every thrust, fresh waves of pleasure rolled in an endless wave through her until she felt as if she were made of the stuff. She was awash with it.

Then at last, he joined her. He let go and let his own pleasure take him; she could see it in his eyes as she watched them go blind. She held him close, and surrendered, body, mind and heart, to desire and to him.

****

Dominic's head was spinning and his knees were as weak as water. Gently, he disengaged from her then he lowered her to the ground. A lock of hair fell onto her forehead and he brushed it back. "Are you all right? I was a bit rough."

Leaning heavy limbs against the door, she opened her eyes and they were still dazed. "Oh, I'm more than all right. That was wonderful even if a bit unexpected."

He felt heat rising up and into his face, but had as little control over that as anything else. He supposed he owed her some explanation, so he gave it a go. "Every time I see you with Elias or hear your reports, I have to keep repeating to myself over and over, 'She's mine, not yours, Elias, and you will never have her, you bastard. She's mine and always will be'. Otherwise… Let's just say that thought is the one thing keeping me from tearing him apart and then picking you up and taking you far, far away from him." He had to clear his throat before going on. "Today, the thought alone wasn't enough. I had to have you. I couldn't wait a second longer."

She gave him an impish smile. "I'm not complaining, far from it." Extending a hand, she stroked down his chest and those beautiful eyes of hers turned sultry. "In fact, I wouldn't mind a repeat performance." Her hand wandered lower, gripped him. "If you're up for it."

He hardened again in an instant. "Oh, I am."

****

Regardless of his anger at her and vice-versa, Elias could not help watching Kate over the next few days whenever he got the chance. That he was consumed with visions of her was nothing new, but once she offered herself to him and he was fool enough to refuse her, he could not get her out of his head. Yet even after that life-changing event, when she held herself aloof and made no further move toward him, he started to wonder why. She still attended the meetings, held daily now, but she never spoke to him directly and was careful never to be alone with him. Curious, he started to observe her more closely than ever before.

In doing so, he learned a lot more about her. She was an excellent student with much ability and natural talent. A quick study, she was hyper-focused during classes. Highly intelligent, she often offered numerous original insights. Yet, there were times when her gaze grew unfocused. Like, now, he realized, as they sat in Advanced Telepathy class. Was she humming under her breath? Christ, she was.

If only he could read her thoughts. But that was impossible; she was a very accomplished shielder, adept at keeping her mind protected even from him. He was dead sure this fact made her a constant fascination to him. With almost everyone else in his world an open book, he found her cryptic words and unfathomable actions captivating. This also made him warier and far more suspicious of her than of anyone else on earth. All this, combined with an overwhelming sexual attraction, made him want, down to his very core, to know her in full then possess her entirely. That translated into keeping his eyes on her when they were in the same room and thinking of her always when they were apart.

In retrospect, he should have known. All the signs were there: daydreaming, fractured attention, soft smiles to herself for no discernable reason. Yet, he had no idea she was in love with someone else until her eyes smoldered and a wave of heated lust broke through her shield and washed over him. It was only for a second, but it was long enough for brief images and sensations to seep through. The sight of hands at her ample breasts, the feel of the skin of her thigh as it pressed to some man's and the sound of her moaning in pleasure at his touch reached him in rapid succession. Then she blinked and shielded her thoughts again. Only years of suppressing his reactions kept Elias from gasping aloud. Only a decade of controlling his emotions enabled him to contain his rage. Because this was no fantasy, it was a memory. He knew it in an instant.

Of whom? Once his anger spiked then dropped to a semi-manageable level and he could think, this was the first thing he wondered. Who the hell was the man in her bed? All he could see was her lover's body, not his face. Face or not, he would find out no matter what it took.

Knowing how unlikely it would be for her to drop her shields again any time in the near future, he didn't let her out of his sight when class was over and they all stepped into the hall. Idly, he wondered how long it would take to figure out whom she was mooning over, but did not care. If he had to wait months or even years to discover his rival, he would.

He had to wait a few days and no more as it turned out. One fine morning as she walked into the corridor after class and out into a bright autumn day, her pretty eyes darted around then landed on Dominic. The way she looked at him, not to mention the way he looked back, was unmistakable and Elias wanted to bash his own head in for not seeing it before. Cold fury filled him as he realized she had never looked at him like that, not even when she had offered herself to him. Dominic was the one she had wanted all along. Dominic was the reason why she held herself away from him, rejected him and the dark gift. Well, no more he decided. She was his, not Dominic's or anyone else's. It was high time she understood that.

As he watched, unable to look away, Dominic approached Kate then drew her into a secluded spot under an archway. As if he were attached to them by some leash, Elias followed. In the dim light, Dominic framed Kate's face with his hands and brushed her lips with his, then settled to feast. Dominic was kissing his woman. His! Right bloody now! Elias's hand was raised and filled with black magic without him even realizing it. The sound of noisy chatter coming closer brought him back to reality however. He couldn't kill the self-righteous prick, not here, not now, he decided. Still reluctant, he lowered his shaking hand, but it took several moments for him to muster the control required to extinguish his power. Soon, he told himself. He would deal with them both very, very soon.

****

It took time but not too much of it for Dominic to find Elias. He was in the corridor between classes with his minions as usual, Dominic saw. He shrugged inwardly. It did not matter. Without warning or even a word, he strode up and punched Elias squarely in the jaw. By God, it felt good. He had been imagining this for over a week, ever since he and Kate had first made love and he could not fight the impulse any longer. He had considered using magic, but this hands-on approach was far more satisfying. Elias didn't only stumble back a step, he lost his footing altogether, dropped like a stone and landed in a heap on the floor. Dominic stared down at him and waited until the younger man met his gaze. Once their gazes locked, he spoke with slow, deliberate care. "I will say this once. If you hurt Kate again, if you touch one hair on her head, I will kill you."

He let that sink in then leaned down to whisper, "She is mine and always will be." Saying the words he had imagined saying to Elias for so long felt almost as good as the punch and he savored the moment.

Even so, the defiant gleam still apparent in Elias's expression did not sit well with him so he continued, "I know what you are. I know what you are trying to do. It's not going to happen."

Elias said nothing, but turned his head and spat out the blood pooled in his mouth in a gesture of contempt.

"Kate is mine," Dominic repeated. "This world is mine. It is mine to protect, mine to defend and so is she. If you think you are strong enough to take me on, go ahead."

He turned to leave and did not stop. Even at the sound of Elias's voice, he kept walking.

"Soon the dark forces will be released and you will die screaming. I'll make sure it saves you to the last. And your pretty Kate? She won't be so pretty once Baylor and I have finished violating her. I'll make sure of that too. In fact, I'll enjoy it."

Blind rage carried Dominic back and each blow he then gave Elias was an expression of his fury. By the time the red haze filling his vision cleared, Elias's face was almost unrecognizable under the blood and bruising. The bastard was semi-conscious and his own knuckles were raw. Panting, Dominic stepped back. Shaking in every limb with the raw desire to finish things once and for all, he walked away. Later, he would wonder if that was the best or the worst decision he had ever made. Either way, it was one of the hardest.

****

When he arrived at his rooms, he had hoped for some privacy along with some time alone to recover a modicum of calm. No such luck. Kate was tucked into a corner of his sofa reading and as the door opened, she closed her book with a bright, welcoming expression. Her smile faded when she noticed his hands. The cut, swollen and bruised knuckles were clear evidence of a fistfight.

"What the hell happened to you?" she demanded.

"I got into it with Elias. I had it out with him. We fought. I won."

His hopes this meager explanation would suffice were dashed when she shrieked, "You did what?!"

"I beat him to within an inch of his life. And don't you dare tell me he didn't deserve it, Kate."

"For God's sake why? Why would you deliberately provoke him like that?"

He whirled to face her. "Why? I can't believe you are asking me that. For Christ's sake do you need a list?"

"Yeah maybe I do need one when you put everything at risk and for what?! You're damned right I need to know why and if there's a list of reasons I want to know every last one."

"That little shite needs to know he will not go unchallenged. He does not have carte blanche. He cannot do whatever he likes and not expect to pay the consequences. That's number one. Second, dealing with him all these weeks has been devastating and not only for you. But most importantly, he put his hands on you. You would still have the bruise if I hadn't healed you. I could kill him for that alone."

Kate blinked. "While it gives me a disturbing thrill to know you mean that, I cannot condone you doing anything like –"

He cut her off with a sharp gesture. "I'm not asking you to condone anything. It's done. Now all that's left is to do our best to finish him."

She wanted to berate him for behaving like such an idiotic Neanderthal, he could tell, but as he had so helpfully pointed out, what was done was done and all she could do was sigh. "I suppose you are right, although you have made things a lot more difficult. He is going to be royally pissed. I'm not so sure he won't kill me now."

"You –" Dominic stared at her face, so calm, so determined. "You intend to go back there?"

"You're damned right I do. I have to make one more try."

"Do you have a death wish? Have you lost your mind?" The question had to be asked in all seriousness.

Kate's shock looked genuine. "What? No! I just have to try."

He took a deep calming breath, not that it helped much, then took her hands in his. "Kate, you are risking your neck for an evil, unmitigated bastard. Why?"

"I know. I'm sorry. I wish I could explain, but how can I when I don't even understand it myself? All I can tell you is I have to take the risk. And, Dominic, it is my risk to take."

"I bloody well know that too. You don't have to remind me." Dropping her hands, he ran his fingers through his hair then took another deep breath. "All right, since you are determined to risk your damn fool neck, what do need from me? I'll do anything, so long as it keeps you alive."

With a rush, she threw herself into his arms and he caught her, as he always had, as he always would. "Stay close," she murmured.

He nodded as he whispered words of reassurance and prayed they would not prove to be empty ones.

Chapter Fifteen

Weeks of hard work yielded progress at last. The updated, redesigned device was far more portable and, Jessilyn believed, more effective. The device, in the end the size of a small power generator, and with much the same function, was a 12" x 12" cube encased in sleek black plastic with venting in the front. The design was simple but powerful enough to effect every dark wizard within a radius of fifty miles with the press of a button. All that was left was to make sure it worked.

"Well, I think we are ready to test it." Jessilyn wiped sweat from her brow and grinned over at Hannah.

The younger girl nodded. "I agree, but how are we going to do that? We have to test it on someone attempting dark magic, but how can we without tipping our hand? The last thing we want is to let the enemy know what sort of weapon we have."

"I've considered that and I think I know just the person to help us." Jessilyn glanced at her watch then rose. "In fact, she should be arriving any second."

Right on cue, there was a tap at the lab door. Jessilyn hurried over to let the newcomer in.

Eager to find out who would be helping them, Hannah turned to see someone she never would have expected: Kate.

For a moment, no words occurred to Hannah.

The silence lengthened until Kate broke it. "Hi, Hannah."

Mind still reeling, Hannah managed a nod.

Jessilyn stepped in. "Thanks for coming, Kate. We are ready at last and I think –"

Hannah found her voice. "What is she doing here, Dr. Matthews?"

"She's going to assist us. She will help us set up a test."

"Set up a test." Hannah said the words slowly, as if not quite able to comprehend them. As the situation sunk in, however, fury filled her in a violent rush. Unable to contain it, she let a little of it out. "Do you have any idea who her friends are?" she demanded of Jessilyn.

"Hannah, you've got this all wrong."

Her rage bumped up another notch as she registered the innocent expression on Kate's face. Unable to stand the sight, she turned her back and faced Jessilyn. "She cannot help us. She is involved. She has been steeping herself in dark magic almost since she got here. She is as guilty as the rest and whatever lies she's told you, you would be as much of a fool as I was to believe them." Something cold and hard settled in Hannah's chest, stronger even than her fury. "She cannot help us unless you want to test the thing on her. I'd be happy to, just say the word."

This time Jessilyn interrupted. "Hannah, enough!" Hannah opened her mouth to continue speaking, studied Jessilyn, thought better of it then clamped her lips shut. "Kate is not involved with dark magic or Elias. She's been spying on him."

"What?"

Kate nodded. "It's true."

Numb with shock now, Hannah asked, "For how long?"

"Since late September. I couldn't tell you. I couldn't tell anyone. I am so sorry."

Hannah took in Kate's pleading expression then Jessilyn's calm one. "I see." She swallowed hard. "I'm the one who's sorry. I treated you so badly. I had no idea you were doing anything like that."

Kate's smile was tentative. "That's okay. That was sort of the point."

Hannah found herself smiling back. "I'm so glad you are not into dark magic. What's it like being a spy?"

Kate grinned. "Not as exciting as you'd think."

Jessilyn cleared her throat, catching their attention. "Okay, now we are all friends here, we should get started."

Kate put on her serious face. "Right. What do you need me to do?"

****

"I'm still not sure this is a very good idea." Kate whispered to Hannah and Jessilyn as they followed Troy and two others whose names Jessilyn didn't know.

Jessilyn glanced over at Kate then shrugged. "Maybe not but it's the only one I could come up with that would give us a semi-accurate assessment of the device. We only have weeks until the solstice. We have to know if it works."

Hannah spoke up. "I promise you we'll be safe as long as we stick to the plan. Test it then erase their memories immediately."

Jessilyn bit her lip, realized what she was doing and stopped. That habit, a holdover from her childhood, wouldn't do, not now. She took a deep breath then asked, "How can we be sure they are going to perform dark magic?"

Kate focused on the figures in the distance. "Oh, they're up to something all right. I'm very familiar with that nasty expression on Troy's face. All we have to do is wait." Quiet and quick, Kate followed as the three headed deeper into the forest with Hannah and Jessilyn right behind her.

"There's one thing I'm worried about," Hannah admitted. "What if they don't do something bad enough?"

"Don't worry. They will," Kate assured her.

"Oh, God," Hannah murmured under her breath.

Jessilyn studied the younger girl's face. Even in the dim light, she could tell Hannah had paled and there was a sickly green tinge spreading under her skin. She stopped walking and the other two followed suit. "Hannah, you don't have to do this. You are fifteen years old and I have no idea what we are walking into, All I know is it's nothing good. It could be very, very dangerous. So, you should go back. Same goes for you too, Kate."

Hannah drew herself up to her full height, shook her head. "No way. We wouldn't even be here without me. The device functions properly because of the work we did together. If you send me home, I'll come right back. I need to see this through."

Jessilyn searched Hannah's eyes then Kate's stony expression. "All right, I'll let you both come on one condition. If I tell you to run, you run. If I tell you to hide, you hide. If I tell you to leave and save yourselves, you do it. You do whatever I tell you, without hesitation or any questions. Understand?"

Hannah and Kate nodded, expressions solemn. "I understand," they vowed, speaking together.

"Okay, let's go."

It was no surprise to Jessilyn when Troy and his companions headed to the circle. Without further discussion, the three women followed. After concealing themselves in the nearby trees, Kate added a quick spell to screen them from sight and sound. Within earshot and able to see well enough, they waited.

They did not have to wait long. After a few moments passed Troy said, "Did you bring us a new toy tonight?" Troy asked Gilman.

"Sure. It was my turn, wasn't it? I wouldn't miss this for the world." He and the others guffawed and Jessilyn struggled not to be sick.

"Well, then bring her out here." Troy's suggestion was met with noises of agreement from the others.

Gilman disappeared to the back of the crowd for a moment then returned gripping a thin arm that belonged to a woman. They could only tell from her figure since her head was covered by a black cloth bag. The girl struggled, but it was no use against Gilman, who looked to be twice her size and weight. The knife he held at her throat also helped. He subdued her with ease then forced her forward.

Troy took the liberty of removing the sack. Her mouth was taped shut and the blood, which ran in a sluggish stream from her freshly broken nose, mixed with her tears.

"Do either of you know her?" Kate asked, communicating mind to mind.

Jessilyn shook her head then glanced over to see Hannah doing the same. The girl was a stranger to them. But she was someone's daughter, someone's sister and there was no way they would leave her to the not-so-tender mercies of these people. Even so, black magic had to be done first in order for them to stop it.

"Be ready." Jessilyn mouthed.

Jessilyn turned her attention back to the action in the circle.

Troy took the girl by the chin, tilted her heart shaped face toward the moonlight in order to study it. Big eyes of indeterminate color, fine cheekbones and light hair could be discerned. "She's pretty. Very nice, Gilman."

Some awful sound between a grunt and a snicker came from Gilman then he grabbed her breast so hard she yelped.

"Enough of that, at least for now." Troy ordered in a sharp voice. "I have something else in mind first." With a sharp gesture, he loosened the zip tie at her wrists.

Gilman shot a startled look at Troy, but Troy never took his eyes from the girl. He gestured to Gilman to back off. With obvious reluctance, the larger man obeyed.

"I think it's time we tried a hunt." Troy looked around, noting eager faces and smiled, all teeth. He fixed his gaze on the girl. Her eyes, though at first still filled with defiance, soon filled instead with utter terror.

His terrible smile broadened further as he murmured, "Run."

For a moment, the girl stayed still, paralyzed with fear.

"Run!"

Troy's shout galvanized her and she sprinted off in the direction of the trees to the right of Jessilyn, Kate and Hannah's position. The whoops and yells of the dark apprentices had another vicious wave of nausea running through Jessilyn. Clamping down on it, she whispered, "Come on." With a gesture, she collected Hannah and Kate and the three women followed.

The world became like a nightmare. It deteriorated until it was like a pack of wild dogs hunting some innocent fox. The three did their best to track the victim, but in such chaos, it was difficult. After some searching, both they and the victim stopped with a small stream between them. Unable to go any farther, despite the sounds of the dark apprentices hunting her, the poor girl fell to the ground. Sweating and out of breath, Jessilyn tried to gather herself.

"We have to stop this before it's too late. Now." Tears flowed down Hannah's cheeks, but her voice was resolute.

Jessilyn, her own eyes dry and burning, nodded her agreement. "That's why we are here. Hannah, you do the honors."

Jessilyn indicated the red, candy colored power button on the CDF. With a shaking hand, Hannah pressed it.

The derisive shouts stopped and the jeering yells dried up. Instead, sounds of puzzlement then fear reached them.

"What the hell?" Gillman cried.

Jessilyn held her breath. This sounded promising but they had to be sure.

"What?" Troy demanded.

"I can't do any magic."

Troy scoffed. "What do you mean you can't do any magic? Of course you can."

"Oh yeah?" Gilman sneered. "You try."

A pause. Then, "What the...?" Another, longer pause. Then Troy shouted, "What the bloody hell?!"

They listened as the dark apprentices reacted to the CDF with confusion soon replaced by anger. As planned, Kate summoned healing magic. The ball of light she conjured in her palm proved only dark magic was suppressed. Jessilyn's grin spread to encompass her whole face. She resisted a whoop of triumph with difficulty. It worked! Hannah had to cover her mouth to stifle a hysterical giggle, stemming half from nerves, half from joy in her accomplishment. Kate went limp with relief.

Jessilyn recovered first. "Come on," she whispered. "Kate, you modify their memories. Hannah and I will find the girl and get her out of here while they are distracted. She shouldn't be far. Be careful," she advised. Kate nodded and started out.

Luck was on their side. Minutes later, a twig snapped and Jessilyn held up a hand to signal a halt. "You can come out now. I swear we don't want to hurt you." She kept her voice low, pitched just loud enough to carry to the woman and not to any dark apprentices, she hoped.

Nothing stirred for some time except the night wind in the trees.

"We want to help. I promise." Hannah called out

At last, a louder rustling was heard and the girl appeared, dropping down from the branch of an oak tree some six feet above. No more than seventeen at a guess, up close the damage done looked severe. Angry welts covered her forearms, there were cuts on her legs oozing blood and there was one shallow slash across her right cheek bone. Her blonde hair was a rat's nest of tangles, her expression was wild and she looked ready to bolt at any second.

Jessilyn held up an unthreatening hand and spoke in a calm, soothing tone, as she might have to a frightened child. "It's okay. Don't be scared. We want to help you."

"How do I know that?" she demanded in a hoarse whisper.

Silently, Kate gave a nod to Jessilyn as she joined them.

Hannah spoke up. "I know these guys. I can't say I like them much. You are going to have to trust us." She held out a hand to the girl. When she didn't take it, Kate said with some impatience, "Do you want our help or don't you?"

The girl took Hannah's hand. Hannah nodded in encouragement. "What's your name?"

"Rose Callahan."

"Nice to meet you, Rose," Kate replied.

Jessilyn said much the same then continued,. "We are going to get you to the main road. It's about half a mile that way. Then we will call you a car. You head home. All we ask is you keep your mouth shut about everything that happened here tonight. I promise you we are handling the situation, but the last thing we need is the police getting involved."

Rose nodded. "They'd never believe me anyway and I doubt they could handle these guys. This situation is way above the paygrade of the local police." She nodded again, this time with an air of finality. "I won't say a word."

"Excellent." Jessilyn beamed at Rose. "Come on. The road's this way."

With a minimum amount of fuss, they made it to the road and called an Uber for Rose, as planned. It wasn't until Rose was safely away and Kate returned to report success that Jessilyn breathed easy. It wasn't until then that she ordered Hannah to turn off the CDF. The night, though unforgettably horrible in its way, had also been productive. They had achieved their goal of testing the CDF without detection. Even better, it worked. Troy and the other dark apprentices would never know what had happened or recall their temporary inability to do magic much less know what caused it. As a bonus, they saved an innocent. Not a bad night when all was said and done. With adrenaline dwindling, Jessilyn led Kate and Hannah back to the safety of the Institute.

****

The next evening, Kate timed her arrival at the circle right in the middle of the ritual so that Elias and his dark apprentices would be distracted and perhaps not kill her on sight. That didn't mean they wouldn't do it later of course, but she had to take the risk. The situation had been deteriorating in a rapid fashion ever since Elias had kissed her. Then when he and Dominic fought, her position became downright untenable for a lot of reasons, her own personal safety being but one. In fact, the whole process was becoming more and more difficult to watch. If leaving the comfort of Dominic's bed and going back to her life and back into danger had been more difficult than Kate ever could have imagined, so was watching Elias lose more and more of himself every night. After this night's ritual was over, she decided, once and for all, no more. She would not sit idly by, not for one more second. Enough was enough.

Too weak to stand after the ritual, Elias sat down and she crouched in front of him, sighed, then stroked a gentle hand over his cheek. At her touch, he looked up at her. When he met her gaze, she saw nothing so much as a little lost boy.

"What the hell are you doing here?" He croaked out.

"Elias, what are you doing to yourself? I know it seems hard and I know you feel like you've gone much too far and there isn't any going back, but that's not true. This needs to end."

For one brief instant, he considered it. For one second he almost capitulated, she could see it in his face. Responding to that, she said her next words without thinking. "Please, Elias, I'm your friend, let me help you."

When he spoke, his voice was low and vicious. "Friends? Is that what we are? Whatever made you think that? The last thing in the world I want to be is your friend."

His kiss then was appalling, rough and passionate, but for one heartbeat, she responded. Then an image of Dominic flashed through her mind and an instant later, she returned to her senses. She wrenched herself away with as much force as she could manage.

"Elias, please don't."

He shook his head. "I will do whatever I choose to do because, like I said, the last thing in the world I want to be is your friend," he repeated. "Especially now you're shagging Dominic after rejecting me."

Her eyes widened in shock, she couldn't help it.

Elias gave a harsh laugh at the look on her face. "What, you thought I didn't know or at least wouldn't say anything? Please. The two of you couldn't be more obvious if you tried. I mean, the way you look at him. Oh, and the fact that he beat the hell out of me might have given me a damn clue. And you convinced yourself I would let all that go? After all of that you have the nerve to come back here!"

"Elias, please, let me explain."

Elias shook his head. "There's nothing to explain. All you feel for me is pity, I know that now, and F.Y.I., pity is another thing I sure as hell don't want from you. I thought you cared for me, but you don't."

Kate gave her head a violent shake. "I do care for you. I love Dominic, yes, I won't lie to you about that, but you do mean something to me. You mean so much to me –"

"Stop lying!" He roared the words and she flinched then stumbled back several paces.

With a wave of his hand, he uprooted a nearby tree and sent it flying. It missed her by inches. The darkest look she had ever seen came into his eyes and for the first time, she was afraid of him right down to her bones. It was then she knew in her heart he could never be saved. Because he didn't want to be.

He stepped close enough that she could feel the electric current of his power in the air surrounding him. "I could kill Dominic. It would be so easy, you know. Kill him then you. You never cared a thing about me. So why shouldn't I toss you aside after I take whatever I want from you?" he finished and extended a hand to her.

This time, when he tried to invade her mouth again, she used her magic to stop him, startling them both. Expending all her strength, Kate held him immobile. Even as angry and afraid as she was, she could not stop the tears rolling down her face. Still, she brushed them away with an impatient movement. "It's over. I may not be strong enough here and now to stop you permanently, but I will. I am going to stop you. I would have anyway for the greater good, but now… It's one thing to threaten me, but you threatened the man I love." Her voice dropped to a whisper and she said, "I'm sorry. I can't do this anymore. I cannot watch you self-destruct and I'll be damned if I'll let you take me, Dominic and the whole bloody world with you."

Wiping her tears on her sleeve, cold and numb, she turned away from him and headed back to the Institute.

PART THREE: CONFRONTATION

Chapter Sixteen

Riding a wave of déjà vu, Kate pounded on Dominic's door without any regard for the lateness of the hour. When he opened up at last she could tell from his disheveled appearance and his drowsy expression she had wakened him from a dead sleep yet again.

"Our little spy game is over," she informed him without preamble.

"What?! Damn it, Kate, you aren't supposed to go anywhere without me."

"It all happened so fast. There wasn't time."

Dominic didn't believe that for a minute, but left the issue alone for the moment in favor of more pressing matters. "What happened?"

He stepped back and gestured her inside while, in a few curt words, she told him.

"I tried to save him," she finished, "I tried, but I couldn't." Now, she broke down into uncontrollable sobs.

He wrapped her in his arms. "Shh, shh. Not everyone can be saved, my love. Not everyone wants to be."

It was strange but, for the very first time she believed him and she was able to let Elias go. In a wash of weeping and pain, and yes, in a storm of emotion, but it was a storm she sensed would, in the end, cleanse her soul.

Once her tears subsided, she put her head on Dominic's shoulder with a little sigh like a tired child. For a long while, he held her, just held her, and did his best to give her what comfort he could. However, after a quarter of an hour had passed he said, "Kate, I hate to have to do this, I hate even mentioning this right now, but we need to let Thomas and Jessilyn know what happened."

Kate gave an audible sniff then grabbed for a tissue from the box on the coffee table. After blowing her nose with an explosive sound like a foghorn, she nodded. With a fresh tissue, she dabbed at her eyes then said, "Right. I'll call them."

Dominic took the phone from her shaking, unresisting hand. "Let me."

****

Thomas was dealing with a lot, administering the school, teaching classes, oh and trying to figure out a plan to defeat Baylor and his dark forces. To be honest he had never been in such a state of exhaustion in his life. So, when his office phone rang at eleven o'clock in the evening while he was in the middle of a very complicated spell, he was tempted to ignore it until the name and number registered on the display.

"Hello, Dominic. What's happened?"

He listened, cursed and gathered the necessary tools for scrying and hunting.

"The last place Kate saw him was the stone circle, but I doubt he'll be there now." Dominic made the comment as he met Thomas at the edge of the woods a bare ten minutes later.

Thomas acknowledged this with a tilt of his head. "I scryed for him and the best I could come up with is that he is still here on the grounds, somewhere in the forest. He's become very skilled at cloaking himself and I couldn't be any more specific."

"All right then, let's do this."

They might as well have saved themselves the trouble; Elias was already far too well hidden for even Thomas to find him. For all intents and purposes, he was gone, at least until he chose to show himself. After hours of fruitless searching, this was the one inescapable conclusion they came to.

"Damn it!"

The heartfelt curse burst from Dominic and Thomas could not help but agree. In fact, it made him want to let fly a few swear words himself. With great difficulty, he refrained. Instead, he clapped Dominic on the shoulder.

"C'mon, let's go home."

"What? I'm not giving up until I find that sod."

"Who said anything about giving up? What we need to do is re-strategize and that's best done inside out of the cold, after a good night's sleep and on a full stomach. C'mon."

Dominic hesitated then, with great reluctance, followed.

****

Minutes after the altercation with Kate, as soon as she released him and he had recovered sufficiently, Elias decided it was time for him to disappear. He wouldn't go far, however. He had to be close to the center, to the place where the dark forces would emerge. Even so, there was no reason to stay at the Avery Institute any longer. He'd learned all he could; moreover, he had gotten what he came for, a direction and a purpose. Now he would devote himself fully to Baylor without any diversions or deviations. There was little time left and he had allowed himself to become distracted by Kate and all his messy emotions for her. Well, no longer. He packed the few belongings he needed for the ritual into his rucksack, magicked the rest of his things over and headed in the direction of the forest and the dark forces.

He was no longer able to resist. If he were honest with himself, he didn't truly want to. Kate had been the one thing holding him back. His feelings for her had been the last true human emotion he had left inside of him. Now, that was gone and in its place, was cold, dark rage, mingled with a desire for power.

It was fitting then, that he should stumble upon a dank cave devoid of light to shelter him and all those he would draw to him. He conjured flame in his hand for illumination and strode inside. As he entered, he noted it seemed sound enough and appeared unlikely to collapse around him. He did a support spell in any case. Inside, he found a circular chamber with a domed ceiling perhaps fifty feet high, with an interior thousands of feet wide and hundreds in length. Several smaller antechambers which would be useful fanned out from it as well. It would do. Darker inside than even the dense forest surrounding it, damp and full of cobwebs as it was, it would suit his purposes admirably. Hidden in the depths of the woods yet large enough to house them all, he was more than satisfied. Yes, this place would do quite well.

****

Dawn was lighting the sky when Thomas and Dominic returned to Thomas's office. Thomas called Jessilyn and Kate and asked them to join he and Dominic there.

"He's gone. Elias is gone," Dominic announced once everyone was settled.

Kate popped up from her chair and jumped to her feet. "What? What do you mean he's gone?"

"We searched for hours last night and could not find him. He never returned here last night. That's confirmed," Thomas explained. "Now do you two want to tell me what the hell happened? All of it please."

Kate and Dominic gave each other a look, but said nothing.

Thomas took a deep breath as he rose from his chair, placed his hands on the desk and leaned toward them. "There are times when I have a very short temper. This is one of those times, so one of you had better start talking. Now."

Kate spoke up. It had all been her idea after all. "It's over. I never imagined he would disappear."

"Nor did I," Dominic added.

"What do you mean it's over?" This question came from Jessilyn.

"There was nothing more I could do, not there with him, not that way. Emotionally, psychologically, he is self-destructing. At the same time, his power keeps growing and growing. He can't be saved and I couldn't watch it for one more second." She took them through the events of the previous week step-by-step. "I've let you down. I'm sorry," she finished.

Jessilyn took her hand, squeezed. "You have nothing to be sorry for. You've done so much. You may have saved us all. And you know what? I trust your instincts. If you think it was time to get out, it was time to get out."

Kate looked Jessilyn straight in the eye. "If I hadn't, he would have killed me. That's how things would have ended. In fact, I think he would have murdered me very soon. I believe that without a doubt."

They were all silent as they took that in.

After a time, Thomas said, "The question now is what next? Do you have any idea where he might go, Kate?"

Kate shook her head. "All I can tell you is he won't be far from the circle. He's so strong now that he can conceal himself even from you. He could be right in front of us and we'd never know."

"Well, we will give priority to finding him then," Thomas said, tone brisk.

"If we can," Dominic muttered. When the others all stared at him, he explained, "If he doesn't want to be found, we might not find him. We need to face that fact."

Kate set her jaw. "I have not come this far to give up."

"Who said anything about giving up? There is nowhere on this earth he can hide from me where I won't find him given time. But if we want to speed up that process, I'm saying we might have to… draw him out."

God, how she loved him, her sexy, fierce, utterly brilliant warrior. In response, she felt more than a little fierce herself. "What did you have in mind?"

He smiled, all teeth. "You as bait."

Shocked, she took in the heated fury and the cool calculation in his expression. "You're sure about that? I have no problem being bait, in fact, I say bring it on, but not long ago you were telling me how you wanted to take me far away where he couldn't find me much less hurt me. I'm surprised that's all."

"That's understandable. I still wish I could take you away from all this, but things have changed. I've changed. When this all started, I wasn't a soldier. Well, I am now and so are you. I am going to be right there beside you. I won't let anything happen to you. What's more, I will find him and I will capture him. If necessary, I will end him." Resolution poured out of him like never before and she already knew him to be more resolute than anyone else she had ever met.

"*We'll* find him and capture him," Kate corrected.

The look he gave her then was one of great admiration. Kate returned it in kind as he nodded then said, "So, what if we started patrolling around the edge of the forest in pairs? Any student of age that would like to volunteer could take a shift."

"I'll do you one better. Certain select teams could be assigned to go in deeper, to the heart of the forest itself, such as you and Kate," replied Thomas in an enthusiastic tone.

Kate all but rubbed her hands together in anticipation. "That is a terrific idea. Dominic and I patrol, but I'm never alone. We'll dangle me in front of him, like a pretty piece of ripe fruit just out of reach." Kate relished the thought.

"Won't he be suspicious?" Jessilyn asked.

"Sure, of course, no question. But after a while, he won't be able to resist making a try for me. It's in his nature. When I left him, I made no secret of the fact that I would do my best to stop him. Not only that, I rejected him for a man who, in his estimation, has a lot less to offer." She turned to Dominic. "You don't have his pedigree, money, or education. In reality, however, you are everything he isn't. You are brave, powerful, kind and loving just to name a few of your best qualities." She paused and took his hand. "He sees you as nothing and yet I rejected him for you. He won't let me get away with that. His arrogance won't allow him to."

"She's right," Dominic commented. "He won't be able to stop himself."

Thomas inclined his head. "I like the idea. Do it." He held up a hand. "But we will add several of our best fighters for protection. In fact, I might join them."

When Jessilyn opened her mouth to protest, he forestalled her. "It's high time I took a more active role in this fight. Besides, I am as juicy a bait as Katherine." He studied his wife's expression then added, "We don't have to decide that issue now. The rest, however, is a go."

"But if he even suspects we aren't alone this plan won't work," Kate protested.

"I'd rather the plan not work than see you dead."

Kate shot a desperate glance at Jessilyn, but the older woman shook her head. "I'm with Thomas on this one."

When she whipped her head around to Dominic, his jaw was tight and his expression was grim, but he said, "We'll make it work."

Kate stifled a sigh then nodded. If there was anything she had learned by now, it was to put her complete trust in Dominic. If he said they'd make it work, then they would. Although she'd be damned if she knew how.

****

The soft whoosh of her bedroom door opening woke Kate. An instant later, the louder sound of the window creaking reached her ears. She saw the white of Hannah's nightgown in the light of the moon, then the flash of leg as she clambered up onto the sill.

Befuddled with sleep and with a voice husky with it, she called, "Hannah? What are you doing?"

When she got no response other than a soft grunt of effort as Hannah climbed down, Kate leapt to her feet, but too late. Hannah was already out of the window and walking across the back garden. Thank God they were on the ground floor, otherwise Hannah might have been hurt and Kate had the distinct impression it would not have mattered to the younger girl. Her friend would have jumped out no matter what. Anything but the ground floor and she probably would have broken her leg, maybe even her neck. Well, she was off to God knows where and Kate had no choice but to follow.

She teleported herself down into Hannah's path and she got her first good look at the other girl. Her eyes were open, but there was no life or sense in them. Her jaw was slack and her stride slow and halting. She most closely resembled one of those zombies on that American television program, The Walking Dead.

Kate wracked her brains trying to decide what to do first to help. She started with the obvious. She snapped her fingers in front of Hannah's face and called her name. No response at all. Not one iota of recognition. In fact, Hannah didn't even blink. Next, she planted her feet directly in Hannah's path. When her friend paused, Kate grasped her by the shoulder with a firm hand. This time she yelled the other girl's name. "Hannah! Hannah! Can you hear me? Wake up! You have to stop this, okay? You have to stay here where you're safe."

Hannah did respond this time, but only to jerk out of Kate's hold, side step her and continue on.

"Christ," Kate muttered. Since this problem was a magical one, it was obvious it would require magic to combat and counteract it. She drew herself up to her full height and took a deep breath. Raising her hand, she conjured power in her palm and sent it toward Hannah. "Wake up!" she ordered. A shimmer of power in the air as it dispersed was all she got for her trouble.

Realizing there was no help for it, she gave in and summoned assistance. She sent out the warning signal she and Dominic had agreed on, adding, "I'm not in danger, but someone else is. Dominic, I need you."

Within minutes, he appeared before her on the lawn. Without delay, he focused on her, looking her over for any sign of injury. "What's going on, Kate? Are you all right?"

"I'm fine. Hannah, unfortunately, is not." She grasped him by the shoulders and turned him around so he could see the other woman.

Dominic narrowed his eyes in puzzlement. "What the hell?" He did much the same as Kate had, waving his hand in front of Hannah's face, calling her name. He got no response of course and asked, "How long has she been like this?"

"Only a few minutes as far as I know. I woke up to see her climbing out of the window. For once, I was in my bed not yours or she'd be gone and no one would know what happened. I tried to stop her but…" Kate waved a hand in a helpless gesture.

"It's easy to tell she is under the influence of something magical."

Kate managed not to roll her eyes, but it was a close thing. "I can see that, Dominic. The question is what do we do about it? I tried using magic to wake her up, but it didn't work. I didn't want to do anything more forceful to stop her, though. I was afraid I might hurt her. But we can't leave her like this and we can't let her go wherever it is she is being pulled." When Dominic said nothing, she asked, uncertain, "Can we?"

Dominic considered for a moment then shrugged. "Why not? Somehow I doubt we will be able to stop this, so let's save our strength."

Appalled, Kate opened her mouth to speak without any idea what she would say, but Dominic spoke first.

"Hear me out. If we let her go, then follow her, at least then we'll know what we are up against."

"Are you mental? It stands to reason whatever it is, it will get stronger the closer she gets to it." Kate shook her head. "Who are we kidding? We both know it is Baylor and his dark forces drawing her to the circle."

Dominic was silent for a moment, considering this. "You are probably right," he conceded. "Okay then, here's what I suggest, you try to wake her one more time. Then if that doesn't work, we could try to build a magical barrier together. We can't use her as bait, not when we might not be able to save her in time. We can't, we won't let it have her, okay?"

Kate gave a decisive nod. "You're damned right we won't."

With all her strength, Kate called up her magic and summoned her power. "Hannah Elizabeth Barnes, wake up, I command you!" Nothing, not a tremor. "Damn it! It's still not working."

"Okay, so time for plan B. Let's form a barrier."

Kate nodded and they stood side by side. Once again, magic rose up inside of her and joined with Dominic's.

"Christ, you are strong," he said.

In spite of the tense situation, she could feel herself blushing at the compliment unable to stop herself being pleased by it. "So are you and thank God, because so is Baylor. In fact, I think he might be too strong."

"I hate to say this, but I think you're right. I don't think we can hold her much longer."

She glanced over and in the spell-light she could see perspiration on his brow even in the frosty air. She could feel the sweat of effort on her own skin as well and wondered what the hell they should do now.

As if on cue, a firm, steady voice said incantations and a new, stronger magical force joined with them. It was Thomas, of course.

In the space between one heartbeat and the next, the wind died and the dark forces released Hannah. Kate's relief was so great the power of it sent her to her knees and even Dominic swayed in an alarming way. As for Hannah, she collapsed unconscious to the ground.

"Do you mind telling me what the hell is going on here?"

Dominic looked Kate over, but quickly, to confirm what he could already sense, that, while she was a bit weak and very shaken, she wasn't hurt. Then he hurried over to tend to Hannah.

Meanwhile, Kate gathered up her scattered wits enough to speak. Once done, she told Thomas, "Hannah spent the night in my guest room. I woke up to find her unresponsive and trying to get out of my bedroom window. The window in the guest room is too small to escape through so I think she proceeded to the next nearest one. I don't think it was a conscious choice at all. Before I could stop her, she was out here. I did my best to wake her and when I couldn't manage it, I summoned Dominic. We tried to create a magical barrier, but we weren't able to do that either. It's lucky you came along." Now the immediate crisis was over she found herself equal to offering him her most charming smile.

"Oh, yes, very lucky," Thomas replied, tone dry as desert air. "How is she, Dominic?" he called.

Dominic hurried over. "Seems to be all right, but I'd like to run some tests on her, magical and medical, if I had my choice. What I wouldn't give for an MRI." This last he said mostly to himself.

"Soon, you'll have it." Jessilyn had joined them unobserved. "I have ordered the most advanced medical equipment Dr. Avery's money can buy and it should arrive in a few days."

"It would already be here, but we wanted certain custom made features added. Ones not needed when testing non-magical people," Thomas explained.

"So what do you think it was? What had hold of her?" Dominic asked.

"Baylor, what else?"

"I was afraid of that." Dominic rubbed a hand over his face. "As far as I can tell she will be all right, but you're the expert on Baylor, what do you think?"

Thomas did a quick scan of Hannah's mind then let out a sigh. "We made it to her in time."

"What about next time? Or the next?" Jessilyn demanded. "We cannot let this go on, Thomas."

Thomas's jaw tightened. "I know. It is twenty days until the solstice. Until then, I will strengthen the wards around this place."

Kate rubbed her hands over her face then looked each of the rest of them in the eye one by one. "Will that be enough?" Before anyone could answer her, Kate went on. "We, all of us, have been studying and training for months. I busted my ass playing spy and still Elias got away. Tonight, the dark forces almost stole someone right out from under us. Will any of it be enough?"

"You want reassurance. No, you want a guarantee. I can't give it you. I can't say anything for certain, Kate. I can't promise you it won't all be for nothing. What I can promise you is we will do everything we can, give everything we have to keep the dark forces from taking over."

"'Return with your shield or on it'. I see." Her voice sounded as cold and lifeless as she felt inside.

"In a manner of speaking. We will not go down without a fight. It's been hard, I know, but please, don't give up now. We need you."

Kate drew herself up, tried to find strength from somewhere. Calling on her severely depleted inner reserves, she managed to say, "I won't let you down."

****

Time passed and the dark forces grew stronger and stronger by the hour. Over the next days, then weeks, Kate searched for any further indication that Baylor and his dark forces were rising. She found no lack of signs. Each time she and Dominic patrolled it was clearer and, particularly after Elias's departure, the state of the forest went steadily downhill. It began with dead plants, the smallest first. Weeks later, larger shrubs withered. Next, one or two full grown trees died overnight. Then, as if gathering strength, the dark forces started on the tiniest animals. As Dominic and Kate walked through the dried leaves, every so often Dominic would have to step over the carcass of a small mouse or inch the corpse of a squirrel out of their path with the toe of his boot. What was most disturbing, however, was the area of damage was in a perfect circle whose circumference was increasing at a steady pace. So, even if they hadn't known what they were looking at, they would not have been able to comfort themselves with the assumption it was some unknown but natural phenomenon.

As they grew closer to the center the smell of decay rose like a miasma to surround them. Dominic and Kate exchanged a glance and picked up the pace. A few yards further on, they found the source. A beautiful deer, a stag in his prime, was dead. Kate's heart stuttered at the sight, but she took a deep breath and when Dominic started a chant of cleansing, she joined him. Together they buried the once majestic animal then walked the circumference of the circle.

"It's getting worse isn't?" Kate asked the question already knowing the answer, but she wanted confirmation.

Dominic glanced over at her then looked away. "Yes."

"Every day it's farther from the center of the forest and closer to us."

"Yes."

"He hasn't taken the bait."

"No."

She grasped his forearm to halt his progress through the bramble. "So, maybe he needs a bit more incentive."

"What?" He glanced in her direction. "You have something in mind?" He drew in a sharp breath as she stepped closer to him, and he realized what she meant to do. The look on her face was unmistakable to him. He'd seen it enough in the past weeks to be quite familiar with it after all. "Kate, I don't think this is a very good idea. It might backfire. He might –"

No longer interested in discussing the matter, she silenced him by the simple expedient of crushing her mouth to his. In spite of his protests, his response to her was as immediate and passionate as always and seconds later, he was tugging her down into the bracken on top of him. As he pulled her shirt up and off, she laughed with the edgy pleasure of it. "Okay, so I guess you are on board with this plan after all."

He shrugged. "If we're going to give Elias a show, we might as well make it good. Besides, I want you. Always."

She put all her own growing feelings into a kiss, stopped thinking and took him.

****

The dark forces were getting stronger. Every indication pointed to that one simple fact and Elias was elated. In the woods, the very air outside the cave that had become home to him and his dark apprentices filled with a scent that was not the natural result of autumn's decline, but an abnormal one, indicative of slow decay. It was cloying and sickeningly sweet, but to Elias it was irresistible. He filled his lungs with it and breathed it in.

He was consumed with preparing for the Winter Solstice, the shortest day of the year followed by the longest night, the time the dark would have greatest dominion. He prayed that with that added power he would be strong enough to take in Baylor fully. Either way, Baylor would take him. He knew for certain it was only a matter of time now and he welcomed it. That being the case, he and his dark apprentices would use every second they had left to prepare.

The vision bombarded Elias as he went through his usual purge prior to the summoning ritual. The purge required a degree of vulnerability he would not in general have tolerated. In the normal course of things, he would never have been so open, but as it was…

Without warning, very similar to the time Kate had slipped and opened her mind for an instant during class, the images came to him in vivid color. It was a thousand times stronger than the previous vision, however, and lasted far longer. Elias knew he ought to block it, but his rage and his craving for her made that impossible. He wanted her, still, and the knowledge humiliated and incensed him to the point that control was a distant memory where she was concerned. Unable to contain his fury, he lashed out at his companions, leaving one wounded with severe burns over most of his body and another dead.

Breathing heavily, he looked over the cowering survivors. When he spoke, his voice was cold. "That traitorous bitch Kate O'Reilly is somewhere in my woods. She is currently fucking Dominic Foster! Find them both and bring them here alive and unharmed." When no one moved, he roared, "Now!" His minions scurried away to do his bidding as all good minions should and he tried to calm himself.

He was making some headway until a second vision hit him, this one a hell of a lot worse. It was from Dominic this time and it was explicit, taunting and triumphant.

"I am hers and she is mine. You will never have her." Dominic's words, the same words he said before, echoed through Elias's brain. As the vision overwhelmed him, Elias let out a primal scream.

****

Elias's impotent yell complemented Dominic's stellar climax very well, Dominic thought as he rode the last of its wave.

As he came down from it, so did Kate. "It worked," she murmured after a few moments.

Dominic nodded against her hair. "We sure as hell got his attention." She caught his eye right as he caught hers and an instant later, they were both laughing like loons, unable to stop.

Wiping his streaming eyes, he shook his head and got control of himself. Despite his bone deep reluctance to do so, he disengaged from her. After he pressed one last, lingering kiss to her lips, he rose and with a few quick, rough tugs, adjusted his clothing. Once he gained his feet, he offered her a hand up. "C'mon, it's freezing. Aside from that, we'd better get you dressed before we have company."

He spoke not a moment too soon. Seconds after Kate made herself presentable, Elias's masked minions teleported in and surrounded them.

"Give us the girl," one growled without preamble.

Far from being intimidated, Dominic strode closer. "Troy is that you? Stupid question, don't bother to answer. I know it is. I recognize your voice. Troy, Kate is not going with you. Neither am I."

"I was hoping you'd say that," another rumbled and made a grab for Kate.

With one swift gesture, Dominic whistled up the wind, which knocked every one of the minions to the ground. Not only that, he held them, some ten people, pinned there.

Dominic strode close to get a good look at Troy. "Tell Elias if he wants my woman, he'll have to come and take her himself if he can. Be sure he knows if he tries, he'll have to get through me." He shot raw electricity through his prisoners for a few long, satisfying moments then released them. "Go."

They ran, disappearing within moments into the dense forest. "I can't blame them for getting out of here, sharpish," Kate commented.

He and Kate waited until all the minions were gone, then she turned to him. Tilting her head in question, she murmured, "Your woman?"

He gave her a look and a simple, decisive, "Yes."

After a moment's deliberation, she nodded in acceptance and they strode back to the Institute.

****

When his dark apprentices returned to the cave, Elias shot an expectant look about for Kate and Dominic, especially Kate, yet did not see either of them.

In a voice of eerie calm, he asked, "Where are they?"

Troy, always the nervous sort, babbled. "They got away, sir. I'm sorry, sir."

"You let them go?"

Troy looked pained. "No, he let us go. Dominic called up the wind to trap us. He is very strong and there was nothing we could do. He told us to give you a message then he let us go."

"A message? What message?"

Troy looked downright panicked now, but when Elias simply waited, Troy had no choice but to speak. "He said if you want his woman, you'll have to come and take her yourself, if you can. He also said to be sure you know if you try, you'll have to get through him."

The edges of Elias's vision went red, but even through the haze he saw Troy cringe.

Troy's voice shook when he said hastily, "Those were his words, sir."

In that moment, Elias's mind blanked, leaving fury. There was nothing else left. Rage filled him and he let it have its head, smashing everything in the immediate vicinity to bits with great ferocity. His underlings, no strangers to such goings on, wasted no time backing away then fleeing to another part of the cave. What he wanted, of course, was someone to vent his feelings on, someone to kill. Not just someone, but Kate and Dominic.

An incoherent roar burst from his throat. They were his, both of them; his to own, his to torture, his to kill. His to do with as he would. How dare Dominic lay claim to Kate! How dare Dominic leave him a message then walk away!

Elias took a deep breath and poured himself a glass of wine. After drinking it all in one satisfying gulp, he set the glass down then stood, hands resting on the table, head bowed, struggling for control.

He had to think before he did anything rash. He went over recent events in his mind, in particular his interactions with Kate and Dominic thus far, and considered the question in an objective light. With slow, painstaking effort, he calmed himself enough to reflect.

"He's trying to bait me."

"Who's trying to bait you?" Troy asked after some hesitation from his position all but cowering in a corner.

Well, at least he hadn't fled like the others. Maybe Troy had a bit more grit than Elias had given him credit for.

Elias got himself another glass of wine and sipped this time. "That's the question, isn't it? I supposed it must be Dominic or even, after everything, that bitch Kate, but I don't think either of them could or would act alone. Thomas?" he asked himself. "Far more likely, but he hates to get his hands dirty." He focused a moment more and knew. Now his mind was clear, the answer couldn't have been any more obvious. "It's all of them. Kate admitted she spied on the ritual that first time. What she didn't say is afterward, she went crying to Dominic then Thomas and she has been playing me for a fool ever since." The decanter and all the glasses smashed with the force of his magic. "They want to be rid of me before the Solstice, before Baylor and the dark forces rise. They hope to take out the servant then the master. They want me to do something monumentally stupid, like go after Kate, and then they'll neutralize me." He took another long, deep breath. "Well, I'll be damned if I'll let that happen."

Ready to give orders, he faced his people, who, now the storm was over, were slinking back. "Right, we continue with preparations the same as we have been."

"Are you certain? You don't want us to make another attempt?" Troy asked.

"After you failed so spectacularly? Hell no. I am damn well going to do what I set out to do and no mere woman is going to stop me. I will rededicate myself to Baylor. I will devote myself to preparing for the Winter Solstice the way I should have done weeks ago. Once I have become what I am set to become, then and only then will I deal with

Kate and her whore." He made an impatient gesture of dismissal. "Go and finish making the arrangements."

****

The days passed and still the ways and means needed to subdue Baylor and all his dark forces eluded Thomas. Until one quiet afternoon in his library when the answer burst upon him at last, found in a little known source. He dropped the small glass he was holding and it shattered, cutting his finger in the process. He looked down at the blood flowing from a small cut on the very tip of his finger. That was it, Thomas realized, that was the solution, the final piece of the puzzle. Blood was required, his blood, and a lot of it according to the text. So much it might mean his life. That was what the spell demanded. How could he not have seen it before? His stomach sank with a feeling of inevitable doom. Perhaps he hadn't seen it because he hadn't wanted it to be true. He had, in fact, searched for another solution, any other solution. But he found nothing except confirmation of what, in his flesh and bone, he already knew. Suspecting was different from knowing and knowing was a far cry from accepting; he understood that now. Without warning, a flair of anger rose in his chest. How the hell was he supposed to accept his highly probable, imminent death when he had only just found something to live for? Jessilyn was his life so how could he leave her? He wouldn't, that was all. He would accept nothing at all about this. The question of how to prevent it? Well, that was another matter. It was one he turned his mind to over the next hours, trying to find an alternative solution with little success.

In their rooms that evening, Thomas was all but silent. Although he had no desire to keep up any sort of pretense with Jessilyn, he wanted to upset her even less. Torn between the two desires and moreover, in turmoil over his new knowledge, in the end he said far less than usual. Jessilyn, being Jessilyn, noticed and after several failed attempts at light conversation, she asked, "Thomas, are you okay?"

He hauled her close and held tight to her. "Do you still want absolute honesty?"

She drew back enough to see his face. "Yes. Always."

He took a deep breath. "Okay, fighting Baylor and his dark forces requires a blood sacrifice. Specifically, my blood."

Her eyes widened in shock for an instant then narrowed in speculation. "You aren't talking about a tiny cut or else you wouldn't be so worried and upset."

"'Whosoever of Merlin's get casts this spell, if he seeks to subdue the dark forces, and Baylor the first among them, must give of his life's blood unstintingly,'" he quoted.

As he watched, helpless, her knees shook then buckled. With a murmured, "Whoa," he grabbed her by the arms to keep her upright then steered her to the sofa.

Once she was off her feet, she put her head between her knees and drew in deep breaths for several long minutes. When she sat up, her face was like stone. "How long have you known about this?"

"Since this morning. Before that I suspected, but I wasn't sure, not until I found this."

He opened the ancient tome, handed it over to her and indicated the quote he had shared with her earlier. After reading the words with great care, she handed the book back to him. "I do not accept this. There has to be another way."

Her jaw set in a mulish line he was all too familiar with and if the situation had been different, he might have smiled. As it was, all he had room for was an impotent rage and a bone-deep despair. "Not that I've found and I have searched all my adult life and in the last few years I have looked extensively as you know."

Although she shook all over, her voice was firm. "Just because something has not ever been done does not mean it can't be. Hell, my whole life is based on that premise and I am not going to stop believing in it now."

Now they were both shaking, because he couldn't seem to keep steady. "I want to believe that but…"

She shook her head. "No buts. You can do anything. You convinced me to believe in magic and if you can do that, well I have every confidence you can do whatever you set your mind to. Besides, Merlin was alone. You are not. In many ways, that was the whole point of this entire exercise. It's the reason you started this school and in doing that, you have gained the allegiance and commitment of every student and teacher here. And best of all, you have me."

Truly, she was an amazing woman. Her utter confidence in him coupled with her unfailing loyalty as well as her formidable brain made him a lucky man and well he knew it. "I do and thank God for that. Let's get started."

****

It seemed getting started meant calling in what Jessilyn privately was coming to think of as Thomas's generals, i.e. herself, Kate and Dominic. At 9 a.m. the following morning, he summoned them to his rooms. Once the two younger people arrived, Jessilyn offered everyone coffee and they all sat in her bright airy kitchen.

Wasting no more time, Thomas began, "By my calculations, it will all come to a head on the Winter Solstice."

Jessilyn studied him in a thorough manner. "December 21. You know this for absolute certain now?" she asked.

Thomas held her gaze. "I'm as certain as I've ever been about anything in my life. The one thing I was ever more certain of was marrying you."

She sent him a brief smile at that and gripped his hand, but soon sobered. "What do we do? How do we prepare?" Jessilyn demanded.

"Are you kidding? I've been preparing for this my whole life. You and I, and especially us four together," here he indicated Jessilyn, Dominic and Kate, "have in fact, been preparing for this for months."

Jessilyn's lips quirked but she said only, "True, but I mean, what do we need to do on the day? We need a detailed battle plan, Thomas, for God's sake."

He smiled and if it was a touch grim, well, it fit the situation. "True. I have the beginnings of one and would like each of you to take a look and give me your thoughts."

As always, they followed his lead. Each of them had strategic suggestions and refinements to make. That day and night, they calculated all they could and did their best to account for the unexpected. Eventually, they had a rough course of action mapped out.

"So, what does everyone think? Will it work? Is there anything we missed?" Thomas asked the room at large.

"I don't think we've missed anything, but I'm no military strategist." Jessilyn glanced at Thomas. "You are the closest thing we have to an expert. You tell me."

"I can't see any obvious flaws, but that doesn't mean there aren't any. Kate? Dominic? What do the two of you think?"

"I'm no military strategist either, but the plan seems like a good one to me. Dominic?"

"We've done the best we can. There's nothing more we can do."

Thomas rose, fetched glasses and poured wine for them all. "Well then, a toast." They raised their glasses. "To light over dark, to maintaining the balance. To victory."

Glasses clinked and they all drank. Ready and willing to fight, kill and die to protect their world.

Chapter Seventeen

The stars burned clear and cold in the winter sky, reflecting on the stones. It was time; Elias recognized it with every fiber of his being. He believed it with every cell in his body. The same body, which now belonged almost totally to Baylor. With the help of the dark forces, he was now more powerful than ever before. On this most sacred night, the Winter Solstice, he had but to open himself. Though he would in any case, there was no need to even call it forth, not this one last time, because Baylor was already there waiting. Tonight, the dark forces would rise of their own accord to pit themselves against the forces of light in an epic battle. How fitting that he give himself over to Baylor completely at the moment of his greatest triumph.

At the appointed hour, his followers joined him and they numbered near to a hundred now. As he had done so many times in the past months, he proceeded to the center of the circle, this time, however, he was dressed for battle. He wore all black (of course) from his simple but functional shirt and pants down to his sturdy boots. His wish to go to war the way the Spartans had, naked, was fleeting. It was not practical after all and all black was the next best thing. He shoved away the random thought and focused. He prepared himself, going through the ritual he had been practicing for months, but he took special care with it tonight, knowing it would be the last time.

"I call to you, oh ruler of darkness, Baylor, I am your willing vessel. Tonight, I give myself over to you fully and –"

Before he reached the center of the circle, a voice, rich, deep and unpleasantly familiar, interrupted him.

"Stop!" The voice ordered in a loud, authoritative tone. As if that indignity weren't enough, the command was backed up by magic and the dark forces receded somewhat in response. Elias was so shocked that for a moment, he did not move or speak. Then he turned to see Dr. Thomas Avery.

****

"Hello, Elias."

"Thomas," Elias hissed. "What are you doing here? I never imagined you would have the courage to show your face, much less try to stop me."

"I may not have challenged you openly, but I have been working behind the scenes since the very beginning," Thomas informed Elias as all their people, both his and Elias's, revealed themselves. "Did you think I didn't know? Did you actually believe I wouldn't be here at this moment? I've been preparing for this since before you were born. Be that as it may, the moment for stealth on both sides is over." Thomas approached. "There's still time. You can help end this. You can choose the right side."

"He's right. Listen to him, Elias. I'm begging you."

Kate's voice rang out, clear and persuasive, but she was not visible until she stepped out of the shadows into the silvery light of the moon. The raw plea in her tone was unmistakable, but Elias shook his head. As the entire company, Thomas included, watched in fascination, Elias rounded on Kate. "First of all, you," he pointed a finger at her, "don't speak to me. Your opinion is the last thing I want to hear and your advice is the last thing I would ever listen to."

Then he turned back to Thomas. "As for you, I am on the right side, the side I chose. And you can go to hell." With no warning, Elias hurled an energy bolt of magic at Thomas, who deflected it without any difficulty whatsoever.

Thomas gave Elias one last look, allowed himself one final moment of pity. "So be it. Let the battle begin."

As planned, he would let Kate and Dominic deal with Elias. From that moment on Thomas's focus did not waiver from Baylor.

The center of the stone circle, the focal point of all power, dark and light, was his destination and he was determined to reach it long before Elias, even if he had to damage the dark wizard to do it. To that end, he unleashed his power, which he had held at the ready, and sent Elias flying sideways to land right at Dominic's feet.

"Dominic, deal with him," Thomas shouted the words as he took off at a run.

"With pleasure."

Thomas heard Dominic's reply even from yards away but he did not stop and wouldn't, not until he reached his goal.

****

Dominic knew his two tasks: neutralize Elias and protect Kate. While Thomas and the others dealt with the dark forces, he stuck as close to Kate as if he were her twin, which he wasn't, or her lover, which he damn well was. He would not fail her.

Deep down to his core, he was a healer. As such, only once had he ever used his magic to harm and never ever had he used it to kill, but he was prepared to do so now. He had, in fact, been training for this for months. He would kill Elias before he ever allowed that man or anyone else to lay a finger on Kate. Nor would he sit back and allow Elias to destroy the whole bloody world either, come to that. In some small part of his mind, it startled him to recognize that, for him, the fate of the world came in a distant second to Kate's well-being and it was even more shocking to discover how little that realization disturbed him.

Instead of confronting the two of them immediately, Elias took his time standing. He sent his people fanning out with a gesture. Next, he turned his attention to Kate and started toward her, magic waiting in his palm. Elias did not halt until Dominic stepped directly in his path.

"So, you're her protector now as well as her lover?" Elias sneered.

Dominic stood still and silent, this response an answer in itself.

Kate sidestepped so she was again in Elias's field of vision and blocking Dominic's body with her own as best she could. "Forget about him. I'm here to make sure you don't do any more harm than you already have."

"And I told you not to speak to me!" He raised his hand to strike her. Acting faster than he ever had in his life, Dominic used magic to block Elias's raised fist before it could connect.

"And I'm here to make sure Kate comes out of this unscathed. If that means taking you out, well, that would be a nice bonus. Either way, if you make any attempt to touch her again, if you so much as look in her direction ever again, I'll break your neck."

Elias jerked his arm in an attempt to free himself, but it was only after two tries that Dominic allowed it and let him go. In one slow, deliberate move, Elias stepped back, hands up in a false, placating gesture. "Fine. I'll leave her alone. At the moment, I don't have time to teach her the lesson she so richly deserves anyway. Right now, I am going to complete the ritual. I would suggest you both stay out of my way."

The last few words ended on a roar as Elias called up his magic and used the air to lift them off their feet then throw them some forty yards. Taken by surprise, Dominic found himself hurled face first through grass and wet earth then he skidded to a halt. For a moment he took a breath, got his bearings, then smacking his palms on the ground, he got to his feet.

Filth covered him from head to toe now, but he didn't give a shit. Unfortunately, the bastard had not stayed to admire his own handiwork. Instead, Elias headed to the center of the stone circle, of course. He strode after Elias without a second thought.

As if from a great distance, he heard Kate ordering him to stop and begging him to wait. When it was clear he had no intention of doing either, curses of startling inventiveness spoken in her pretty Irish brogue reached his ears, but he ignored them.

Mere feet from his goal, at least twenty members of Thomas's army blocked Elias's path. Dominic found it difficult not to laugh in triumph when he realized. Why fight it, he decided, and gave voice to the full-throated sound. A heartbeat later, however, his smile faded when Elias's minions appeared out of nowhere. Damn teleporters!

As he stopped and planted his feet, ready to use his power, Kate rushed up to his side. They stood together as if they had done so many times before. It felt natural and right to Dominic, as did the quick grin he tossed her. "Hi."

For a moment, her mouth worked silently trying to find words, as if she were going to say something, perhaps something rather uncomplimentary, then thought better of it. Jaw set, she said, "Hi."

As the minions surged forward coming closer and closer to them, Dominic took one last moment to memorize her face. "I love you."

"I love you too."

"Let's fight."

Kate nodded and conjured a shield with her magic to hold back the tide while Dominic did the same.

****

Jessilyn was far from satisfied with her assigned role in the battle. She was to wait, concealed, for the battle to begin. At Thomas's signal, she would activate the CDF, bringing all the dark magic conjured by dark wizards to a halt, winning that part of the battle at least. This would, in turn, give Thomas the time to wrestle with Baylor and his dark forces himself and subdue them. One part of her was proud of her achievement and was well aware the CDF might turn the tide, save many lives and perhaps even save the world. On the other hand, she wanted to be by Thomas's side, physically there, fighting with him. It was unfortunate she could not be in two places at once. Even with all the magic she had learned about over the past year, she had come across nothing which could accomplish that.

So, her impatience notwithstanding, she took up her post and waited as instructed. After what seemed to be an interminable amount of time, things began to happen. Elias and his minions arrived. Jessilyn could not seem to take a full breath, so worried was she that they would be discovered and lose the element of surprise. Nor did her tension ease once Thomas revealed himself. If anything, it ratcheted up several large notches. As she watched, Thomas held a brief conversation with Elias then took off like a shot.

When her husband's hand lifted then lowered in the universal symbol for go, Jessilyn activated the dampening field as planned. The sound of it was at first a piercing shriek, then a deep rumble which soon became deafening. It caused utter chaos in the ranks of the enemy and seeing it, Jessilyn wanted to cheer.

However, before she could make a sound, everything went dark.

****

Time did funny things during a battle, Hannah discovered. Waiting to begin, seconds seemed like hours. Now, those same seconds flew by. In a blink, she found herself in the thick of the fighting. Baylor's dark forces rushed toward her. Elias's dark apprentices wreaked havoc all around her. Their elemental magic, the churned earth, hurricane force winds and wild fires they conjured were more than enough to deal with.

Then there were the demons. The dark forces were, Hannah realized, in a word, dark. Darkness too dense to be of the air and too porous to be solid permeated the area. One tentacle slithered up her ankle while she stared fascinated, mouth agape. Coming to her senses when sharp pain flared on her skin, she cast a shield charm and did her best to push the dark forces back.

She ducked a flying tree limb then pivoted in time to avoid being consumed by a demon. Adrenalin surged at her narrow escape and her soul turned to steel. Time to use some magic of her own. Instinct had her relying on what she did best. Telepathy. She sent her mind into the minds of as many of the dark apprentices as she could. For the first time in her life, she used her gift to cause pain. All the dark apprentices within fifty feet of her shrieked in agony. Most fell to their knees and covered their ears. Right when she was beginning to appreciate the sight, the world spun.

She hit the ground hard and her breath was knocked out of her. "What the?" she gasped. She looked around, dazed, trying to figure out what hit her. Over her head, a demon shrieked and passed right where she had been standing seconds before. A young man was shielding her body with his own. He was vaguely familiar and she studied him a moment. He was sixteen years old at a guess. He was also tall, with that skinny, just beginning to grow into his adult body look. Chocolate brown eyes shined out from behind horned rimmed glasses. She had noticed him right away and considered him both attractive and kind but she had never believed he would speak with her. And wasn't she lucky, it was Jason Montgomery, the one boy she had a crush on. Great. He had to see her screw up and then make sure said screw up wasn't fatal. He was wonderful and perfect and he would never notice her, beyond saving her life that was. He saved her life. As that thought sunk in, she wondered how the heck was she going to keep from falling in love with him now.

"Are you okay?"

Being so close to him, his big brown eyes filled her vision and she could count the freckles on his nose. Dazed, it took her a moment to process what he said. She tried to formulate some intelligent response but all she could come up with was, "Uhmm." She blinked and at last managed to murmur, "I'm fine. You?"

He grinned. "Yep." He rose, then held out a hand to help her up.

She took it in a firm grip and found her palm engulfed in his warm one. On her feet now, she tried to think of something intelligent to say, but all she could come up with was, "Thanks for saving my life."

His grin widened. "No problem."

Unfortunately, demons chose that moment to race between them. An instant later, dark apprentices approached from behind and they were separated.

"Thanks," Hannah murmured again.

She focused once more on the task at hand, i.e. not getting herself killed, and cast another spell.

****

Knocking Dr. Matthews out with his magic had been easy and smashing the machine had been plain fun in Troy's opinion. For the space of about thirty seconds, the dampening field had worked, however, and Troy saw he had lost several of his comrades even in that short amount of time. As he continued to observe, however, his fellow dark apprentices regained some of the lost ground. Even as they did, the enemy fought to prevent them from getting the upper hand. One of them, seeing what Troy had done, raced toward him to exact a penalty. With a reckless laugh, he faced his new opponent, ready to take on any and all comers.

****

With a groan, Jessilyn surfaced. Regaining consciousness was no picnic. Her head throbbed and she probed then winced when her fingertips grazed a large knot forming on the back of her skull where she had hit her head on a small stone half-buried in the ground. The blurred vision she faced when she opened her eyes was a damn dangerous nuisance and she blinked and blinked trying to clear it. After far too much time passed, she was able to see the remnants of her work lying in bits all around her. Lucky for them all, there was a spare hidden not ten feet away. Within moments, the second CDF was up and running and ready for action. All she had to do was connect one last wire. As she did, she said a prayer to a God she had long since lost faith in, shut her eyes and completed her work.

This time the element of surprise was lost. Even so, the CDF did its job. Again, all dark magic ceased. Only light magic, the dark forces and Baylor himself remained. This time Jessilyn could appreciate the results of her efforts. Spells cut off mid-sentence, power frozen in mid-air. It was all most impressive and she had a terrific view of it.

Then Jessilyn saw the love of her life standing there, jaw slack, watching her. A small triumphant smile played on her lips until one of Elias's minions headed straight for him. Appalled, she signaled to him. 'Go' she mouthed.

****

Thomas saw it happen as if in slow motion. Troy Evans hit his wife with a rather large burst of power, one strong enough to knock her unconscious. Even though it seemed to take forever, in reality, it happened so fast, he had no chance of stopping it. Nor could he stop Troy a moment later and keep him from smashing the dampening field Jessilyn had worked so hard to create.

Every instinct he had screamed at him to go to her, but he couldn't. More than anything, he wanted to stand in front of her and protect her with his life, but he had other duties to perform first. For now, the best he could do was throw out a shield around her to protect her. He was responsible for saving the whole damn world and he had never felt more torn. Frozen to the spot, he waited in agony until she regained consciousness. When her eyes fluttered open, a profound sense of relief shot through him. He could not take his gaze off her as she powered up the replacement CDF.

Even dazed as she still was, she must have sensed his attention, because she started to shout at him. Although her voice did not carry over the din, he did manage to see her lips form the word, 'Go,' and, as ever, he obeyed, narrowly missing a direct hit from a demon meant for him when he dodged to the side.

****

Even with the chaos of a battle involving several hundred people, give or take, surrounding him, it still surprised Elias to discover so many of his dark apprentices in retreat. He lost about half of them outright at the first proof of Thomas's strong light magic and Jessilyn's dampening field. Finding themselves powerless and, what was more, defenseless, sent more than a few of them into shock. Seeing the dark forces fully rise sent most of the rest running for their lives. Some simply could not cope with Baylor's full power. Cowards, he decided. If he'd had the time he would have spat the word into every face before he killed them with his own hands, each and every one.

Now, however, he was alone. Not that that was a problem. Alone was the way he had always been, why should it be any different now? He would do what he set out to do and bring the dark forces to fruition. At last, he took the final step toward that worthy goal and entered the center of the stone circle, the epicenter of the portal. Baylor was more tangible than ever before, especially to him. He could feel the ruler of the dark forces in the very air around him and each cell in his body reacted. He did not even try to fight it. No, he let the familiar, searing, forbidden pleasure flow through him unchecked for once and at last.

Then he saw them, Dominic and Kate. Kate was his and he, Elias, would take her with him wherever he meant to go, even if it was to hell. As for Dominic, whatever hell waited for the three of them, Dominic deserved it for stealing what did not belong to him.

With a roar, Elias scrabbled for them both, determined to take his revenge or die trying, but Dominic was stronger than Elias had ever given him credit for. Dominic forced Elias back, well away from the woman that was his rightful prey.

Unwilling to give up, he tried again. Whoosh! Crackle of power! Smack as he hit the ground! Again, Dominic forced him back. Again, he got up. Whoosh! And again. Crackle! Again. Smack! Unable to concentrate on both Baylor and Dominic, Elias was well aware he was losing. On his knees now, Dominic stood over him, eyes calm yet fierce, prepared to kill him.

Before that could happen, however, he was lifted off his feet and the dark forces took him out of Dominic's influence.

He chanted the words so familiar to him. "I call to you, oh ruler of darkness, Baylor, I am your willing vessel. Tonight, I give myself over to you fully."

Brought into the whirling maelstrom that was its very heart, Baylor penetrated him entirely at last. For one blinding instant, the pleasure of it was more intense than anything he had ever experienced, better than any drug he'd ever taken or any orgasm he'd ever had. It was so amazing that he screamed at the top of his lungs in unmitigated pleasure.

He was still riding high on it when the pain started. Slow at first, it built at an astonishing rate, until within seconds his scream evolved to one of agony. If the pleasure had been beyond anything, so was the pain. As the sweet sensation faded, the pain left in its place turned scorching. It was brutal, far too brutal to withstand, so brutal he expected to pass out. Denied that small mercy, he remained conscious for every instant of it. This was all too much; it was going wrong and he knew it.

It came to him then that he was being eaten alive. At the thought, shock gripped Elias first. In utter panic, he realized Baylor was in fact devouring him. The demon king was in the process of swallowing him whole and would continue to do so until there was nothing left. Foolishly, he had assumed he would retain his own consciousness, if not his body or soul, once joined with Baylor. Well, that theory was being disproved right this very moment. Baylor wanted his body and even more his magical energy, to strengthen himself for the battle with the forces of light and he had played right into his hands. Fury roared through him alongside Baylor. For the first time, he comprehended how much of a willing participant he had been in his own destruction.

In trying to strengthen himself, Baylor consumed more of Elias every second. Blinded and maddened by the pain, it was only then, at the last, that Elias entirely comprehended he was going to die. Not a trace of him would be left when it was done and it was far too late to stop it now. Feelings of betrayal mingled with a dark thrill. Yet, he could not bring himself to feel any remorse over any of it, nothing but acceptance.

"I regret nothing! Je regret rien." He didn't merely say the words, he shouted them into the vortex because he damn well meant them and because they would be his last.

And so it proved. Baylor utterly consumed him and the demon king's terrible flame turned his body to ash.

****

In her heart, Kate still wanted to save Elias, even knowing deep in her soul that it was impossible. Even knowing full well he was a lost cause, she could not help wishing things could be different. Watching him give himself to Baylor yet again, all she could think was, 'He has lost. He just doesn't know it yet.'

Elias gained the center of the circle and within minutes, Kate realized what was about to happen, but could think of no way to stop it. The burning began at Elias's core and spread with startling rapidity to consume him.

Kate took an instinctive step forward to help him, but Dominic forced her back. "No." When she pushed at him and struggled, he held her in place, keeping his grip gentle but firm and his hold unbreakable. Even though it was not painful, it was like iron, and she was unable to free herself.

"No, it's too late. It's been too late for him for a long time, you know that."

Her breath left her lungs in labored gasps from the scuffle with Dominic and from something else. It writhed inside her chest trying to break free. She'd failed. She'd failed Elias. She had also failed Thomas,

Jessilyn, and everyone attending the school, perhaps even every magical person living, maybe even the whole world. The weight of it all brought her to her knees.

Even then, Dominic didn't let her go, but dropped to the ground with her. His strong, loving arms wrapped around her were her one comfort in a bleak world.

****

The dark forces rose up from the depths of the earth, greater than ever before. Thomas watched in horror as Baylor consumed Elias, knowing any interference at this point would mean his own death. Once it was finished, Thomas steeled himself for an attack, an outright physical assault, instead aside from its presence and a lot of damn wind there was nothing. This state of affairs was not what he had expected at all and it chilled his blood and bone.

There was nothing, that is, until a voice, dark and seductive, whispered in his head. "Stop fighting me, Thomas. I am stronger than you think and I will win. Give up and I will spare you and these few you call friends, students, and army. Your wife will live to bear the child she carries even now, but only if I allow it and only if you stand down now.

Join me and I will make you my general and together we can rule this new, dark world we will create."

Thomas didn't even have to think. He never hesitated. "No. I'd prefer to send you back to hell where you belong, Baylor. Back into the void for another thousand years. I am Merlin's heir, not this world's ruler. I am its guardian, the protector of its people and as such, you should know I would never trade one life for another or even for a thousand others. Unless it's my own." In one deliberate, decisive move, he slashed himself with the knife he carried, ripping a wound straight from his palm down his wrist. Clenching his fist until the blood welled, he let it drip onto the ground.

A simultaneous roar rose within his head and assailed his ears from without and that was when all hell broke loose.

"Well, that sure got his attention," Thomas quipped to no one in particular, already feeling rather woozy.

Baylor and the dark forces whirled everywhere around him now and he himself was all but lost in the vortex. Lost until he saw a tiny pinprick of light at the center of the stone circle and he stumbled toward it. Instinct had him reaching out for it with his own power. In an instant, it responded and he recognized it as something deeply familiar to him, a part of his very core. It dispelled the cold and the chaos and the more he clung to the light the stronger he felt.

It drew on him, but not in the same way that Baylor had drawn on Elias to drain him. In a flash, he understood in the most practical, primal way that light creates more light, while darkness destroys, consuming everything and yet never satisfied. So, he focused every particle of his being on the light in front of him and on finding examples of that same light in his own life. The Institute, his power and his family were shining examples, but it was Jessilyn who was the brightest example of all. The love they shared and the beautiful child they had created (because he was certain that in this Baylor had spoken the truth for once) were everything that was light and all that was good in the world. Holding that knowledge close to his heart and letting it infuse his very soul, he took a deep breath and called on the forces of light from whence all his power emanated.

It surged up in a rush to fill him as never before and he knew himself to be no mere conduit, but an integral part of the deep interconnection running through all living things in creation. An interconnection Baylor and his dark forces wanted to sever in spite of being as much a part of the universe and as crucial to the balance as each and every tiny grain of sand.

At last, he entered the center of the stone circle and was engulfed in light. He lifted his hands high and spoke the ancient words in Welsh, then Greek then in his native English.

Come light, come dark, come balance to renew.

Let good spark and begin anew.

Replenish the strength of those who live true,

So darkness may be given its due.

Let centuries pass in peace, one hundred years by ten,

Until the dark forces must rise again.

Together with mine and me,

This I, Thomas, son of Merlin, will, so mote it be.

The very foundations of the earth shook. Baylor screamed, whether in pain or fear or anger, he had no idea. For one heartbeat, he saw deepest dark and brightest light somehow mingled together and he had no idea which would be the stronger or emerge victorious. Then he saw nothing more.

Chapter Eighteen

Jessilyn rushed to him so quickly it felt as though her feet never touched the ground. "Help!" she roared as she did her best to staunch the blood pouring from his wrist. "Someone help!"

Someone must have heard her even over the din for mere seconds later Dominic appeared with Kate by his side.

She tore her gaze away from Thomas's bleeding form and locked it on Dominic's face. "Please, you have to heal him."

Dominic crouched down beside her, his manner soothing and calm. "I'll do my best. But you have to let me work." With gentle fingers, he pried her hands away from the terrible wound.

Wasting no time, he used his power to close the gash. Jessilyn breathed a sigh of relief which choked her before it could be released when the cut reopened seconds later.

Dominic cursed. "This is no ordinary wound."

"What?" Jessilyn managed the one word as she stood poised on the cusp of utter hysteria.

"It was created to stop dark magic, but also to balance the scales. It's part dark magic, part light. I'm trying to find the right balance within myself in order to heal him, but it's taking some time," Dominic explained.

"He hasn't got any time!" Jessilyn's voice rose in panic, but she didn't care.

"You think I don't know that?" For the first time, Dominic's voice was sharp. "Be quiet and let me work."

Jessilyn obeyed.

****

The first thing Thomas registered was her voice, Jessilyn's voice, begging him to stay with her. Then he came all the way back in a rush. With a gasp, he sat bolt upright. His head had been in her lap and he wished idly he'd stayed for a moment to enjoy the sensation, but he had far greater concerns.

"Did it work? Did we subdue Baylor and the dark forces?"

A strangled sob issued from Jessilyn then she managed to croak, "For the next thousand years. Look."

She gestured to the horizon. With great care and with her assistance, he got to his feet to get a better look. He found it hard to believe what he saw. A wave of pure magic surrounded them and raced away from them, a wall of brilliant, vibrant pale blue that traveled over the land like a scanner onto printer paper. This aura of undiluted enchantment spread over them and would encompass the whole world. Every last member of his army bowed their heads at this incontrovertible evidence that light magic and all the forces of good still ruled the earth.

Then someone, Thomas was never sure who, let out a whoop and the whole company erupted into cheers. Triumph filled him. It was done by God! Light magic would rule for another millennium. He had lived up to the promise of his ancestors. He had discharged the duty placed on him by Merlin, the greatest magician of them all, and now he could claim his birthright. All the tension, tension with him all of his life, tension with him so long he barely noticed its weight, lifted from him, leaving him feeling lighter than air. His heart and soul soared. Utter relief and unmitigated joy rushed up from deep inside of him and he had to share it with the person most important to him. He pulled Jessilyn into his arms and held her as close as he could. For a long moment, he clung to her as waves of varied, sometimes conflicting emotion battered him. "It's done. We did it." He whispered the words into her hair.

She drew back enough to look at him. "We did."

Then they were both smiling. Feeling stronger by the moment, he picked her up, then whirled her around and around, filled with some sort of crazed exuberance, then kissed her. He put his whole heart into the kiss, all of his gratefulness, his joy and his deep, abiding love. She kissed him back and it was glorious.

****

As everyone around her shouted out their joy, Kate's eyes filled with tears. All her hard work, all the sacrifices, all the months of abject fear and frustration had not been in vain. Even though she was not able to save Elias or his minions, all the rest, all those she loved, were safe. For the first time in months, her heart lifted and the burden she had carried for so long lightened.

In her blurry peripheral vision, movement caught her eye. She blinked to clear away her tears and watched as Dominic walked straight toward her. As soon as he got within arms-reach, he hauled her to him and, without preliminaries, he took her mouth in a wild, fierce kiss. It was the sort of kiss that said, I'm still alive and so are you, thank God, so let's bloody well take advantage of that fact and celebrate in the best possible way.' Dimly, she registered the even louder shouts of the crowd as everyone looked on, but she didn't care. She returned the kiss with abandon.

****

In the aftermath, the rush of their utter victory, of using his powers to heal, still filled Dominic. Kate could see it in his every move. There was much to be done, lots of injuries to set right. It had been a long time since he had been able to use his powers in the way he was born to and she could tell it felt amazing. From triage, to treatment, to surgery, she knew he relished all of it.

"Shouldn't you rest? You've been at this for hours."

He glanced up at her and grinned. "Are you kidding? Tired is the last thing I am and rest is the last thing I need. We won and it feels so damn good to be a doctor again." He grabbed her wrist, jerked her against his chest then planted one hot kiss on her pretty mouth. He didn't rush, but let himself enjoy her and their whole life with all its possibilities before them. When their lips parted, he chucked her under the chin and rushed to his next patient.

Kate stood there blinking and bemused for a moment then a slow grin spread across her face. She scanned him, took in his handsome features, so tired yet so satisfied, and spoke the words in her heart with no reservation. "Marry me."

Dominic's head whipped around so fast she was sure his neck would be sore. "What?"

"You said you wouldn't ask me to marry you, remember?" Her cheeks heated at the recollection and, while he looked adorably bewildered, he nodded. "So, *I'm* asking *you*. I may be only nineteen, but I know what I want. I always have."

His body was tense and there was a certain wariness in his expression. Behind that though, deep inside, something flared, a mixture of hope, pure desire and the emotion she'd at last learned to put a name to: love.

After a long moment, he said, "We're both so young. I shouldn't even consider it. We will both change; no doubt about it. Are you certain you want this? There is a chance our feelings for each other, even as strong as they are now, may change." He was as close to babbling as he had ever been in his life, but he rushed on. "Having you then losing you, or worse if either of us ended up regretting this, it would destroy me. But if it's what you want, I'll take the risk because I believe down to my soul that my feelings for you will remain as strong as they are now. You are part of me and you always will be. I know that now." With a gentle hand, he caught the tear sliding down her cheek and wiped it away. "Are you willing to take the risk?"

"I am. So, you'll marry me?"

"Yes." His face broke into a grin. "Yes, I will definitely marry you."

Dominic wrapped his arms around her and kissed her. Even though they were quite used to the spectacle the two of them made by now, the people in the immediate vicinity clapped and cheered.

****

For once Hannah did not feel separate and detached from the others. Instead, she felt part of it all. As she and dozens of other onlookers watched, Kate and Dominic became engaged. Rushing forward, she squeezed through the crowd to congratulate her friend.

As she turned to let other well-wishers speak with the couple, a tap on her shoulder distracted her.

"You're Hannah Barnes right?"

Her head was still muddled from the battle and she studied him a moment before placing him. She tried to formulate some intelligent response but all she could come up with was, "Yes, that's right and you're Jason Montgomery. You saved my life."

The young man nodded and the expression that crossed his face was a pleased one as far as she could tell. He was happy, she assumed, that she not only remembered him, but that she even knew his name.

He cleared his throat. "I hear you helped design the CDF." It was Hannah's turn to nod. "That makes you pretty and smart." His fair complexion pinked and there was a long pause. A full thirty seconds passed before he cleared his throat again. "I was wondering, would you like to go out sometime? With me, I mean."

Pink morphed to bright red, but he met her gaze and there was something in his which drew her. Heart all but flying, she replied, "I would love to."

****

"So, you did it." A few hours later Jessilyn stood beside Thomas observing the wild celebratory mood of the students, but apart from it. In this sweet little bubble of isolation, just the two of them, she let all the tension and terror of the last months, days and hours go and allowed herself to enjoy being with him. She savored the simple fact that they were both still alive and well.

Thomas shook his head. "No, *we* did it. Me, you, Dominic, Kate and every other person here did it."

Standing behind her with his arms around her waist, he held her close. Jessilyn leaned against him and let the feeling of safety his nearness brought flow through her.

"So, there was one thing Baylor said to me, one truth among a lot of lies."

Jessilyn raised her eyebrows. "Wow. Baylor spoke the truth? I find that hard to believe."

"He said you were pregnant."

Jessilyn stilled and words, always at her command, failed her. At first, all she could manage was a rather incoherent stammer then after one stunned moment she was able to get out, "What?"

He turned her to face him so he could study her. "Are you?"

In order to focus on her body and its inner workings, she closed her eyes. "Yes, I am." She turned to him, the joy filling her all but overflowing. "I will have to take a test to confirm it and make it official of course, but I am, I know it." Then she stiffened and she grabbed his hand. "I swear I had no idea until this moment. If I had, I would never have risked going into battle. I never would have risked myself or our child, certainly not without discussing it with you. Do you believe me?"

"Of course." He pressed his lips to hers in a gentle kiss. "I am a bit surprised neither of us noticed before now."

He gave her a rueful smile she returned with interest then she shrugged. "Well, to be fair, we have been busy, saving the world and all that."

He grinned. "True. Not to mention building a school, teaching, battle planning, and oh, shagging every chance we get, to great effect it seems." He looked down and placed gentle hands over her stomach. "A baby."

"A baby. Wow, I am so happy, but I can't take it all in. I think it's going to take some time for me to process this. I mean so much has happened so fast. A baby," she said again in wonder.

"I feel the same way. Well, I guess we'll have seven months or so to get used to the idea, right?"

She beamed at him. "Right."

With a tilt of his head, he indicated the revelry. "Do you want to join in? Dance?"

She studied the general merriment, smiled in approval, but shook her head. "No, I would rather have a little time alone with you."

Heat shot down her every vein as she took him in. "Some privacy does seem like a great idea." Arm in arm, he led her to their bed.

****

"I can't believe it's truly over," Kate admitted to Dominic as the sun rose. They had spent the day dealing with the wounded then been up all night celebrating and now she was crashing. After being awake for a full twenty-four hours, who could blame her? Dominic, on the other hand, still seemed to have a bit of energy left, though not as much as before when she'd asked him to marry her. Had she really done that? Her cheeks heated at the memory then she stuck out her chin, squared her shoulders and brushed any lingering embarrassment aside. She loved him and could not find it in her heart to regret any of it, particularly not one of the most precious moments of her life. He had said yes after all and every bit of her warmed at the thought.

"I find it hard to believe too, but right now I'm tired and I'd like to take my gorgeous, kick-ass fiancée to bed, make hot, passionate love to her and then sleep for about eighteen hours, if that's all right with you?"

"Oh, that sounds wonderful to me."

His eyes fixed on her with an intensity that made her shiver. "Good," he said. "Let's go then."

Chapter Nineteen

Things returned to normal with a swiftness that surprised Thomas. A week after the battle classes resumed. A week after that he called Dominic and Kate into his office. As usual, Jessilyn joined them.

After exchanging greetings all around, Thomas settled back into his chair. "So, I have called you two here today because I am in a bit of a quandary."

Comfortable in the chair opposite, Dominic eyed Thomas. "Oh? How can we help?"

"Well, you two are the quandary in fact."

Intrigued, Kate raised an eyebrow. "Are we? Do tell,"

"Both of you were instrumental in making sure this world is still ruled by the light. You did this with compassion and bravery. You did this without a care for your own lives and at great risk to your own personal safety."

Kate stole a look at Dominic then answered for them both. "We did what we could, what needed to be done."

"Indeed. Yes, well, you will receive the highest honor Jessilyn and I can devise. An honor created for and named for you both as well. The O'Reilly-Foster medal for bravery, for your unselfish devotion to England, the world and light magic."

Dominic sat up straighter and Kate's fierce eyes glittered with unshed tears. This time Dominic spoke first. "It would be our very great honor."

Kate cleared her throat as she searched for what to say. "I am grateful beyond words for this recognition. But what about you? As Merlin's heir, it was you who sent Baylor and all his dark forces back into the abyss."

"Being Merlin's heir is honor enough. Knowing I did my duty is all the recognition I need," Thomas said. "That said, I could not have done any of this without the two of you and I will see you honored. On the tenth of this month we will have a formal celebration of this new era and you will receive the award then." He paused a moment, considering. "Over these last months, it has been my pleasure to get to know the two of you. Apart from Jessilyn, there are no two people I trust more, both personally and professionally. It has been my very great privilege to serve with you both and I look forward to letting the magical world know how instrumental both of you were in winning this battle."

Again, Dominic and Kate glanced at each other, then spoke as one. "The honor has been ours," they chorused together.

Thomas acknowledged this with a nod then leaned forward once again and steepled his fingers on the desk. "However, this is not the primary reason I called you both here today and brings me back to my quandary. Going forward, where do you see yourselves?"

Dominic hesitated for a second before responding. "Healing, medical and magical. It's what I've always seen myself doing."

Thomas smiled. "That sounds wonderful. We would be lucky to have you." He sent Dominic a steady look before he added, "In that or any capacity."

"I appreciate that."

Thomas nodded then directed his attention to Kate. "What about you?"

"I don't know," she said, considering the question for the first time.

"Have you ever considered recruiting?" Jessilyn chimed in.

"There are still many descendants out there," Thomas elaborated. "We need to find them and bring them here. We think you would be the perfect person to help implement that project."

"Really?" She tilted her head, mulling over the possibilities. "It does sound intriguing. Only –"

"Only?" Dominic asked.

Kate glanced over at him. "Only I can't imagine doing something like that without you." The two of them shared a long, serious look. Already it was apparent to them both that going forward wouldn't be without its complications.

After a time, Thomas cleared his throat to regain their attention. "It seems you both have a lot to think about. Take some time. Decide what you want as well as what you need. As I said, the Avery Institute will be happy to employ both of you in any capacity. On a personal level, I would be grateful, pleased and honored to work with both of you."

Thomas rose to escort Kate and Dominic out and, taking this as their cue, the young couple got to their feet as well.

****

One evening a week later, Kate sat down to think about her future while Dominic sat beside her at the kitchen table with his laptop writing out some final reports for Thomas. Did she want to recruit? Always one for lists, she fetched paper and pen then wrote 'Pros' on the right side and 'Cons' on the left.

Under pros, she listed going out into the world and helping others like her find this place. The idea sounded rewarding and she had the feeling she would need that after saving the world. Nothing could be more fulfilling or worthwhile than helping to restore the balance had been, but now she would need to be a part of something that would come close. Also under pros, she had the feeling she would be good at it. In the past months, she had discovered so many qualities within herself she had never believed she possessed, such as compassion, an ability to read people with great accuracy and unshakeable nerve. These qualities would serve her well if she decided on this path.

Now for cons. First, it would be unpredictable work, if not downright dangerous. Second, all too often she wouldn't be here at the Institute, the place now like a second home to her. She would be traveling a lot for the next God knows how long, certainly for the next few years. Of course, she did enjoy travel, at least on a limited basis, so she listed that under pro as well. Connected to that issue, was the biggest con of all. Dominic could not be with her. As a healer, he would need to remain in one place to complete his training. Or maybe not, at least not all the time, she mused, as an idea took shape in her brain.

Excited by the notion, without preamble, she asked Dominic, "I think I want to recruit. What if you came with me on the more dangerous missions as a sort of combat medic? There are bound to be missions with a certain element of risk where a highly trained, prodigiously talented healer such as yourself would come in handy. Think about it, frightened kids not altogether in control of their powers, not to mention panicky parents and terrified neighbors to deal with. I can guarantee you'd still be using your skills."

Glancing up, his eyes narrowed in speculation. "I would. In fact, I'd be getting experience in the field as it were. Also, I'd be back up for you."

He sounded captivated by the concept and Kate's heart lifted. Even more eager and enthusiastic now, she added, "Best of all, we could still work together. What do you think? I know it's a lot to ask, but would you consider it?" She tried to prevent it, but she couldn't stop both hope and plea from infusing her voice.

"I'll do more than that. I will say yes right here and now."

"Seriously?!"

Dominic nodded. "Mmm hmm."

"You're sure? This is what you want? Because if it doesn't suit you we can try and figure out something else."

"Are you kidding? It suits me down to the ground. What I am at my core is not only a magician or a doctor but also a trauma medic. That is what I do. To be able to see you, work with you and still continue my medical training, I can't think of anything I'd like better. I've been racking my brains for the last week to come up with some sort of solution and here it is and it is brilliant. You are brilliant." The smile he offered her then was blinding.

She preened a bit at the compliment then beamed up at him. "So my Gran says. Thank you for saying the same. It is a good idea even if I do say so myself."

"It is and I am so glad you thought of it."

"Then we're agreed? We'll bring the idea to Thomas and see what he thinks?"

Dominick nodded. "Yes, as soon as possible. He and Jessilyn might even have improvements to add. We'll see what they say and go from there. I can't imagine they wouldn't love the idea. I know I do."

He pressed his mouth to hers and she knew she could ask for nothing more in life.

****

Jessilyn was as big as a house and still the babies – there were two for the love of God – refused to come. So what if her due date was still three weeks away, twins were supposed to come early, right? A strange mix of irritation at her children's stubbornness and bone deep contentment with her growing family filled her.

Expectation and abject panic also played a part, if she were being honest. Becoming a mother was something she had always dreamed of, but now the time was almost here, a part of her wondered whether she was cut out for the job. Was she capable of doing the most important job on the planet, being a mom? To prepare, she and Thomas had read as many books about birth and child rearing as they could get their hands on. It helped to know what to expect, but the most important thing she learned from all her reading was that raising her own children would be a challenge like nothing else she had ever taken on before, including Noble prize winning research, defeating dark forces and restoring the balance of light and dark magic. She was determined to do the best job possible. Nothing had ever been more important and while a part of her was scared to death, another stronger part couldn't wait to get started. As if in response one baby kicked right beneath the hand which rested absently on her rounded belly and she smiled.

Without warning, her entire body was in a vise and pain radiated from the inside out. Contraction! Her mind screamed the word even as her body registered the slow ebb of the agony. She glanced at the clock, noted the time and sat down to wait for the next. Eight minutes later another contraction gripped her. As she stood to stretch her back after the end of the second pain, an unfamiliar wetness poured down her legs. For a moment, she stared down in astonishment, her mind blank, then her heart kicked into high gear and her synapses resumed firing.

"Thomas!" she yelled at the top of her lungs.

The terrified, urgent tone of her voice brought him running and he raced in from the kitchen where he was making breakfast without wasting a moment. When he gained the door, he took in the scene in an instant: his wife standing over a puddle of liquid, clutching her belly and in the midst of another contraction. "Oh God, it's time."

She nodded as she panted the way she had learned in Lamaze class. He took a few deep breaths of his own then pulled himself together. "The plan," he muttered, eyes a little wild. "We have a plan for this. If only I could remember it." For a moment, he stared at nothing, wracking his distracted brain, until it came back to him. "Okay, let's take this one step at a time. Like we practiced."

"Okay."

"Right. Step one, make you comfortable."

With gentle tenderness, he helped her into dry clothes, then cleaned up the mess. That done, he guided her to a chair.

"Step two, get your bag and head to the clinic. You sit. I'll be right back." He gave her a swift kiss on the top of her head and rushed to grab her packed suitcase from the bedroom closet.

Following the plan step by step seemed to calm Thomas a considerable amount and soon enough they were ensconced in the state of the art birthing suite adjacent to the clinic. Then the waiting began. Minutes that seemed like hours passed, each filled with tension broken only by the misery of yet another contraction until Jessilyn feared they would both go mad. She was also reconsidering her decision to give birth without the help of any drugs.

After two hours of torture, the longest two hours of her life and, she would bet, Thomas's as well, her husband blurted, "Let me take some of the pain."

What?" Jessilyn gasped. "You can do that?"

"I think so. I can't take it all away, but I am pretty sure I can take some of it."

"Is it safe?"

"As long as I don't try to take it all at once it is," he assured her. "Will you let me?"

The offer was a lifeline. Still she asked, "Are you sure? It hurts like a son-of-a-bitch."

"I'm sure. I can't bear to see you in pain. Besides, I'm this baby's father. I should share the pain if I can."

Moved beyond measure, tears prickled in Jessilyn's eyes and she pressed her mouth to his. Their lips met in a kiss strong and loving but brief. "You are the most wonderful man. Yes, please do what you can as long as it's safe for you."

A moment later, Thomas, already with her hand in his tight grip, entered her mind. A heartbeat after that, he gathered as much of her pain as he could toward himself. Her agony lessened, she could feel it in her mind as well as her body. Without any apparent embarrassment whatsoever, he screamed with it, but as the contraction eased, the pain dialed down to what she hoped was a dull, throbbing ache for him. Even so, cold sweat broke out all over his body and his chest worked like a bellows.

"Christ," he mumbled when he managed to speak. "I have never felt anything like that in my life. It was like being ripped apart. How the hell can you stand it? I only took half your pain and I still thought that contraction was going to kill me."

"We girls are tough," she claimed. "I just thought of something, you will be the first man to ever experience childbirth, mentally if not physically. Congratulations." She let out a giggle bordering on hysterical, which turned into a groan as another contraction started.

"Thanks," he said, tone dry, but he repeated the same procedure as her pain grew.

Time seemed rather endless after that, what with the ceaseless repetition of pain, relief, pain. Until at last, things sped up. "All right, Dr. Matthews, I can see the head. When I tell you, push as hard as you can." Dr. Santos gave Thomas a quick glance. "Both of you." Santos took a quick look at what was going on between her patient's legs then said, "Okay, push."

With a groan, Jessilyn did as instructed. After a count of ten, Santos told her to stop. Then she pushed again when told.

At last, in a tone of repressed excitement, she ordered, "Okay, one more time. Push!"

With an almighty yell, Jessilyn did. Her shout mingled with the cries of a newborn baby and it was the sweetest sound she had ever heard.

"You have a son," Dr. Santos announced.

At last the pain was gone for them both and in its place there was a level of euphoria like nothing Thomas had ever known. He could hear the baby crying and felt torn. He wanted so much to hold his son, to see his child's face, but leaving the child's mother was unthinkable. Luck was with him and so he did not have to make the choice. Soon enough, the nurse brought a tiny wrapped bundle over and placed him in his mother's arms.

Thomas put a trembling hand to the baby's head and caressed the delicate cheek with a finger, already captivated. When the little one reached out blindly, grasped his thumb with a little hand and held it in a tight grip, he fell hopelessly in love and he knew he would protect, honor and cherish his child all the days of his life.

"What should we name him?" Jessilyn whispered.

When he glanced over at her, she seemed as dazed and dazzled as he. "How about Daniel?"

"That sounds wonderful." She smiled then asked, "Do you think he'll have powers?" No nerves came along with the question, only avid curiosity.

Thomas shrugged. "I don't know for sure, but it stands to reason. One thing I do know, he won't be alone. He'll have me. He'll have his beautiful mother and all the people here."

"And a wonderful world, full of joy and magic. Oh and love, above all, love. So much love." Jessilyn smiled down at Daniel and Thomas had never seen a more beautiful sight.

Thomas nodded in agreement. "Yes, love above all, as much as we can give him."

Love filled Jessilyn's heart to overflowing. Love for this man who had shown her in every possible way how magical life could be. And that was nothing compared to her love for her son. Jessilyn never expected she could love one tiny little person so much, that her heart could be so full, but it was. And that was the greatest enchantment of all.

About the Author

Shirley grew up in Baton Rouge, LA and started writing at an early age. Always talkative, when she was eleven she began to put her thoughts on paper, writing stories inspired by some of her favorite writers, Laura Ingalls Wilder and Madeline L'Engle. As she grew older, she developed a love of romance and in 2009 she decided to try her hand at paranormal romance. The result was the self-published title The Smoke and the Flame and its sequel, The Wind and the Fire. Her novel, If the Shoe Fits, published by The Wild Rose Press in 2016, was featured at the 2017 Louisiana Book Festival to Shirley's great delight. Her most recent novel, The Crystal Flame, was published in 2017.

Shirley graduated from Nicholls State University where she majored in History and minored in English. Since graduating (she doesn't like to think about how long ago that was) she has worked at some of the best libraries in the Baton Rouge area. She makes her home there and enjoys spending time with family members. She also loves seeing movies, reading, and going to the park with her niece in her free time.

Currently, Shirley is hard at work on her newest venture, titled DragonSong in which a princess turns the tables on the dragon hunting her with the help of the best dragon slayer in the world and She has also narrated and produced her self-published novella, Awake, in audio format. To learn more check out www.shirleypmccoy.com , or follow her on facebook at https://www.facebook.com/shirlmccoy50 or twitter at . https://twitter.com/Scifigirl20